The Milk Market

Dennis Leger

This book is a work of fiction. Names, characters, businesses, places, events and incidents either are the product of the author's imagination or are used fictitiously. Any resemblance to actual persons, living or dead, events or locales is entirely coincidental.

ISBN 1-434-81196-4
EAN-13   9-781434-811967

All rights reserved

Copyright ©2007 by Dennis Leger

Cover design by Joel Leger

For my wife, Lynn

The Milk Market

CHAPTER 1

The red alert telephone rang in a back office at Fire Station 9. Adam Bennett fumbled for the receiver, picking up before it could ring a second time. Still nearly asleep, he listened to the message and slowly pulled himself up to the edge of his bunk. Across the room, his partner Stewart stirred and stretched. It was just before 2 a.m.

"OK, got it! Arson is responding." Adam put the dispatch telephone down and stood up. "House fire. Eighteen hundred block of Ridgedale."

"What have they got?" Stu, with his feet on the floor, tried to rub the sleep from his eyes.

"One victim. The fire is under control." Adam slid into his shoes and reached for his jacket. "Let's go!"

Stewart stood next to the bed, cursing softly as he tried to get his right foot into his left shoe. It was going to be another long night.

They trudged across the darkened apparatus floor of the station to an unmarked blue Ford. Adam pulled the timer cord to open the big door as Stewart started the car. With a red light flashing on the dashboard, the drive through quiet neighborhoods brought them to Ridgedale in less than 10 minutes.

They parked a block away from the fire trucks and bright lights. With their boots pulled up, they walked toward the scene with their flashlights, notebooks and a camera. Adam reported, "Arson unit on Ridgedale," on the portable radio.

On the street, firefighters and paramedics were working desperately to save a male fire victim. The stretcher was still in the street behind the ambulance allowing room to set up oxygen and intravenous lines. Their patient was not breathing. CPR had already been started when the heart monitor confirmed there was no pulse.

Neighbors stood around in nightclothes, shocked by the gruesome sight. The victim's face was ashen gray except for dark smoke stains around his mouth and nose. In the glare of spotlights the body on the stretcher was not human, not real and certainly not the neighbor they knew.

It became less frantic when the patient was moved into the ambulance and a discreet radio call was made to the emergency room asking for further instructions. Nothing more could be done. On the doctor's advice, paramedics pronounced the victim dead.

Adam and Stewart ignored the crowd on the

sidewalk as they walked past. The neighbors would be interviewed later. The investigation had to begin in the fire ruins before evidence was lost in the ashes and debris or shoveled away by firefighters trying to find the last ember. Because of the fatality, this would not be a routine case. Arson had become murder if the fire had been set.

It was dark and smoky inside the front door of the house. Stewart went ahead, stepping carefully over the hose and equipment that cluttered the front stairs. They greeted the firefighters who were moving in and out with tools and equipment. Adam and Stewart knew most of them by name. Arson investigators were promoted from the ranks.

"Where did you find this guy?" Stewart asked no one in particular.

"Upstairs, bedroom on the left," came a reply from the semi-darkness. "Watch your step."

A few firefighters were still in the bedroom, flashlights pointing out the grim outline of a human form in the heavy soot on the carpet. It was a photographic negative of the victim's death, as he struggled for breath during his last moments.

"Didn't make it very far did he?" Adam said, shaking his head. Death from smoke inhalation was every firefighter's nightmare.

Stewart went to look in the other bedrooms while Adam used his flashlight to search for the victim's personal effects. Fumes from burned wood and plastic were still strong enough to sting his eyes. Eerie shadows from a spotlight crossed the bedroom's front window. In spite of the tears in his eyes, he could see forms moving back and forth in the dark, firefighters at work in the hazy smoke, hanging fans in doorways and windows to get fresh air into the house.

In the nightstand drawer Adam found a wallet, a checkbook and a title for a car, the Thunderbird parked in front of the house. The billfold contained some bills, a pilot's license folded up in a plastic sleeve and a Georgia driver's license with a photograph. Anthony L. DeLuca had been 31.

His house, its interior blackened with soot, was no longer a home. All that remained was a pile of stained and melted furniture, ruined as much by smoke and grime as by the heat of the fire. Mr. DeLuca no longer needed the house. Had he planned to fill it with a family? Would a wife or girlfriend find her way into this room asking for him? Adam hoped that it would fall to someone else to tell her the news. She'd be in shock when she learned that her hopes and dreams had been incinerated.

Adam stood in the dark, in the mess of soot and ashes and ruined life. Everything had ended in a few minutes for Mr. DeLuca. Who would ask about him in the morning when he missed work or an appointment? What were his plans for tomorrow? Or for the rest of his life?

"Where did the fire start?" a young firefighter asked from the hallway, bringing Adam back to the investigation.

"Basement. Extended up into the kitchen," another firefighter responded before Adam could reply.

"Let's have a look." Adam and Stewart met outside the bedroom door. The point of origin would help determine the cause of the fire and whether it was an accident or arson. They made their way down to the basement where a team of firefighters was searching for hidden embers.

"Did your crew force the back door?" Adam had noticed splintered wood and a broken deadbolt on the back door near the basement stairs.

"Hello Bennett." Captain Hogan stepped up to answer their question. "No, it was open. We think the neighbor who called the alarm tried to break in up there."

Adam didn't voice his suspicion. Even if the neighbor had been physically able to force the door, he would not have tried to get in where the fire was raging.

While Stewart returned to his search of the upstairs rooms, Adam examined the rubble in the basement. He could easily identify the point of origin but not an ignition source. Imagining the course of the fire, he focused his eyes in the half-dark basement. His flashlight traced the fire's path. There was nothing unusual, except he could not tell how it started.

"How did it get going?" Stewart wondered when Adam climbed the basement stairs to the kitchen.

"Late at night, I suppose no one spotted the smoke."

"What about...?" Stewart looked around the kitchen then up at the ceiling.

Adam was looking up too. He should have noticed sooner. "The kitchen smoke detector is disconnected."

Stewart whistled in surprise. "Too many false alarms?"

Upstairs, they found another disabled smoke detector, its cover hanging down into the hallway. It could mean everything or nothing, but the covers could be removed and checked for fingerprints. First they would be photographed as they were found.

"We better make sure our guys didn't touch them," Adam warned.

"Jackpot. Looks like we might have hit the jackpot." Stewart was excited. "Arson, murder, maybe robbery."

"Do you see anything missing, or out of place in this mess?" Adam was wide-awake. They were not just going through the motions. This was a fatal fire with possible foul play, not the routine cause like smoking in bed, shorted electrical wires or other random misfortune.

The back door had been forced. Had there been a burglary, or had the victim come home late without a house key? Did someone break in and start the fire? The smoke detectors were disabled. Could there have been too many false alarms? There were too many unanswered questions to assume the fire was an accident.

"Let's see what the neighbors can tell us," Adam suggested.

Even considering the late hour they expected the neighbors to be cooperative. For now there were only a few questions. A thorough investigation would start in the next few days, but it was vitally important to collect information while memories were fresh. They needed to find out what the neighbors knew about the victim and if anyone had seen him come home.

Although they were eager to help, the neighbors had little to tell. They had never even learned his name. He had lived in the house for a few months. They supposed he was a traveling salesman because he was not home very often. When they saw him he never gave more than a polite greeting. He had declined an invitation to a neighborhood party, saying he would be out of town.

Stewart soon found the neighbor who had called in the alarm. The man's poodle had jumped on the bed, barking excitedly. Opening his front door, he couldn't believe his eyes. Heavy black smoke poured from every part of the house across the street. Shouting for his wife to call 911, he had run barefooted across the street with the poodle nipping at his heels.

Pounding on the door and ringing the bell, he had heard no response from inside. In the back of the house there were roaring flames in the basement windows and in the kitchen. He had run back again to the front and banged at the heavy front door. Then finally, after what seemed like an eternity, he heard fire sirens in the distance.

Relieved that help was on the way, he had backed out to the street to see into the upstairs bedrooms. His neighbors, in their slippers and bathrobes, had joined him on the boulevard, anxiously awaiting the fire trucks and wondering if anyone was at home, and if they were, how they could survive the inferno.

Stewart joined Adam in front of the house with the neighbor's story. The work was just beginning. "What do you think, Stu?"

"I can't figure the back door. None of our guys broke it down."

"Right, they thought the neighbor..." Adam began.

"Right. No way, too much fire back there." Stewart shook his head.

Tired firefighters went about their business,

picking up equipment, lights, fans and hose. A few remained inside wielding axes and shovels to help the arson investigators search for clues.

There was a procedure to follow. Adam began taking careful notes while Stewart photographed every detail of the ruins. Adam stood on a kitchen chair and removed the covers from the smoke detectors.

They searched for an ignition source and gathered samples for the crime lab to analyze. An arsonist had to have used something like fuel oil or paint thinner to get the fire to extend quickly, preventing the victim's escape. If traces of an accelerant were found, the fire was arson.

"Did you see anything that says family?" Adam asked.

"You mean pictures of the wife and kids?" Stewart had looked in each of the bedrooms. "Nothing."

"Really?" Adam had found little more than the billfold in the nightstand.

"Nope. No pictures of anything, not much personal stuff at all."

"Did you look in the refrigerator?"

"A few cans of beer, a bottle of wine. Not much." Stewart smiled. Once in a while they could learn about a victim or suspect's lifestyle by checking the refrigerator.

"Anthony DeLuca. We don't have much more than the name at this point." Adam was puzzled. They had a mystery victim.

"I don't know, maybe we can get something from the autopsy," Stewart said.

"At least fingerprints."

"Don't worry, someone will show up. Family,

Milk Market

girlfriend, someone..."

"Did the neighbors give us anything?" Adam asked.

"Nothing helpful."

They walked back toward their car after the front and back doors of the house were nailed shut and the last of the fire trucks drove away. A few hundred feet from the fire ruin, they reviewed their notes, sharing ideas and doubts. Their report would have to include every detail, so they would not leave the scene until they were sure every base had been covered.

Although they knew where the fire started, they were not sure how it had begun. With both arson and accidental fires, too much evidence was destroyed by the fire itself and by water during extinguishment. They needed to find the ignition source.

"First, can we prove that it's arson?" Adam posed the question.

"Depends on the lab work, partly, but we already have the busted back door and the smoke detectors," Stewart speculated.

"Depends on the lab work," Adam agreed. "We need traces of accelerant, gas or fuel oil or maybe something more sophisticated."

"If it's arson, it might be a good one. Unless this guy busted into his own house, we could be looking at intentional murder."

"But we might never know." In seven years Adam had known a number of cases that were never solved.

"Yeah, so we could work it from the other end. Find a motive, an enemy. Or," Stewart added, "we could find something missing..."

"Well, I'd rather get some sleep without thinking

about it," Adam said with a yawn. "There's a fresh crew coming in the morning."

"It's morning!" Stewart yawned too. "Can I go home now?"

"As soon as the little hand gets to the eight."

"Do you think the other shift will get into this?" Stewart wondered.

"They have to!" Adam insisted. "This could be the best case we've had in a long time."

"But they'll just tell us to leave it to the homicide investigators."

"We still have to establish that it was a set fire," Adam said.

"If everything we've got here isn't probable cause for homicide, I don't know what they want."

For months they had endured a routine of writing reports about accidental fires. A fire with a victim was unusual enough. They had to try to be objective, but it certainly looked like the fire was set. Even if arson had been used to cover a lesser crime, like burglary, it became murder when there was a fatality. That was the law.

Adam was sure that the police department's homicide detectives would help the arson division. But first, the cops would demand proof of arson. Everyone knew that evidence was usually destroyed in the fire. Their next question would be about the victim. Everything would be on hold until a relative came forward, or until the arson investigators came up with a motive for murder.

As they were leaving Ridgedale, the radio crackled and the dispatcher ordered them to a fire on the east side of the city. After a quick ride across the river they determined that the fire in an overstuffed chair was the result of careless smoking. Hours after an ember had dropped into a cushion in the living room, it had burned into the clear, scaring the smoker, his wife and their children out of their beds. There were no injuries or fatalities. Howling smoke detectors had done their job. The family was wide-awake and assembled in front of the house when the first fire trucks arrived.

The eastern sky was bright when Adam and Stewart returned to their station. In the dark and quiet firehouse, Engine Nine stood ready. A sleepy firefighter on watch closed the big door as soon as they backed into their place next to the Engine. It was 5:30 a.m.

"Don't you guys ever sleep?" The night watch firefighter complained.

"Not really, no." Stewart was now wide-awake and excited about the case. He followed Adam back to the arson office.

Adam wanted to finish the reports and lie down again for an hour or two before their relief arrived. His body ached for sleep. As usual he was ready to go home long before his shift ended. Now there was something he cared about more than this sad and dirty work. Out in the country, his wife was sleeping quietly, safe from the chaos of a dark neighborhood and its dismal burned-out house. Their baby was due within a month.

"Do you ever wish you were back on a rig, fighting fires?" Stewart asked as they started to type their reports.

"At least I'd get some rest," Adam responded. He thought of his warm bed at home and the quiet of the countryside at night.

"Yeah, but you'd be bored, right?"

"Stu, I've been doing this for seven years. Some of the fun has worn off here too." He wondered why Stewart would ask. Perhaps he had somehow signaled that he was losing interest or that he was getting emotionally burned out.

"Well, if this case turns into something, it will be worth it."

"That's for sure." Adam planned to be excited too, after he got some rest.

There were times when he longed for the simpler life of a firefighter. Arson investigators worked the same 24-hour shift, but they couldn't expect to get any rest during the night. The beds that folded up into the office wall came down, but they were rarely used for more than a few hours at a time. Arson responded to every fire in the city to determine if it was accidental or intentional. Most fires were just accidents, but arson investigators had to make the call.

Adam's day off was usually spent trying to make up for lost sleep. He wondered if he would be tired for the rest of his life. At times his body felt older than his 35 years. He tried to stay in shape by playing racquetball once or twice a week, but often he was too tired after his shift to go to the gym.

When the reports were finished Stewart went in to take a shower. Adam went back to his bunk. He dozed and tried to dream about the country, about Carol and the baby. She was there sleeping on her back, propped up on pillows. Whenever she tried to make herself comfortable it seemed the baby would wake up and begin kicking. They were thankful that her first pregnancy had been normal so far, but it was dragging on and on, not only for her but for Adam. Together they wanted it to be over. They wanted their baby and to be able to hold each other close again.

He tried to concentrate on his wife and the baby, but his mind kept coming back to the fire victim, DeLuca. The name came up too often on the fire report and there were too many unusual circumstances about the fire. They had a broken door and disarmed smoke detectors, but there was much more to be learned before they could make a case.

The victim would have been fast asleep in his upstairs bedroom, unaware of the monster in his house. He probably twisted and turned in the bed sheets, dreaming of fire and smoke as he buried his head in the feather pillow. Then the carbon monoxide deepened his dream, and he could no longer sleep or breathe.

Firefighters found him on the floor, so he had tried to reach the door or the window. He might have gained a few minutes of breath on the floor, but by then his limbs would not obey his commands. After crawling a few feet, he had slumped down to take his last breaths just as help arrived. He probably never heard the crash of splintered wood when the front door was forced from its hinges or muffled voices of firefighters as they entered the burning house with a hose line.

To the public it was routine news, a short headline in the back section of the morning newspaper: "Man dies in house fire." The evidence was in a test tube at the crime lab or on a stainless steel table in the morgue. For Adam and the police investigators who would take over, it began at least a week of gathering information and filing reports.

Their preliminary paperwork said that the fire was of suspicious origin with murder as the motive. It included a request for a thorough investigation by the police homicide squad. The cops had the resources to aggressively work the case. They would have ultimate responsibility and would not share the credit if an arsonist were collared.

In a trial that involved arson and homicide, the arson investigator's part was usually limited to technical matters. Proving arson was always hard enough, and proving the identity of the arsonist was even more difficult. Finding a suspect with a good motive and enough other circumstantial evidence would give them a chance, but if the arsonist was a professional, or even just lucky, they might find neither.

Adam drifted into uneasy sleep. An hour later, when a locker door slammed in the next room, he got up and walked into the kitchen for a cup of coffee. Stewart followed a few minutes later. By 7 a.m. firefighters from both shifts sat at a long coffee table, talking and joking. Word of the suspicious fatal fire had already spread around the department.

Adam and Stewart sat at the end of the table. They laughed off curious questions about the case. The only discussion would be with their relief, the investigators who needed to pursue the investigation during the next 24 hours.

Back in the office, they sat quietly while Tom Vogel and Al Jensen scanned their report. After a few minutes of reading they knew all the news from

Milk Market

Adam's shift, including what they had found out and what still had to be done.

There was plenty of work for everyone. Film in the camera had to be developed and samples in an evidence container had to go to the crime lab for analysis. The most important thing was to find out about the victim: his identity, his occupation and his enemies. They had not yet established whether there had been a burglary. Finally, the autopsy would determine if there were any other injuries besides smoke inhalation. When they had the answers, they could start putting the evidence into a tidy bundle for homicide.

"If you guys get busy, just leave it for us. We'll pick it up tomorrow." Stewart was new to the arson division.

"Don't make it too easy on them," Adam warned as they walked to the parking lot.

"Try to stay awake on the way home," Stewart answered. He lived only a few miles away in a suburb.

"Thanks. If you have nothing to do today, you can drive out and help me do some brake work on my car."

"I'll be too busy." Stewart laughed as he drove away. "I'll be sleeping."

"See you in the morning." For Adam, getting into his car and driving home was a relief. He wished he could just stop and sleep, but in less than an hour on the interstate he would be in Riverton. Carol would be as anxious to see him, as he was to see her.

Adam loved his job. He was happy to have an exciting case to work, but he expected to leave it all behind on his day off. That was the beauty of it.

Jensen and Vogel would take up the investigation, then he would return in 24 hours for a fresh start. But this case was not easy to leave behind. Who was Anthony DeLuca? Why had he been murdered?

CHAPTER 2

The Crow River, brown and lazy in the summer morning, drifted close to the highway then wandered away to join the Mississippi a few miles downstream. On its banks, tall oaks and elms shaded favorite fishing and swimming holes. Beyond the thick woods of the river valley were hundreds of square miles of rich farmland. To the west, mile after mile of family farms stretched into the Dakotas.

Nearing the stop sign at the bottom of the Riverton exit ramp, Adam lowered the windows to let fresh air blow through his sandy hair. Away from the rush of interstate traffic the countryside smelled fresh and green. Fluffy white clouds floated overhead, here and there casting shadows on the black asphalt and green cornfields.

At the corner there was a Perkins restaurant where Carol worked as a waitress four days a week. When she worked on the early shift, he usually stopped for breakfast. But this morning she'd be waiting for him at home. When she was at work she was too busy waiting on other tables to give him any attention. She'd glance his way as he sat alone in a booth. "Sorry," her eyes would say, "I'm busy." After being apart for 24 hours during his shift, they would have to wait for hers to be over to be together.

Past the restaurant, Adam turned left, back under the freeway. The county road dipped down to cross the Crow River near Riverton Dam and its deserted mill. It had once been the center of commerce in the county, where the local farmers brought their wheat to be ground into flour. All but a few of the buildings had collapsed years before. Only the old stone dam remained to slow the lazy river.

A few blocks away Riverton struggled to remain a small town. It was a losing battle. The freeway brought change, good and bad. The village was no longer isolated by distance from jobs in the city. Working people were willing to suffer a long commute to leave big city problems behind. If the children were going to ride a bus anyway, they said, let it be to a small-town school.

But some of the problems followed families to the country. Riverton had built two new schools and needed a bigger high school. The board of education tried to plan for the future, as more old farms became housing developments for new families from the city. Many longtime residents lamented the change, but businesses like the Perkins grew and prospered.

Away from town, Adam enjoyed the quiet order of the river valley. Life was better here among the farms and fields. Each morning when he came home from work, he got out of his car, stretched his arms and legs and took a deep breath of fresh air. The noisy fire incidents, the smell of burning wood, urgent radio calls, interviews and reports were left behind in the big city. Like leaving the dark and coming into the light, he felt the difference between bright mornings in the country and the squalid hustle of the city at night.

This morning there was a difference. Even invigorated by the country air and anxious to get home to Carol, he was an arson investigator with a mystery fire victim. Someone started the fire that resulted in the death of Mr. Anthony DeLuca. That was murder. There were plenty of leads to follow, so even if Al and Tom didn't work the case today, he and Stewart would start putting together information tomorrow, on their next shift, which would lead to the truth. A dozen different angles crossed his mind, but until they knew more about the victim, speculation was a waste of time. There would be relatives and friends gathering to grieve, and someone could try to answer his questions.

Adam tried to clear his mind. After another left turn, it would be less than a mile to his driveway. He would be at home where he could put the DeLuca case away. As he approached the little farmhouse, he could picture Carol waiting for him. She would have a bright smile, her hair pulled back in a ponytail and both hands locked together supporting her stomach.

Turning into the driveway he saw Mickey, their Labrador retriever, sitting on the porch. The old dog stretched slowly, getting up to meet him as he turned off the ignition. When he opened the car door the only sounds were a breeze through the trees, a bird singing for the joy of it and the distant hum of a tractor in the cornfield a mile away. Mickey wagged his tail vigorously in greeting. Carol appeared on the porch looking just as he had expected,

"Hi, honey, how are you feeling?" he asked.

"OK, now that you are home. Just fine." She smiled.

"Baby awake?" he wondered.

"Oh yes, he's awake and kicking his mom."

"I will have to have a talk with her, as soon as she is born." He laughed as he walked up the steps to the porch. They had asked the doctor not to tell them whether the baby was a boy or a girl.

"What's new in the big city?" Carol asked as they hugged and kissed.

"Fatality during the night. Probably arson and homicide."

"One for the police department?" She knew he hated to turn his cases over to them.

"Probably. But we will have a shot at it first," he replied.

She poured two cups of decaffeinated coffee and they walked back onto the porch, their favorite place to sit and talk. Carol had found two old wooden rockers at a farm auction and painted them in bright colors. They leaned back in the creaky chairs and enjoyed the view.

Across the road, the river valley was green and thick with hardwoods. Just above the trees they could see the steeple of the old Catholic church a few miles away in town.

The Crow River valley gave them a home, their own place in the world. They had been drawn to the

Milk Market

little town, allowing its prairie friendliness to swallow them up. Local people easily accepted them in church and on Main Street. Carol quit her city job, tired of commuting after only a few months, and started her job at the restaurant. They felt as if they had lived in Riverton all their lives.

"You really don't feel like going to work do you?" Adam knew that she'd prefer to be home with him on a warm summer day.

"I'll probably be back by two, but people need to have lunch you know."

"We can get along just fine without the money, anyway." Adam would not tell her what to do, but he wished she would just stay home. The doctor had convinced her that if she stayed active during the pregnancy, her first delivery would be easier.

"I know, Adam. Don't worry, I'll know when it's time," she assured him. "Trust me! When it gets too uncomfortable, I'll just come home and do nothing."

He knew that she enjoyed her job. She was a small-town girl who loved meeting people, finding out who was related and where they lived. Adam marveled at her memory for details about people she didn't really know. "Are you going to run for mayor?" he sometimes joked when they were alone.

She changed the subject. "Are you going to be able to prove arson?"

"I think so. We'll have to work at it. We need the other shift to work at it."

"You'll do it, I know." Carol was confident.

"We don't know anything about the guy yet, just a name." Telling her about the case didn't make it easier to put away until Tuesday morning.

"No relatives or friends?" she wondered. "No one at all?"

"Not yet." He shook his head. "Someone should show up today."

"I hope so! I can't imagine anyone being so alone." Carol frowned.

"We will know a lot more about him tomorrow. Then we can figure out who wanted him dead."

"So you have a real case to work." She gave him her supporting look.

"Today I'm working on my brakes," Adam reminded her.

"Well, do a good job on that, too. I have to get ready for work."

She was scheduled to work the lunch shift starting at 10 in the morning, so he made his own breakfast while she got ready. He ate cold cereal and toast and watched through the screen door as she drove away.

He couldn't convince her to take it easy. Last fall, before she was pregnant, Carol had worked tirelessly to help shingle the roof, shore up the foundation and tear off the old siding. Now she had a mission and a deadline. The big jobs in the house had to be done before her due date. Most of her earnings seemed to go for decorating supplies at the hardware store. She painted and wallpapered, climbing up and down a stepladder in spite of her condition. After the baby came, she didn't want to be distracted by projects. The house had to be as perfect as they could make it.

Only a year ago they had spotted the abandoned farmhouse in a field of tall corn. Hiking through the rows of corn and the thick black soil, they found a dilapidated little house in an island of weeds. Window glass had long since disappeared and years of weather had eroded the paint. The siding was cracked and gray. A wide front porch sagged precariously above a dangerous step of broken and rotten boards.

Within a few minutes Carol had adopted the house. She was everywhere at once, inspecting every nook and cranny, stepping through the kitchen doorway and chattering about all of its possibilities. Adam, who often tramped through fire ruins in burned-out slum apartments without giving it much thought, had been reluctant to enter. She saw possibilities. He saw hard work, but she countered his every doubt and pointed out the huge kitchen, the straight roofline, the shady porch and the view of the river valley across the county road.

Her chattering amused him. It was unlikely that the farmer would be willing to give up part of this rich cornfield. But he knew that Carol had made up her mind, so the farmer was in for a battle.

He was wrong, of course, and Carol was right. Albert Johnson had delayed razing his grandparents' house, planting his crops around it year after year, because it was part of his family history. His sons had wanted to burn the old house down, offering it to the local fire department for practice. Instead, Albert had let it stand in the middle of the field, occasionally getting down from his tractor to walk around and remember the old folks. He said he was a sentimental Swede who would be happy to see the old house restored. Besides, nearly retired, he didn't need the land. Most of his acreage was rented to neighboring farmers.

Carol's enthusiasm finally rubbed off on Adam.

Together they began planning what they would do when their offer was accepted, when they could begin building their dream home from the gray farmhouse. She was choosing paint colors and window curtains while he worried about a new roof and the foundation the house needed. He convinced her that they needed to build a garage to store building supplies and tools before they did anything else.

They had never been so happy, working on the house day and night for almost six months before moving from a rented house in Riverton. Finally, they had danced in the construction debris that littered their very own living room.

There were jobs yet to be done. Most of their three acres were in corn stubble. In the spring Adam had planted pine seedlings and laid sod until he thought his back would break. There was never enough time to do everything on his day off, and too often he needed to sleep for two or three hours before he could begin to work.

Today, after he slept, his old BMW would come first. It had been stored in the garage for the winter while he saved enough to buy parts for its restoration. He had hoped to have it ready in the spring so he could start driving it back and forth to work. Carol could have the Saturn and they could sell the old Chevrolet truck that Carol drove back and forth to town. Although she wouldn't be working much longer, it had become important for her to have a dependable car.

He passed up the sofa in the living room, still cluttered with wallpaper and tools. Instead he went to bed and fell asleep almost as soon as he stretched out.

Milk Market

Mickey sighed and settled down in the doorway of the bedroom. It was past noon when Adam awoke and wandered into the kitchen to fill his coffee cup from the thermos on the counter. Before backing the BMW out of the garage, he sat on the porch with his coffee while thinking over the brake repair procedure step by step. By 1 p.m. he had started the job. The car was up on jack stands with both front wheels removed.

As he worked, he could hear kids yelling from the river bottom across the road. Riverton kids spent their summers along the river, playing, swimming and smoking cigarettes. In the fall he and Carol had hiked the river trail all the way into town. There were swimming holes where rope swings hung from the elms that leaned over the water. There were kids playing down there now, without a care in the world: no job, no house, and no car.

He was removing a brake caliper from the right front when four or five boys came up from the river. Adam kept working. Out of the corner of his eye he could see that most of them were walking back toward town except for two, who came hiking up the driveway. Mickey barked a few times without enthusiasm.

"Hey mister, can we get a drink?" They pointed at the garden hose in the grass.

Adam nodded. He was dripping with sweat, bent over inside the wheel well.

"Wow, cool car." One of the boys stood in the yard admiring the BMW. "Need any help?"

Funny, even Adam didn't think of his old BMW as a cool car. It was a great driving car, of course. What would a kid know about how a Beamer drove? He smiled and asked for a different wrench from the toolbox. He had new friends. They crouched down nearby and talked as he worked, helping whenever he needed an extra hand. Nice kids, 13 or 14 years old, two buddies with nothing to do on a summer day but keep him company and work on a cool car.

They had been swimming. Their hair was wet and slicked back, but their shorts and shirts were dry and they had no towels. They had been skinny dipping, no doubt. Thank goodness there were still places where kids could be kids.

"How's swimming down there?" Adam asked.

"Great, really great." Both boys agreed.

"Water warm?" Adam wondered.

"It's pretty warm. What year is this?" One of them asked, pointing at the car.

His friend laughed.

"I mean what year is this B whatever?"

"1967, that's BMW," he gave the two boys a closer look. "It's older than either of you, I suppose."

"No sh.… No kidding." The boy corrected himself, not sure whether this adult would approve of the language he used with his friends. "Hey, cool dog. Does she bite?"

"It's a he, and he doesn't bite." Wiping sweat from his forehead, Adam concentrated on the brakes. "His name is Mickey."

"Here girl, er, boy."

The dog slowly got up and came to visit. Then one of them threw a stick and made a friend for life. Mickey loved to retrieve. They played until Mickey barked when Albert Johnson's pick-up truck turned into the driveway.

Milk Market

The old farmer always appeared when Adam was in the middle of something. Carol loved to have coffee with Albert, and the old man always had time to visit. Adam liked him too, but he believed the farmer was a little nosy. Albert was interested in everything they did to the old house. He had a story to tell about each room. They had heard some of his tales over and over again. Adam wanted to be polite to his neighbor, so he stood as they talked.

"Thought I should warn ya." Albert took off his hat and scratched a nearly bald head. "It could get stinky around here tomorrow."

"Oh? What's going on?" Adam asked.

"They're fertilizing that 80 behind you. If the wind stays northwest you might want to keep your windows closed. Ammonia, you know."

"Hello, Bobby." Adam was always polite to Albert's youngest son.

Bobby had been driving the pick-up. He was Albert's slow boy, probably the only reason Albert stayed on the farm instead of retiring to a lake cabin or a trailer home in Florida.

"Hello, Mr. Bennett." Bobby never stopped grinning as he took a ball from the bed of the truck and started throwing it for Mickey to retrieve. He played with the dog and the other boys while Albert talked.

The boy was slow and clumsy, but big and strong. At about 19 years old, Adam guessed he was stronger than most men. Bobby had his father's disposition. He was so eager to help that he was worth more than his keep around the farm. Like his father, he worked hard without complaint. Although Bobby could not get a driver's license, Albert allowed him to drive the pick-up around the farm on country roads.

Albert was unshaven, his beard gray as his thin hair. There was always a twinkle in his eye, as if amused by city people working so hard on the house his family had abandoned. Adam knew that the seeming amusement was kind. As near as he could tell, Albert accepted everything, including all that was old and new and every opinion. He accepted having a son he would need to care for all of his life. Years of farming, taking the good with the bad, had made him easy-going. Carol and Adam agreed they had never heard him say a bad thing about any other person. He liked to talk about the weather, the crops and the hard times.

"So you want us to wear nose plugs, is that it?" Adam teased. Then he thanked Albert for the warning and they talked about the weather for a while. If Carol were home, they would be having a cup of coffee on the porch by now.

"The Mrs. must be working today." Albert sensed that Adam wanted to get back to his car. "Tell her to be careful. And call up if you need anything."

"Thanks, Albert." Adam waved as Bobby backed the truck out of the driveway.

The boys remained to help. One of them said he loved to work on cars. Adam called him Ace. The extra hands helped, if for no other reason than to pick through his disorganized toolbox to find a particular wrench. Nothing on his car ever went as well as he expected, but the front brakes were finally good as new.

Carol came home at three. She looked tired. "So

you've finally made some friends around here."

"Hired hands." Then he asked, "Tips?"

"Are you with the IRS?" she questioned back with a grin. She said "hello" to his new friends and went in the house to start laundry.

One of the boys lost interest in the job and started back to town. Ace helped Adam get the rear wheels up onto the jack stands. Working hard, they found less and less to talk about. An hour flew by before Carol came out on the porch to ask if they wanted something to eat. She brought hot dogs in buns, napkins and two cans of Pepsi and sat with them. Adam ate quickly and went back to work on the car.

"Don't you think you better be heading home?" Carol didn't want Adam's friend to get in trouble.

"Naw, no problem," Ace responded.

"Won't your folks be worried about you?" she asked.

"Nope, they don't worry about me." He was his own boss.

"I'll bet. Why don't you call them?" Carol suggested.

The boy agreed to call home, but no one answered. He guessed that he should be getting home.

Carol was concerned. "It's two miles back to town, and it's getting late. Adam, why don't you drive him?"

In another 15 minutes the BMW would be back on the ground. They agreed that Ace could help finish the job and go for the test drive on his way home.

The boy lived in the Homewood division, a row of houses built on an open field that had probably been planted with corn or beans a few years before. When they reached the entrance to the development, the boy asked Adam to stop.

"This is close enough."

"I can take you right to your door," Adam offered.

"Naw, this is close enough, thanks." Out of the car as soon as it came to a stop, he yelled over his shoulder. "Thanks for the hot dog. See you later!"

"Thanks for the help, Ace." Adam watched the boy cross the road and walk toward the Homewood entrance. Then he drove some of the country roads, running the BMW up to its redline a few times before giving his brakes a real test. Happy to have his car running again, he went home to Carol.

* * *

Robin Anderson was in trouble. The boy was supposed to be home to baby-sit his two little sisters at 3 p.m. His mother had missed her dental appointment. Now it was suppertime, 6 p.m. and Robin wasn't home yet.

"A little too much freedom. That's what it is!" Bill Anderson became more irritated with each passing minute. He had never touched Robin, but he was tempted now to pull out his belt as soon as the boy came home. His father had done the same for him more than once.

Robin and his friend Billy Mayes were usually inseparable. When Marilyn called the Mayes' house, no one answered. In frustration, she kept trying the number until Billy himself answered. It was all she could do to get Billy to admit they had been swimming in the river. He had not seen Robin since late afternoon. As far as Billy knew, Robin was on his way home to baby-sit.

When the Mayes boy didn't know where to find Robin, Bill started driving around town looking for his son. Marilyn began calling neighbors who quickly volunteered to help look for the boy. By late evening, they made the call to Sheriff Knowlton, an old family friend.

"Don't worry, Marilyn. We'll find him," he reassured her.

Within a few minutes every policeman and deputy in Crow County was looking for Robin Anderson. He was nowhere to be found.

CHAPTER 3

Carol didn't stir when Adam reached over to shut off the alarm clock. She needed her sleep so he quietly closed the bedroom door and dressed in the bathroom before going into the kitchen for orange juice and toast.

It was Tuesday morning, and DeLuca was on his mind. In the middle of the night, he had been wide-awake thinking about the case. Fortunately, he drifted off to sleep again before the alarm went off at 6 a.m. He was anxious to get to work. Getting an early start, he arrived at Fire Station 9 well before his shift began.

Al Jensen quickly closed the trunk of his car when Adam drove into the parking lot. Nobody needed to see his private property, especially a bottle of vodka. He waited for Adam to get out of the car.

"You'll never prove arson on this one," he said.

"Is that so?" It was not the first thing that Adam wanted to hear, at least not from one of the arson investigators on the other shift. He tried to keep his sense of humor. "So I might as well go back home?"

Milk Market

"No way. It's my turn to go home, soon as I finish entering a report," Jensen grumbled.

They walked into the side door of the station together. Al sauntered back toward the arson office. Adam intentionally went in the other direction. He was not ready to hear why he would not be able to make a case for arson. Instead, he detoured around Engine 9, draped with fire coats and helmets, toward the noisy laughter coming from the kitchen.

Nines, as the station was called, had the familiar smell of drying hose, clean as detergent but mixed with smoke. There was a lingering odor of long extinguished fires, of history. Framed newspaper photographs, yellowed by time, lined walls and hallways. There were pictures of ice-covered firefighters battling flames in the night sky and hose lines that covered the street in a tangled mess. The tangled hose was referred to as spaghetti by firefighters old enough to remember the big fires.

As a rookie Adam had listened to endless stories. There was old Captain Weston, blown out of his boots by a backdraft, accounts of tragic loss of life in old hotel or apartment fires and the firefighters lost in a sudden collapse or explosion. There were tales about the ladies of the night who came by the fire stations and the other lonely souls who valued the friendship of firemen. There were stories about pranks and jokes that were played, and about the characters and drinking in the days when they lived and worked in the fire station for a week without a day off.

The photographs showed the bitter cold of long winter stands, pouring water into all night warehouse fires. They couldn't show the long hours of boredom followed by moments of terror in which a firefighter's strength and courage were tested.

Captain Bennett, Adam's father, was in some of the old photographs. Growing up, Adam had known little about his father except that he had a bad temper and he drank too much. Howard Bennett had been a stern parent at times. After Adam joined the department, he learned that his father had been an iron man. Captain Bennett had stayed on the front lines more than 40 years; so long he enjoyed only a few years of retirement before his death.

The old timers claimed the days of wooden ladders and iron men were gone. They had been replaced by iron ladders and wooden men, and of course, women. Young firefighters didn't take offense; they could only imagine how iron men entered burning buildings with nothing more than a mitten in their mouth to protect their lungs. Now firefighters carried a supply of fresh air in tanks on their backs. But even with that advantage, Adam knew it took courage and strength to enter a burning building, to put water on the seat of the fire and to rescue those who couldn't save themselves.

In the kitchen, two shifts of firefighters passed a blackened pot up and down a long table. Adam put his cup on the table and it was quickly filled. It was easy to see who was coming on duty and who was going home. After a 24-hour shift, those on the way home looked tired and disheveled. The rest were in their blue uniforms, clean-shaven and alert.

"Hey Bennett, did you know old man Hayward?" Dick Swenson had worked at Station 9 for most of his career.

"Sure, but he retired the year after I got on the job." Adam laughed. "I never had a chance to work with him."

"You heard the story though, right?" Swenson now had an audience.

Adam nodded. He knew what was coming.

"This old guy, Hayward," Swenson continued, "he'd put a row of raisins on the window sill. Then when a bunch of school kids came in with their teacher to see the fire station, he stood next to the window with a fly swatter. He'd slap a fly on the window, then pop a raisin into his mouth."

There was laughter around the table. A cup was spilled when the table rocked.

"Kids loved it, naturally." Swenson had his day. "No one knows how many of them tried it at home, you know, eating flies instead of raisins."

"The class always sent thank you notes the next day," Adam added. "They liked the fireman who ate flies."

Adam still enjoyed life in the fire station. Fourteen years had slipped by quickly. He had gone from rookie firefighter to seasoned arson investigator in the blink of an eye. The big fires he had worked in his early years were now part of his own history. There were experiences from those days that he shared with few others on the job. He remembered crawling blindly into heat and smoke, between a sagging floor and an uncertain ceiling, dragging his hose line, hoping to reach the seat of the fire before it chased him and his crew out of the building.

Struggles that had seemed epic at the time were fading into proud memories. He had started taking them for granted, but he knew that he had been brave. He had proven himself in the face of the orange devil time and again. Perhaps he had been more foolish than fearless, but he knew his father would not have thought so. Captain Bennett would have been proud.

A few more fire station stories went around the coffee table before conversation changed to fishing, sports, or the latest from the morning newspaper. Adam topped off his cup and walked back to the arson office. It would be easy to stay and talk, but he had to relieve his counterparts on the other shift. Whether Al and Tom believed arson was provable or not, he had to hear what they learned about DeLuca.

He walked past the pumper, as Engine 9 was called, to the back of the station. Their office had been a training classroom until it was remodeled to provide desk space and folding beds for the investigators. As usual the beds were folded down, but Tom and Al had slept very little during their tour of duty. They had been called several times during the night to investigate routine fires. Folding their blankets and sheets, they briefed Adam and Stewart about the night's fires and the work of the day before.

Tom looked tired as he quietly closed his locker. He was ready to go home. A firefighter in the old days, he had joined the arson division after being injured in a building collapse. His back troubled him after a busy 24 hours, and the rumors circulated constantly that he expected to retire soon. When asked about it, he was noncommittal, but Adam knew Tom was just putting in his time.

Al, his partner for years, lit a cigarette next to the open window. In a casual show of respect for the rule

Milk Market

against smoking in the fire station, he blew the smoke outside. "You'll never prove arson in this one," he repeated.

The state crime lab had found no evidence of an accelerant, the flammable liquid that could get a fire going quickly and fatally.

"Now, with no accelerant, unless you can find something, a motive, an ignition device, at least a suspect, you've got nothing. I mean squat." He flicked ashes into the nearby wastebasket.

"Did you find any prints on the smoke detectors?" Adam asked.

"Disabled smoke detectors!" Al declared. "You can find them in about half of the kitchens you see. And who knows who forced the back door? Or when it was done?"

Adam looked to Tom. "Good morning, Tom. Have a bad night?"

"Average." Tom yawned. "Looks like your fire victim doesn't have any relatives or friends."

"Really?" Stewart heard Tom's comment as he walked into the office. "Good morning, Tom."

Tom continued, "Maybe you guys can find out more about him. There's no criminal record, at least not under that name. The autopsy will give you fingerprints today. We put his name out on the FBI wire. Maybe something will turn up there."

"How about telephone records?" Adam was glad that Tom showed some interest. "There should be something there."

"We didn't get out to the house." Tom shifted in his chair and changed the subject. "How long do you suppose he lived there?"

"The neighbors said a few months." Adam expected to know a lot more by the end of the day.

"Maybe a relative will turn up today." Al spoke up, afraid of being left out.

"That's all you got?" Stewart was clearly discouraged.

"Went to his bank, got nothing there either," Al responded. "None of the officers at his bank could remember opening the account. The records showed an initial deposit of a few thousand dollars. He deposited four more times, brought his balance up to over $11,000 when he died."

"What kind of deposits? Payroll checks?" Stewart asked.

"Didn't find out."

"Did you ask?" Adam persisted.

"Adam, we had a bad day."

Adam had heard the excuse before, but he was grateful. They had done the basics and started the file. Other investigations and a training session had kept them busy. Adam knew that a long lunch was part of their day too. At least they had found the time to fax an inquiry to the Federal Aviation Agency to get details about DeLuca's license. Perhaps they would learn about his employment, former address, relatives, or something that would lead to the discovery of a motive for arson and murder.

"The autopsy is this morning, in case you want to be there." Tom spoke to Stewart while Adam looked through the file.

"No arson, no murder. I don't see any way to prove arson." Al was done with the case. "Unless you come up with something today, it would be a waste of time to keep this open."

Adam didn't want to show his irritation. It was too early to write off a big case. If the fire was set, the arsonist was guilty of murder. If the fire was an accident, then the death was an accident. The easy solution was to call the fire an accident and kick back. But Adam was angered by the idea that an arsonist, possibly a professional, could commit murder in his city with no chance of being caught.

"Thanks for your help." Adam was sincere. Even if Al and Tom did not want anything more to do with DeLuca, he might need their help again. They would be back tomorrow, and there might be something important that carried over to their shift.

In the past, everyone in the arson division would have been enthused about a case like DeLuca. Since criminal investigation had been turned over to the police department, morale had slipped lower and lower until some fire investigators just went through the motions. Adam and Stewart tried to work every case as if it was their own. The other investigators were not as dedicated. Still, with a case like this, everyone had to be involved. It could make up for days and months of boring routine.

The veteran investigators who had trained Adam would have done anything to solve an arson murder. They had known and respected his father, Captain Bennett, so they had taken his son under their wing, teaching him how to conduct interviews and how to gather evidence. They had taught him to trust his intuition and fire experience, the skills that could not always be learned from books. Adam tried to teach his partner, Stewart, the same things.

When they were alone, Adam and Stewart concentrated on the case file. There was no new information about the fire victim except the bank balance. Aside from that, there was only DeLuca's driver's license, auto registration and pilot's license. It was skimpy information.

First, they had to prove arson. As usual, there were no eyewitnesses. Without any solid physical evidence, they had to look for a motive. If there was a lover seeking revenge or maybe a business deal gone sour, they could sometimes trap a suspect into admitting guilt. In this case, until they learned more about the victim, there was no one to suspect.

There were few true facts. Interviews with the first firefighters at the scene and with the neighbor who had called 911 were consistent. The smoke detectors in the house were not working, and the back door had been opened by force. They had the photographs from the night of the fire showing the smoke detector covers hanging from the ceiling, disabled.

There was always the chance that Adam and Stewart had missed some detail in the dark on Sunday night. Back at the fire station they could test the smoke detectors and dust the covers for fingerprints. Today they intended to revisit the scene to look for evidence of an incendiary device, an effort the other shift should have made on Monday morning after the fire. They hoped that daylight would reveal something obvious.

Neighbors might be interviewed again to see if they could remember anything about the victim. It was unusual that there were no relatives or friends interested in the DeLuca death. Someone should have

Milk Market

come forward.

"Everybody has somebody, right?" Stu wondered.

"Maybe they just don't know yet," Adam speculated. "If we could find out more about the guy, maybe we could tell somebody he's dead."

"You know we could just file this one." Stewart was discouraged, influenced by the other shift.

"Yes, we could. But then the city could just mail out our paychecks. We would never have to leave home." He looked to see if Stu got his point.

"Why don't we just file a report on what we've got and let the boss tell us if he wants us to do more?"

"The boss wouldn't know a set fire if it was going on in his kneehole," Adam answered.

"What's a kneehole?" Stewart asked.

"Under your desk." Adam pointed.

"Well, no one is asking us to be heroes here, to break our asses for nothing. We've got to chase fires all day and night."

Adam could hear Al and Tom as if they had never gone home. "You're right. Almost no one gives a shit one-way or the other. Except for us. It's our job."

"All right, all right. We go for it. So what's our first move?" Stewart was a poor actor. His face turned red under his red hair.

Adam could see that the other shift had been convincing. This case could go nowhere. It might be a lot of work for nothing.

"Stewart, we'll make an arson investigator out of you yet."

"Right," Stewart said, sarcastically. "What's the next move?"

"There are a lot of things to check out before we

give up. Did DeLuca own or rent? Who did he buy the house from? There had to be a real estate agent who knew something about him. Let's see. Are there county records for the purchase of the house? There should be telephone records. And we haven't even talked to all the neighbors yet. Maybe someone was out walking the dog, saw something, or saw him come home. Anything!"

"In the meantime," Adam continued, "we're waiting for a fax from the FAA on the pilot's license. Then we make a trip to the coroner's for the autopsy report. Fingerprints, remember? See if the FBI's got anything on the guy. Who knows? Maybe DeLuca is an alias. Has he got a record? There has to be a lead somewhere. He bought his car somewhere."

"It's going to be a long day." Stewart started putting on his sport coat. "So let's get to work."

"Now you're talkin'." Adam could act too, but the job would be easier if their hearts were in it.

Adam was still enthusiastic about his job, and loved the department, even though it was run by a few political hacks. The only blessing was that arson investigation was technical. They had to be left alone to do their work, even though it annoyed the micromanagers. Adam liked the independence. He and Stu could move around the city as they wished as long as they could respond to investigate every fire.

Investigators tried to follow a routine each day, but accidents and suspicious fires came at random times. They could be called away by radio at any moment. There was always a fire somewhere in the city to be investigated. Even in the middle of the night it was busy in one neighborhood or another.

Milk Market

Fortunately, most of the fires could be easily explained. Most of them were accidents. Once the determination was made, there was little left to do but file a report. If there was a scorned lover or the possibility of insurance fraud, there was a lot more to do. Suspicious fires usually had to do with money or revenge.

This morning their first stop was downtown at fire department headquarters to deliver hard copies of the reports from the previous shift.

The medical examiner's office was only a few blocks away, and the autopsy was nearly done. Fingerprints had already been taken and sent to the FBI. The cause of death had been determined. It was asphyxiation from carbon monoxide, but the victim was also intoxicated. There would be more lab tests before a final report was issued. DeLuca's blood alcohol level was so high that he probably wouldn't have been able to save himself, even if the smoke and carbon monoxide had not impaired him. Adam wished they could find someone who had been drinking with him.

An Assistant Medical Examiner wanted to show them the body. While Stewart satisfied a morbid interest, Adam waited in the office.

"Our best bet now is for the prints to get us something from the feds," he told Stewart on the way to the car.

On the way to revisit the DeLuca house on Ridgedale, they were dispatched to a fire on the north side of the city. They established its cause and point of origin even before going in the house. An elderly woman had left food cooking on the stove while she went to work in the yard. The grease fire had gone unnoticed until it was too big to be put out by a neighbor's garden hose.

By the time they returned to Ridgedale, it was lunchtime. The cold fire ruins revealed no more than before and so they had made little progress on the case. Adam admitted there was a long way to go without enough time in the day. Stewart had stopped talking.

"Let's go see Owens after lunch. Maybe we can get some help with this." Adam had to try to keep Stu interested.

Deputy Inspector Owens ran the homicide squad from his office on the second floor of the courthouse. He knew something about every murder and murderer in the past 30 years. At times he was loud and obnoxious, but he knew his business and was highly regarded at police headquarters. As usual, his office was neat and clean. Owens was good at preventing the stacks of papers and files just outside his door from coming inside. He was an expert at delegating in his own department so he could deal with trouble from the fire department.

Adam knew they would have a hard time getting any help on the case, so he went to see Owens by himself and Stewart stayed near the coffee machine downstairs. Owens had already seen the preliminary report that emphasized the smoke detectors. Adam explained that they were battery operated and the batteries were still connected. If there had been false alarms, DeLuca would have removed the batteries to shut the detectors up. Instead, the covers were left hanging down.

"You don't have much here." The Deputy Inspector was a busy man, and beyond being polite. "You don't even know who the guy was."

"There are a lot of things to look at," Adam answered. "The back door was forced too. This was murder, so it will end up here anyway. We just need some help on it before it goes cold."

"Come back when you can show me the fire was set," Owens snorted.

It was the brush-off that Adam had feared.

"I'll let you know right away if we get a fingerprint I.D. for your victim, though." He handed Adam a crumb. "Check in with them downstairs."

The detectives downstairs made it just as clear. Adam and Stewart had more work to do. Prove it was arson, they advised over coffee in Styrofoam cups, and we can give you some help. It was too common to see disabled smoke detectors. It didn't mean a thing.

"You don't know anything about your victim." They echoed their boss. They repeated Owens' invitation to stay in touch, empty words that meant they were too busy to help.

Homicide wanted everything wrapped up in ribbons and bows. They would never waste their time on an accidental death just because the fire department thought it was murder. They would be happy to take the glory of the arrest and the conviction if arson would just do the legwork. Like everyone else in the city, they were understaffed. Uniformed cops on the street satisfied the voters and the politicians, but there were not enough detectives. Homicide had more than they could handle.

"Christ, Adam! Let's just hang it up." Stewart was

discouraged. "You said yourself, we needed the lab to find an accelerant."

"Let me know if you've got something better to do." Adam was irritated. "I thought this was our job. If you want, I'll drop you at the station so you can take a nap. It doesn't take two of us to do this."

"Don't get pissed," Stewart whined. "But you're the only one who gives a shit."

"That's not a first. I'm sorry buddy, but it's just the way we've got to do it."

Now more than ever, Adam was determined to put the case together. Even if he was the only investigator to believe it, this was a case of arson and murder. He would stick with it until there was no doubt that it was an accident. And that was too unlikely.

He had not enjoyed being sent out of police headquarters like a dumb schoolboy who forgot his homework. Adam knew about doing the homework. He had simply asked for help. More and more the case was looking like a private mission. That was fine. There was nothing to lose if he was wrong and if he was right they could all kiss his ass.

Stewart fell back into his quiet mood, staring straight ahead as they drove through town. At least the day was going by quickly. They were in and out of the car, checking leads, talking to people, finally returning to their office late in the afternoon. There was a fax from the FAA with an answer to the previous day's inquiry about DeLuca. There was nothing new.

Adam called homicide late in the afternoon. Anthony DeLuca had a clean record. His prints dated back to his military induction in Georgia. There were no arrests, no convictions, but he was a commercial pilot who made numerous trips to Mexico. Drug Enforcement maintained a file on him. Finally, there was a break in the case.

The report included the name of the DEA agent who was supposed to be familiar with the file. Adam wanted to talk directly with anyone who knew anything about the fire victim. The area code was from Chicago. Dialing the phone number late in the day, Adam was not surprised by several minutes of transfers and holds. But it was rare luck that he reached Agent Rich in his office. Finally, Adam was talking to someone who knew about the pilot.

DeLuca flew a business jet with passengers who had business in Mexico. He had been carefully scrutinized and was clean as far as DEA was concerned. He was not on their "A" list. But they were curious, "Let us know if you find anything on this guy."

"Well there's not going to be more to find. He died in a fire a few nights ago. Can I get a copy of your file on him?"

"Sure, it's not active, but I'll see what I can dig up." Rich seemed helpful.

Adam updated his notes. There was little to show for a day of work except that he had alienated his partner. That too, would pass, and the case would come together. It might take a few days or weeks, but he was convinced that he was working on a murder case. He put his head down on the desk for a moment to rest his eyes when Dick Swenson knocked on the door of the office.

"Adam, did you hear the 6 o'clock news?"

"No, is it already 6?" Adam yawned.

"All about your home town! Something's going on out in Riverton," he warned.

"Riverton?" His first thought was for Carol. Was she in an accident? Was she all right?

"There's a kid missing," Swenson said. "I didn't get it all. We just got in from a car fire."

Adam heard the full story on the 10 o'clock news. A 13-year-old boy had not come home the night before. His parents had spent the early evening calling his friends and looking everywhere. Finally they had called the local sheriff. Neighbors and friends searched through the night, along with on and off-duty Deputies. Then by 8 a.m. they had organized on a large scale to walk every street, road, yard and every inch of shoreline on both sides of the Crow River.

The search had intensified during the day. More volunteers, along with deputies from surrounding counties, were walking the woods and the river bottoms. They fanned out through the country adjacent to Riverton. Detectives were questioning everyone who might have seen something or someone. As the day went on, searchers and the family grew increasingly desperate, caught in a cycle of worry and hope.

The conventional suspicion was that the boy had been lost in the river. Over the years the Crow River had taken many swimmers, most of them children.

Divers were being called in to search the muddy water, but visibility was poor and the Sheriff's next plan was to begin a dragging operation. Interviewed on television, he said they had done this sad work before, pulling skids with hooks along the bottom of the river. It rarely had a happy ending.

Milk Market

Adam knew that Carol would want him to help with the search. She would expect him to volunteer when he came home in the morning, but he hoped they would have found the boy by then. At 10:30, after the evening news, he called her to say goodnight.

"Adam, I think the missing boy is one of the kids who was helping you work on your car yesterday!"

CHAPTER 4

"The sheriff's here!" A neighbor watching from the Andersons' front window sparked hope that Robin had been found. Bill Anderson went to the front door, anxious for word about his missing boy.

Sheriff Knowlton had turned his patrol car onto Homewood Lane. The street was nearly blocked by television trucks, their towers and satellite dishes broadcasting to every corner of the state. The sheriff climbed slowly from the car, looking the part of a country lawman. A crowd of news people pressed excitedly around. This would be great television.

Knowlton stood tall and gray-haired with tired eyes set back in an experienced face. He fingered the brim of his white Stetson as he spoke. Politely, but in his best political tones, he took command.

"Please understand what these people are going through and please back off a respectable distance." He cleared his throat. "Now, don't you know you're disrupting a nice quiet neighborhood here? If the

Andersons want to give an interview with anyone, I will let you know. If they don't care to, then leave them alone. Even if they choose not to talk to you, I will give you everything I have. I will be holding a press conference back in my office at 10 o'clock this morning. Let these folks have some privacy. Think about what they are going through and think about your own families."

His appeal had little effect. Questions were shouted at the sheriff, microphones reached out and cameras followed him to the front door of the house. He had promised a news conference just to see if he could get them away from Bill and Marilyn's house.

"Leave these folks alone!" he turned to say. "There are some new developments you will hear about at 10 o'clock."

The reporters assumed this was a great career event for Sheriff Knowlton. After all, public officials usually begged for media attention. They couldn't know that Knowlton was an exception. His career had gone well without media circuses like this. Of course, he stood for election in the fall. A little publicity never hurt, but all that was far from his heart and mind. None of that really mattered now. He would be as polite as he could to the press, but he had a boy to find.

He was a parent too, and in times like these he did not feel like a tough old cop. It was not as if the Andersons were strangers from the city. He knew both of their families. He was there when Bill and Marilyn got married, and he was even at the house when Marilyn brought Robin home from the hospital. "Let's see, that was 13 years ago." His own son had been about twelve at the time.

Inside, the family knew by the look on his face as he plodded up the front sidewalk that he didn't have good news. He didn't need to say the words. So far, the search had been futile. Strangely, the news left them some hope. There could be only one discovery worse than finding nothing. At least there was still the possibility of a miracle.

"I just want you to know, again, that we're doing everything we can do," Knowlton sadly reassured them as he came in the door. "Just about everyone in town is out looking for your boy. I asked for the National Guard, but they're having trouble gettin' together, 'cause most of them are already out searching."

He was extending the search to a five-mile radius around town. After that they would go as far as they had to go. There was nothing else to do but encourage the Andersons and provide some hope. He had to tell them their boy would be found, but in his heart he felt only despair.

A persistent belief held that the boy had been abducted. And other wild tales circulated, some suggesting his parents were somehow responsible for his disappearance, he was simply a runaway or drugs were involved. A few even heard that aliens had landed nearby and taken him away. Some mean-spirited people said the family had abused the boy while maintaining a respectable front. These were whispered rumors that parents would never hear.

The search would have created enough interest by itself, but the abduction rumor brought intense media coverage. There were newspaper reporters, of course,

Milk Market

and four television stations flooded Riverton with satellite trucks and teams of photojournalists. Cameras recorded every event, every public prayer and almost every coffee shop conversation that included talk about the boy. Many residents were stopped for interviews on Main Street.

To the assembled media it was better than a high profile murder trial. To Robin's parents it was the worst of all possible nightmares. Other parents kept their children from the streets and playgrounds, protecting them and cherishing them in their homes. Sheriff Knowlton couldn't blame them.

He was happy to see that friends and family of Bill and Marilyn had gathered in support. Everyone tried to be encouraging and hopeful, bringing up better possibilities to take the place of their most dire thoughts. Some even tried to be cheerful, until they lapsed into the quiet that filled the house. Except for Robin's sisters, ages 4 and 7, no one in the family had been able to sleep since his disappearance. There were only short restless naps interrupted by the arrival of new rumors.

One of the sheriff's suspicions, after a lifetime in Riverton, was the possibility that the Crow River had taken another child, this time a boy from a family he knew well. For the time being, he would not tell them that a diving team from the city was going to do an underwater search of the millpond and the river below the dam.

The sheriff's other suspicion was worse, involving the unthinkable: abduction, sexual assault and murder. His investigators were interviewing a farmer who thought he saw a boy matching Robin's description as late as Monday afternoon. They were following up on every lead. Until there was better evidence, he was not going to tell the Andersons that a witness claimed to have seen a boy get into a car down on the county road. He didn't intend to tell them they were going to interview a suspect who might have kidnapped their son.

The sheriff endured another encounter with the press before he escaped from Homewood Lane. He drove to the river and parked by the old mill site. Stepping over the rusty railroad tracks near the river's edge, he stared into the turmoil of waves and eddies at the foot of the dam. The water recirculated constantly, in a whirlpool that did not allow the escape of snags of driftwood or anything caught in it, not even a body. He stared into its brown roiling mystery and wondered if it held the body of a boy.

There was a van parked at the water's edge. Huddled around were divers in black rubber wet suits arranging their equipment, getting ready to search. He worked his way down the steep bank past a few spectators who greeted him and a television crew setting up their camera. They had followed his car.

"Hello boys. I'm Sheriff Knowlton. Thanks for coming out to help us."

"Hello sheriff. We aren't going to be able to help you much, though. Over there by the dam the water is too fast. The rest of it is just too brown. You can't see your hand in front of your face down there. Same as above the dam in the millpond. Just too murky."

"You goin' to give it a try?" He knew they would.

"We'll sure go in and take a look, but don't expect too much." The divers looked at each other.

Milk Market

"Anything else we can do?" Knowlton asked.

"Nothing we know of, except dragging it. You know, the old-fashioned way."

The sheriff did indeed know about dragging. He hoped to avoid it by using the divers. It was bad business either way, fishing for something he didn't want to find. Using his cell phone away from the news people, he notified his chief deputy to organize a dragging operation.

Chief Deputy Holmes was in charge of the search command post. Although friends and neighbors had initially looked for Robin in the obvious places, Knowlton and his deputies had started over from scratch.

The command post had been set up in the conference room to make sure nothing was missed. Holmes coordinated the effort, carefully marking progress on a large pull-down county map. He had to keep track of volunteers who came to help, local policemen and deputies from nearby towns and counties, volunteer firefighters and more friends and neighbors than he could keep track of in all the excitement. The Crow County Saddle Club was mounted, sweeping roadsides inch by inch. When the National Guard unit arrived, Holmes met with the troop commander to assign search zones for a hundred soldiers.

At first, the official search had concentrated on the river valley, away from the openness of the prairie and farmlands. It began in the city park at the river's edge, then followed the paths north and south that led to the favorite haunts of town boys. And when they met no success, they continued along the country roadsides, overgrown with weeds. Finally, faced with the hopelessness of searching thousands of acres of cropland, they began resolutely to walk each field.

The FBI routinely assigned two agents. The child might have been taken across state lines in violation of federal law. And because it was a high profile case they were more than anxious to help. With the county investigators, they interviewed Robin's friends. In particular, they questioned two boys who had been with him earlier in the day, Billy Mayes and Tim Nelson. The boys had split up in the late afternoon.

Out in the field, the searchers found nothing, and authorities were losing hope. It had been almost 40 hours. Nothing.

"Disappeared into thin air," said a searcher to a television camera.

* * *

Bill Anderson moved slowly as if in pain, a young man grown suddenly old. He had been strong and self-assured until a few hours ago, when reasonable hope was lost. In place of his heart there was a desperate, silent scream that gripped his chest like a vise. In 40 years of life he had never been so helpless. His only son was missing.

He had never realized how big the world was and how easily it could swallow up a little boy. It was already Wednesday morning. Robin had been gone since late Monday afternoon. He had been down in the river bottoms with Billy Mayes and some other boys, but they had not come back to town together. Billy reassured him that they all left the river at the same time, and he was sure Robin wouldn't have gone back to swim alone.

As much as Bill wanted to simply walk out the door and find his boy, he could not search by himself. Where would he start? Neighbors and friends had come to help, going out in groups to look in every obvious place. Now that Sheriff Knowlton had taken charge of the search, hundreds of volunteers were out there too, lining up in rows to hike through fields and along the river bottoms. As they searched, they looked at the Crow River, suspicious of its dark brown menace.

Bill had to trust that everything possible was being done to find Robin, but he was desperate for a new idea. They had called the players on Robin's baseball team and every student in his class, hoping that he would be found in a safe place. But no one had seen him. Bill searched for another answer. He needed some new hope that would explain what had happened and how Robin could be found. His boy could be fast asleep somewhere safe, or playing a bad joke. These things happened; sometimes they made the evening news. Bill wanted all of this to be a mistake. Yet he knew it was not.

His wife sat in her chair at the dining room table surrounded by worried friends and close relatives. Marilyn managed to control her tears somehow, but she couldn't hide the sobs that came from deep within her every time she tried to speak. Each sob was like another knife in her husband's heart. She knew this, but she couldn't stop or explain, so she just stopped talking.

Instead she stared at the oak tabletop, tracing its

wooden grain with her finger, idly trying to make sense of the random pattern of light and dark, spaces empty and full, lines that made no more sense than the evil that had taken her only son.

The stricken parents were struggling to deny their own morbid imaginations. True, he was 13 years old, but he was their baby. Growing up, changing month by month, Robin still needed them every day. No adolescent voice change, no teenage rebelliousness, no growing tall, no peach fuzz on the chin changed that feeling.

They couldn't accept the theory that the river had claimed him. Robin was an excellent swimmer, and he knew the river. They tried to avoid the darkest thoughts. Why would someone take a little boy? For what purpose?

By maintaining a facade of ignorance, by asking righteous questions, above all by trying to remain positive, they could avoid thinking about the terror of a sexual assault. Putting it out of their minds, they just hoped the search parties combing the woods and fields would not find their son, that instead he would be found alive somewhere, anxious to come home.

When the time came, Bill and Marilyn walked out the front door and stood together on their front step, nervous under the harsh lights of the television cameras. They never wanted or expected to be at the center of this attention. Nearby, their pastor stood in support. He had been with them all day.

Bill stood just behind Marilyn, hand on her shoulder for reassurance, while she wiped away tears and tried to be brave. Through her sobs he tried to be the strong one, for her sake and for the girls. He held

Milk Market

back his tears too, trying not to yield to a secret panic that made him want to run out into the street to find his boy.

They couldn't believe this had happened. They lived in a small town where children were safe. There was no crime. Most people didn't even lock their doors at night. Many city people thought small towns were a curse, where everyone knew what everyone else was doing and where there was no privacy. To those who lived in them, that was a blessing. Without big city anonymity, people were responsible for their actions and their children, and with that came trust.

But the interstate highway had brought the city to small towns like Riverton. Now anyone with a car could be miles away in just a few minutes. Perhaps now they understood that there were no more small towns.

Their statement before the cameras was simple, expressing hope and love. Even forgiveness. Pastor John had quietly helped them with the words at the dining room table. They were not going to answer questions. They just wanted their son back, at any price. As his wife read the statement, Bill Anderson felt a wave of nausea. He closed his eyes and swallowed hard. "My Robin! Oh God! When will this end?"

* * *

"Sheriff, we're ready at HQ," came the radio call.

Knowlton had just climbed back into the car to return to his office. He and Holmes had agreed that the word "suspect" was not to be used on the air.

There were too many people with scanners listening to every word. The searchers, if they found anything, even a clue, were ordered to avoid talking on the radio.

"If you find anything, send a runner," the sheriff told them. He had learned how to avoid the television stampede.

Now what did they know about this suspect, really? He had been around for a couple of years, but that was nothing. Even most of the new folks in town had lived here longer than that. Many more were like the Andersons, lifelong residents he had known most of his life. "These new people," he wondered, "who really knows anything about them?"

Arriving at his office, Knowlton walked straight to the interrogation room. Sitting at the long table were Chief Deputy Holmes, two FBI agents and Bill Brooks, his chief investigator. Sitting alone on the other side of the table was a suspect, their only suspect, in the abduction of Robin Anderson.

CHAPTER 5

"Mr. Bennett, we would like to talk to you about what happened here the other day."

They had been waiting for him to get home from work. Even before Adam turned into the driveway, he noticed the Ford sedan parked in front of the house. There was a sheriff's cruiser parked on the other side of the garage.

Carol was on the porch talking with two plainclothes investigators. A uniformed deputy stood a few feet away playing with Mickey. Adam got out of the car quickly to make sure nothing was wrong.

"These people want to talk to you," she said, a hint of worry in her voice.

Adam ignored them until he greeted her with a hug. This was to be the start of their two days off together. She called it a weekend even though it came on Wednesday and Thursday.

"What can I do for you?" He asked the detectives.

"My name is Brooks, with the Crow County

Milk Market

sheriff's department. This is Detective Peterson and Deputy Heff." He cleared his throat. "Mr. Bennett, we would like to talk to you about what happened here the other day."

"What other day?" Adam didn't know Brooks, but he recognized the deputy. He had seen him around town.

"Some boys came by here Monday," Brooks began. "You know, I suppose, that one of the boys who spent some time here with you is missing?"

"I sure heard about a missing boy," Adam answered.

"His name is Robin Anderson."

"I didn't get any names." Adam tried to remember if he had ever heard either of the boys call the other by name. There had never been a formal introduction. He knew the nickname he had given his helper, Ace.

"We want to know what you know about it," Peterson declared, with emphasis on the "you."

"They left here about one or two in the afternoon, I guess," Adam replied. "Except for one of them. He stayed and helped me with a brake job. I drove him home later, sometime after five."

"It looks like the boy was abducted." The investigator named Peterson was abrupt.

"Is there evidence of that? How about the river? These kids spend half the summer in the river." Adam looked back at Brooks.

"I know. We are checking that out. But we have a witness who saw Robin getting into a car like yours." Brooks was almost apologetic.

"I dropped one of them off on the county road by Homewood Lane." Adam was trying to be helpful.

"At this point, we only want to talk to you," Brooks said. "We'd like to go over this in the sheriff's office."

"I don't see why that would be necessary. I just told you everything I know." He had not even had breakfast, and this was supposed to be a day off.

"We would like to get it all down for the record," Brooks responded.

"Am I suspected of something?" He knew that it sounded weak, but they couldn't really think he was involved with anything like the abduction of a boy. He was irritated. "There are a lot of cars that look like mine."

"Mr. Bennett, you have the right to remain silent..." Peterson was impatient.

"That is not necessary," Adam barked. "I'll go in and tell you what I know. I did not have anything to do with a missing kid."

Peterson continued with the rest of the Miranda statement then he said, "Do you understand your rights?"

"Of course," Adam snapped. He could see that Carol was upset.

He was not under arrest, but he was going to be interrogated as a suspect in the abduction of the boy he had befriended. If he were just providing some information, they would have asked him a few questions and left him standing in his driveway. He had no choice but to leave Carol alone on the porch and go with them, like a criminal, in the back seat of a police car.

Adam knew the truth. There was no evidence against him. Yet his experience told him that he should not treat this lightly. This was going to be a desperate investigation. There would be intense pressure to find the boy or someone who was responsible for taking him. Of course they would pursue every lead. He was the suspect because someone had seen him drop Ace off at the Homewood addition. Is that why they assumed that the boy was kidnapped? Perhaps he had simply run away from home. Maybe he had gone for a swim by himself and been lost in the river.

As much as anyone, he hoped the boy was not in danger. They had been friends for only part of an afternoon, but Ace was a good kid, friendly and eager to help. Adam would be relieved when the boy was found, for the boy's sake and now for his own.

Carol was standing in the kitchen door as the investigators drove away with her husband. Although it was unfair and embarrassing for now, the truth would soon come out. She was confident that this was a simple mistake. Adam would never do anything to harm a child. Still, she thought it was serious enough to call their attorney, John Chambers, the only lawyer they knew in Riverton. He had handled the purchase of the land and the farmhouse from Albert Johnson.

* * *

Adam had been in Crow County courthouse a few times to pay real estate taxes. It was a modern building, beautifully landscaped, with enough parking spaces for every car in the county. Offices and courtrooms were on the upper level. In the back, the lower level housed the law enforcement center. It held the sheriff's department, the jail and the county emergency communications room. An underground garage with automatic doors provided security for transferring prisoners and bringing in suspects for questioning.

Adam was ushered into the interrogation room. He expected the mistake to be cleared up quickly. He would soon be back home with Carol to begin enjoying their weekend in the middle of the week.

Brooks came into the room and reintroduced himself. He was nervous. "I need some routine information, just for the record."

The reason for delay was apparent when the sheriff himself arrived just a few minutes later. Adam had never seen Knowlton in person. The sheriff was an old-time lawman, still dressed in the uniform, even though he could have worn a suit and tie. Detective Peterson soon followed Knowlton into the room. Behind him were two unidentified men in dark suits.

The sheriff knew what he was going to say. He introduced himself and assured everyone that he was just an observer and that he would not be conducting the interview. Investigators on the case would ask the questions.

Sheriff Knowlton reminded everybody in the room that it was Wednesday morning. The boy had been gone since Monday afternoon, over forty hours. Imagine how the parents feel! He knew them personally. Of course they were distraught, worried to death. The rest of the community was worried and agitated because one of its children was missing. He would appreciate it if Adam gave the investigation as much cooperation as possible.

"Of course," Adam agreed.

Peterson asked him to recount the events of Monday afternoon. When Adam was finished Brooks laid out the evidence.

"We have a witness who saw a green foreign car pick up a boy who looked a lot like Robin Anderson on Homewood and County Road 7."

"Do I really need to tell you how many green foreign cars there are?" Adam responded.

"The other boy says you were the last adult they were with on Monday afternoon," Brooks continued. "He thinks you're a great guy, but you touched one of them on the leg."

"I can't believe this!" Adam was getting more impatient. "I'm at home, working on my car and these kids come in the yard. They helped me do a brake job, that's all!"

"I don't doubt what you say." The calming words came from one of the blue suits.

"Who are you?" Adam asked, unable to hide his anger.

"I'm Don Magee, special agent."

"What's the FBI doing in this? The state line is a hundred miles away."

"Well, we're not sure where we are going to find this youngster, so we're just here to help the local boys." Magee played to the sheriff and the investigators.

"I'd like to see you come in on arson cases this quick." Adam was really trying to keep his composure.

"Well if you think a Federal law has been violated in one of your cases, you can get help from the bureau or ATF. But let's get back to these boys who came to see you the other day."

Adam asked if he should talk to his attorney before they continued. The question only made them more suspicious. He understood their reaction.

"Mr. Bennett, you are a suspect," Magee said firmly, "unless you can account for your time Monday. You know you have the right to remain silent, you have..."

"They already gave me Miranda," Adam interrupted. "Are you arresting me too?"

"Not at this time. What's more important is that we find Robin Anderson. Can you tell us anything..."

"Mr. Bennett," Sheriff Knowlton made the plea. "Do you know where he is? I have to ask you, for the boy's sake and for his parent's sake. They are desperate!"

"I've told you everything I know," Adam answered, trying to be calm. "I wish I could tell you where he is."

He was embarrassed and angry. People who knew him would see him on television and in the papers, the only suspect in a horrible crime. He could imagine the talk in the fire stations. His mother would see it on the news and have to explain to her neighbors that her son would never do such a thing. And no one even knew for certain that a crime had been committed.

His friends wouldn't believe a word of it. There were others, he guessed, who would be happy to see that he was a suspect. Carol was the only one who mattered. Anyone else could think whatever they wanted to think. Adam knew he was innocent, and Carol knew it too. He just wanted to be back at home with her, away from all of this.

There was nothing more to tell them, but he would have to be careful. It was dangerous to submit to an investigation that had a foregone conclusion. In this case it appeared they were going to make the evidence fit the accused.

The investigators, Brooks and Peterson, went in and out of the room consulting with the FBI agents. When they played good cop, bad cop, Adam was amused.

"Sorry, cheap tricks will not work." He had to remind them that he too, was a criminal investigator.

Peterson, the younger detective, enjoyed playing bad cop when the FBI agents and his boss, the sheriff, was watching from the back of the room.

Adam's association with the two boys and his green foreign car, the BMW, made him their prime suspect. He could account for most of his time on Monday, but not completely. The minutes between dropping the boy near the entrance to Homewood and getting home for supper could not be explained. He had gone for a ride, testing his new brakes on the back roads.

"Anyone else with you when you went for this test drive?" Peterson already knew the answer.

"No."

"How long were you gone?"

"10 or 15 minutes," Adam guessed.

"So you just dropped the kid off without taking him all the way home?" the detective asked in disbelief.

"Right."

"Why wouldn't you take him all the way home?" Peterson snarled.

Milk Market

"He didn't want me to take him all the way home." Adam told the simple truth.

"Did you touch any of these kids?" Peterson stared intently into his eyes.

"No, no way." Adam sounded as positive as he could.

"Are you sure?" Peterson persisted.

Adam remembered that he had Ace help him put leverage on a wrench, trying to loosen a tight lug nut.

"You touched one of them on the leg. He was wearing shorts." Peterson was ready for the kill.

"He was helping me." Adam knew again that he sounded weak. He suddenly felt like throwing up, even though he had missed breakfast.

"Did you notice what they were wearing?" Peterson glanced back at the sheriff.

"They both had shorts on." Adam replied. "They had been swimming."

"Did you watch them when they were swimming?"

"No."

"But you've been down there. You know where they swim," Peterson stated.

"Sure, everybody does." Adam insisted.

"Everybody?"

Adam knew that he was not doing himself any good by cooperating. All of this could be used against him. He had said enough.

Peterson was not satisfied. This was a challenge. "So these kids must have looked pretty good. Like a dream come true. Tight little asses in their shorts! Hard bodies! Did you try to get one of them alone with you? Did you touch one of them?"

"You sound like a pervert to me. Where were you

on Monday?" Adam resented the prodding. "Why don't you ask those kids if I messed with them? I was working on my car for Christ sake!" He paused, and then said, "I'm not answering any more questions."

"That's enough boys, that's enough! Let's all calm down." Sheriff Knowlton now asserted himself. He was in charge.

There was a knock on the door and a young deputy announced that the attorney wanted to see his client. John Chamber's appearance was a surprise to Adam and the sheriff's investigators. The investigators gave each other knowing looks and left the room.

"Hello, Adam. What is going on here?" Chambers noticed the surprise in his client's face, so he explained, "Carol called me."

He listened patiently to Adam's story, paying particular attention to the line of questioning from the investigators. Adam had no alibi for the time that he had spent driving his car after delivering Ace to his street. They had repeatedly questioned him about that.

"Don't say anything, that's all I can tell you. You should know the routine Adam. You do this for a living. They'll have to release you. Suspicion is not enough to hold you, unless they have some evidence..."

"They say there's a witness who saw a kid get in a car like mine."

"Who's the witness?" Chambers asked.

"I don't know. A farmer in his field, I guess." Adam had not heard a name.

"They're going to need more than that, anyway. And they have to find Robin, one way or another." The attorney closed his briefcase.

Milk Market

"Well, they're wasting time on me. They should be dragging the river." Adam was tired and hungry. He wanted to go home.

"I'm sure they are doing that too. They always do." The attorney pushed his chair back and stood up. "Adam, there is one more thing. You'll need a criminal attorney. You know I don't handle this kind of case."

"Jesus, John, are you against me too?" Adam was feeling alone.

"No, I think they got the wrong suspect, but I can't help you on this."

"I didn't mess with any kid!" he insisted.

"That's not it! Adam, I'm definitely not a criminal defense attorney. It isn't even ethical for me to take a case I'm not qualified to handle. I'll help you get the right guy. Stevens! Stevens would be the best around here. I'll call him for you. In the meantime, you know the routine. Don't say anything to anyone."

Adam couldn't tell whether he had been brushed off or honestly referred to another attorney. He knew that Chambers' practice was divorce and civil cases. With a sick feeling, Adam wondered what it would cost just to talk to Stevens. He might wake from the nightmare any minute, the sooner the better, but he would probably be poorer. His only choice was to trust Chambers.

Back in the interrogation room, the investigators asked a few more questions. With Chambers sitting at the table, they were cautious. "Did anyone else see you with these kids?"

"Albert Johnson was there for a while. And his kid, Bobby," Adam said.

"The slow one?" Brooks took an interest.

"Yeah, Bobby. He was playing ball with the kids and the dog."

"I know the one." Brooks looked at the others. "About 18, can't get a driver's license. Old Albert lets him drive around the farm once in a while."

"Does he have a green BMW?" Peterson asked.

"No, I guess not." Brooks admitted.

Adam started thinking about Bobby. The boy was considered harmless, but what if he had taken an interest in one of the boys in the yard that day. Everybody knew that Bobby drove around the countryside all alone without his Dad. At least there was someone else to suspect, if they ever determined there had been a crime.

Although the investigators were convinced that Adam was their best suspect, they could not hold him. Without better evidence, just as Chambers said, he had to be released.

After the attorney left the room with their suspect, Brooks turned to Peterson, "Do you think he'll take off?"

"Where's he gonna go? He's got a job and a pregnant wife. If he runs, he's guilty as hell." Peterson was sure of himself.

"That doesn't find us the kid."

"I think you can quit worrying about the kid." Peterson was realistic.

"Fuck you!" Brooks snapped.

"I'm sorry, but you know as well as I do, it isn't looking too good." Peterson softened. "Sometimes they're just never found."

Brooks nodded. He was realistic too.

"Anyway, we got this guy. He'll stay put or run. If he stays put we've got our work cut out for us, if he bolts, he's guilty!"

* * *

Adam walked out of the courthouse with John Chambers. Both were surprised at the crowd of reporters and television cameras lined up at the jail entrance. When they reached the steps they were surrounded by the mob. Some of the shouted questions were simple. Others were just rude.

"Why did you do it?" The horde followed them to Chambers' car.

"No comment. My client has no comment."

Adam refused to try to hide his face as the cameras recorded the scenes that would appear on the 6 p.m. and 10 p.m. television news, and in the newspaper the next morning.

There were long shadows outside. It was still sunny, but the better part of the day had passed quickly during his first experience as a criminal suspect. He had not looked at his own wristwatch.

"Thanks for driving me home, John." At least Adam was spared the additional embarrassment of riding like a prisoner in the back of a squad car.

"No problem," Chambers replied. "I'm sorry you're in this mess."

There were cars and television trucks parked along the road in front of the farmhouse. Crews were set to watch and televise anything that happened at the Bennett home. The attorney stopped at the end of the driveway to tell the reporters that there would be a statement in a few minutes, but only if they promised to stay off of the Bennett property.

Carol was waiting for them in the kitchen. "What's going on?" she asked.

"They think I did it." Adam hated to tell her that he was a suspect.

"Did what? You didn't do anything!" She wrapped her arms around him.

"They think he was abducted, and I am their suspect."

"What? I can't believe this." Carol started to cry.

"I can't believe it either. I didn't do anything wrong." Adam felt his heart start to break as the tears streamed down her cheeks. They could accuse him of anything, but he wouldn't allow them to make his wife cry. Yet he could only try to console her by holding her close and wiping away her tears.

"I just can't believe this. They will figure it out, I know they will," she cried.

Chambers assured her that everything would be all right. The truth would come out. "And I'll try to chase those TV cameras away."

"It's so unfair," she said. "We were just being nice to a kid. Can't people even relate anymore? One of the reasons we moved into the country was because people are not totally paranoid out here. Apparently they are!"

"This is someone's kid. We would be paranoid too, you know that." Adam tried to calm her.

"I know, but that doesn't help," she frowned and wiped away her own tears.

"I don't know where these guys get off." Chambers was peering through the kitchen window at the line of

Milk Market 75

cars and television trucks along the county road. "They're like vultures out there!"

After leaving Adam and Carol at the back door, Chambers drove to the end of the driveway and got out of his car. Immediately surrounded by cameras and television lights, he cleared his throat and in his courtroom voice addressed the reporters and television news photographers.

"My client denies having anything to do with this crime, if indeed a crime has even been committed. He is himself a hard-working criminal investigator. He hopes that foolish effort expended in trying to prove that he, an innocent man, is guilty, will not prevent investigators from pursuing other leads to find the child, and if a crime has been committed, to arrest the offender and save the child before it is too late."

He continued, "In the meantime, considering the sensitive condition of his wife, who is eight months along, we request that reporters and television cameras stay at least one mile away from his home. Failing that, we intend to file trespass charges against any members of the media who step onto Mr. and Mrs. Bennett's property. Thank you."

He got back in his car and drove away without answering questions.

Adam and Carol watched from the kitchen, hiding behind the curtains. They could hardly hear what Chambers had to say before he drove away, but some of the trucks backed out of their driveway and turned around. They didn't leave.

"Before you came back they called from Perkins." Carol was dejected. She had tried to avoid giving Adam more bad news. "They don't want me to come to work until this is cleared up."

"Well, you weren't scheduled to work again until Saturday. Everything will be fine by then." Adam tried to reassure her.

"Don't worry," Chambers had told them, "you didn't do anything wrong. The truth will come out."

At first it was comforting to hear the words, but then Adam realized how easy it was for the attorney to tell him not to worry. Chambers didn't have a pregnant wife to protect. Lawyers could afford to just wait and see what the investigation turned up.

Adam had to face the hard fact that in spite of his innocence, this could turn out to be even worse. Carol and the baby would have to be protected. He hoped her emotional state would not affect her health. She could go to Green Bay to stay with her parents until the baby came. He promised himself to sell her on the idea, for her sake and for the baby, and for his own peace of mind.

The next few hours were like a bad dream. Adam and Carol wandered around the house with nothing to do, afraid to step out onto the porch. The phone rang constantly.

If not a reporter asking for an interview, it was a deranged and anonymous caller threatening to burn them out or worse. There were some obscene calls. Reporters knocked on their door or called on the telephone requesting interviews with either Adam or Carol. Some tried to be friendly, but most were abrasive, as if they were due a press conference. They had satellite trucks and a deadline. Unconcerned with guilt or innocence, their job was to make pictures and stories out of an abduction and lurid suspicion.

Carol soon learned to leave the telephone off the hook.

They couldn't bear to watch the 6 p.m. news. The missing boy had been the lead story even before Adam was a suspect. Every parent in Riverton would be hearing news and rumors. The entire community thought Adam had taken one of their children. "Have they checked the river?" Carol wondered.

"I don't know," he answered. "I just know they are wasting time on me. If the kid has been kidnapped, they should be trying to find him. At least they should be dragging the river."

Adam felt worse for Ace than he did for himself. He was sure of his own innocence. The teenager, on the other hand, was either dead or in deep trouble. Adam could imagine how horrible it was for the boy's parents, yet he couldn't even express his sympathy to them. If people believed he was guilty, any attempt to tell them he cared about the boy would be treated with contempt.

At dusk they decided not to turn on the lights. They tried to avoid being seen in a window as if there were snipers outside ready to shoot at them. This was what had become of their day off. There had been no plans, but neither had expected it to end like this, under siege. Instead of indulging in a shopping trip and having lunch together, they were prisoners in their own home.

Hiding at the corner of the kitchen window, Carol watched the lights of the cars and vans in front of their house. Even if the press didn't intend to stay the night, it looked as if they had been joined by a traffic jam of sightseers driving slowly by. Suddenly, life in the country was not friendly. Just a day ago, their lives had been simple and serene. All that they loved and enjoyed had been turned upside down, inside out. They took refuge together in the dark living room before going to bed.

"Do you want to watch the 10 o'clock news?" Carol asked, exhausted.

"You know what they will be saying. I don't want to see or hear it. I just need some sleep." Adam had slept little for two nights. Now, there was a nervous hole in the pit of his stomach and a cloud in his head. He went to bed but he couldn't sleep.

CHAPTER 6

Ron Wells finally caught a break. Sort of. After six months of searching, he had found Tony DeLuca. Unfortunately, DeLuca was dead, and that was a problem.

"I suppose," Wells muttered to himself, "he won't want to answer any questions."

He had rushed to the airport as soon as he heard Deluca had been located. Official Business Priority put him in the first available coach seat. Now he couldn't even remember which airline he was flying. Not that he was particular. So many flights were overbooked, he was just happy to get a seat on a morning flight. With a little luck, he would be in Minneapolis before lunch.

DeLuca was not going anywhere, but there were other reasons to hurry. Wells was running out of time. He had to find out what the local authorities knew about the pilot. Success or just another stonewall, one way or the other, this was his last chance. It was his best and only bet. Anthony DeLuca had been impossible to track while alive. Now that he was dead, he could be investigated.

"Welcome to the Twin Cities. Thank you for flying Delta. It has been our pleasure to serve you...please remain seated until..."

He didn't have the patience to stay seated. As soon as the 727 stopped moving, he stood up and pulled a small bag out of the overhead compartment, only to wait in line as passengers slowly exited.

"Thank you for flying with us. Have a nice day."

At least he didn't need to wait for luggage. The small overnight case had everything he needed for a few more days. Away from the arrival gate, the crowd thinned. Walking quickly, he followed the signs to the car rental counters. In just over 20 minutes he was driving away from the airport and checking into the nearby Holiday Inn.

"How long will you be staying with us, sir?" the desk clerk asked. She seemed relieved when he handed her the federal agency credit card.

"Just tonight, if all goes well, but maybe tomorrow too. Just have to see." He didn't expect to spend much time in the room or around the motel. How much he would sleep tonight or tomorrow night depended on whether there were more answers than questions about DeLuca.

The room had a full-length mirror. He threw his bag on the bed and took stock of himself. His dark skin hid the fact that he had not shaved in two days, but the midnight blue suit looked as if it had been slept in, which it had. He had been back in his apartment in Arlington just long enough on Sunday to pack clean shirts and underwear. After three days in

Milk Market

Atlanta, the bag that had been so carefully packed was now a mess, clean and dirty mixed together.

"Today is Thursday," he said to the black face in the mirror. "Let me see, where am I? There better be a laundry or they're not going to like me very much here in Minneapolis."

He thought about changing shirts before going down to police headquarters. The locals wouldn't be looking at his shirt, not after they saw his skin. There was no use in trying to impress them. If he were lucky, they would have the time and inclination to help. Usually his homeland security identification got him past any bad first impressions. For his part, there were more important things to worry about than making an impression.

The telephone book in the nightstand was his starting point. It was easier to make some contacts by phone from the room than to call from his cell phone. He jotted down a few phone numbers, and then studied the metropolitan area map. The map was a quick lesson in local geography. It was a trick he had learned to get his bearings and find his way around a strange town. He could get the lay of the land and, this time, an idea of how to get to the city courthouse without asking anyone for directions.

There was still time to see Chief Inspector Owens before lunch. The head of the homicide unit was a little short over the phone. He intended to be out of his office precisely by noon.

By 11:15 a.m. Wells was on the downtown freeway, grateful that everyone else seemed to be late for an appointment too. Driving north from the airport, traffic moved too quickly for anyone to enjoy a view of the city skyline. He didn't get lost. A few minutes after leaving the freeway he was circling the courthouse looking for a place to park. He drove into the "Police Only" lot, intentionally acting like he was supposed to be there. The plain-looking rental car helped. On the dashboard he placed a crumpled sheet of paper that had been folded up in his coat pocket:

Official Business-Homeland Security Department Immigration and Customs Enforcement

On the second floor, Captain Owens came out to meet him. Satisfied that Wells would not interfere with his lunch hour, he relaxed and offered his hand. First he had a question. "Are you going to tell us how to reach this DeLuca's family?"

"I wish I could, but I know less about him than you do."

"So what does the ICE care about his guy? Is he an illegal alien?" Owens parked himself on the edge of a nearby desk.

"I've got him as a suspect in a smuggling operation, but he has been invisible for at least six months. Probably longer," Wells admitted.

"You mean to tell me with all the federal agencies and resources you couldn't locate one little wop?"

Wells ignored the smart taunt. "He was a commercial pilot, so I had his last address from the FAA. He had to take a flight physical every year, but he just disappeared in between."

"What about the drug enforcement agency? Sounds like this is their kind of case," Owens suggested.

"That is where I got him in the first place," Wells countered. "Just the name."

"He's not going to tell you anything now. So you

Milk Market

don't know anything about family either?"

"Nothing." Wells shook his head. "I looked at just about every DeLuca in the country. And there are quite a few of them."

"Well, we've got no one interested in claiming him. No next of kin, no friends, nobody." The inspector was ready to finish the conversation.

"Just my luck," Wells responded. "Anyway, I need to get all that you folks have on him to see if it goes anywhere. I hope I can find out that he was working with someone who can still answer questions."

"Do you think this guy was connected?" Owens would take an interest if the feds thought DeLuca was a hit man.

"I don't think so. This stuff would be too ugly for the Mafia. But you never know."

"Now what could be that ugly?" The inspector was curious.

"I'll get back to you on that." It was Wells' turn to be evasive, a payback for the wop remark.

"Good luck." Owens shrugged. If he was not going to get something juicy, he had better things to do. "How did you find out he was dead?"

"The FBI computer pulled it up. I had a permanent inquiry over there."

"They got that from us, through arson," Owens said. "Anyway, you got the wrong department. Fire handles arson until it's a homicide. They are trying to prove it was arson and murder instead of just an accident. If they can make that case for us, of course we'll start a murder investigation."

"Thanks for your help. Just show me the way."

Owens ordered a clerk to guide him to the fire

Milk Market

department offices on the other side of the building. From the doorway he had a suggestion, "The guy you want over there is Bennett. He's their best man."

"Thanks!"

Wells had been able to keep the lid on his investigation one more time. It was hard to avoid giving it away. He needed witnesses and victims to prove a case, to prosecute a crime so evil it had to be stopped. Until he had proof, his investigation was top secret. It was so secret it didn't even exist unless he was right. His supervisor and the department head had made it clear. There were politicians, particularly those who hung their hat on family values, who would tear the agency apart if they found out why he was looking for DeLuca. If the media found out, they would have a field day and heads would roll.

He had begged for this special assignment because he was sure he could make the case. His own supervisor, sticking his neck out uncharacteristically, was at risk for supporting the project. Travel expenses were carefully scrutinized every month. The investigation was not in the budget and wouldn't be budgeted at all next year. The fiscal year ended in the fall. After that dollars were going to be more important than preventing terrible crimes. It was his fault. He had promised that there were crimes being committed. So far he had not been able to prove it, no matter how hard he tried.

In between answering calls, the fire department receptionist tried to contact the on-duty arson investigators. She sensed his impatience.

"They work on a 24-hour shift, just like the firefighters. They are out on calls a lot of the time," she apologized, "but usually I can get them on their cell phone."

"All right, how can I find them?" Wells wondered if he was going to get a bureaucratic runaround instead of the answers he needed. Right now he needed results, something he could bring back to his own agency and the State Department.

The receptionist drew a simple map with directions to Fire Station 9. "They are in and out of there all day, but someone should be able to help you."

This was his last hope. When DeLuca's name turned up, he was certain he had found the lead he needed. Then DeLuca disappeared from the face of the earth. He had tried everything he could think of to track him down. Gaining access to every government database had been useless. If he was alive, he was not paying Social Security or income taxes. He had no criminal record, at least under the given name. DeLuca had a commercial pilot's license, but the address listed by the FAA brought Wells to a vacant apartment in Atlanta without a forwarding address at the local post office.

A week and a half in Atlanta trying to locate Rainbow Aviation Charters had been a waste of time. The firm was listed as DeLuca's employer. They were not in the Atlanta phone book. It was just bad luck that Atlanta had three major airports and several smaller fields. There were hundreds of places to hide an air charter business. Rainbow was not to be found without weeks of legwork or some dumb luck.

DeLuca himself had to burn up in his bedroom to be found. Thank goodness for dumb luck. Wells had been notified when the name turned up on the FBI database. Last night he found a message at his Atlanta motel to call one of the agency secretaries.

"I'm supposed to let you know that a Mr. Anthony DeLuca died in a fire at his home in Minneapolis." If there was sarcasm in the message, the secretary was not transmitting. There was no hint of emotion in her voice. She could have said, "You are looking in the wrong place, stupid. Mr. DeLuca was living in his own home in a city a thousand miles away from Atlanta."

DeLuca could have been a victim of foul play. It sounded like the Minneapolis arson investigators were coming from that angle. Still, maybe Investigator Bennett was an over zealous arson guy so bored that he saw crime everywhere.

No matter, it was still the best shot. If DeLuca had been murdered, a homicide investigation would reveal something. Wells could use anything that would tell him where to go next. There had to be a lead after half a year of facing brick walls. No one, not even DeLuca, lived in a vacuum. There had to be friends or business associates who knew what he was doing, or even what he was not doing. If he was involved in crime, his friends might be hard to find, or just gone.

Wherever it ended, Wells might be too late. If he didn't bring something solid back to the agency this time, he would be reassigned. His investigation would be abandoned.

At Fire Station 9 a uniformed firefighter answered the door. The arson investigators were out of their office. The station captain tried to reach their car phone without success. He offered to take a message. Wells instead asked for Investigator Bennett.

"Sorry sir, I believe today is his day off."

"Can I have his phone number?" Wells pleaded.

"It's long-distance. He lives out of town." The captain explained that they were not permitted to release a telephone number to a stranger.

Wells tried to control himself. He presented his Immigration and Customs Enforcement badge and patiently explained he was working on a case involving a fatal fire that Bennett was investigating. It was important that he exchange information with their investigator. Reluctantly, it was agreed that he could see Adam Bennett's address and telephone number.

"He should be working tomorrow. If you are here in the morning, they work on writing reports until about 9 a.m." They were still trying to be helpful when a plain blue Ford backed into the station. "Here's the arson car. Maybe these investigators can give you what you need."

Al Jensen and Tom Vogel had started walking back to the office when Wells intercepted them. They looked him over and asked a few questions. He had to offer his identification and explain again what he was doing. It seemed to spark their interest. They walked him back to their office and offered their notes on the DeLuca case.

"Not much here," Wells commented as he looked at the record.

"Bennett and his partner are working this one pretty hard," Jensen responded. "I'm sure they have more notes than this. They will be here in the morning."

"I'm on a short leash, supposed to be on a jet back to D.C. in the morning. Think I can get him at home?"

"Sure, but he's in a little trouble himself. He might be preoccupied." Tom looked at Jensen.

"If he gives me half an hour, that would help." Wells was puzzled. "What kind of trouble?"

"Some problem with a missing boy. He's been questioned about it," Jensen answered.

"You're kidding, right?" Wells could not believe what he had heard.

"I wouldn't kid you. Here's his card. I'll write his address and phone number on the back. Good luck."

"Thanks, I appreciate the help." Wells had been delayed long enough. He had to talk to Bennett. But there was something about a missing kid? That was impossible!

After he left the arson office he sat in the fire station parking lot and tried again and again to call Adam Bennett. Each call resulted in a busy signal. He was not going to wait until morning. If he couldn't talk to Bennett on the telephone, he would find his house and knock on his door.

It was early afternoon when he found his way out of town on the interstate. The village of Riverton was only 40 miles away. At least driving there gave him something to do. Unless Bennett had some answers for him, waiting around would only be a waste of time. And wasting time just guaranteed reassignment to some routine job in the agency. He'd have failed in his mission.

Otherwise, some monotonous relief might not be bad. How about a nice routine life with a wife and kids at home? A decent job that was not too stressful and a fishing boat in the driveway, or even a cabin up north in the woods. A regular job and busy weekends at the cabin. A family at home that cared whether you lived or died. He tried to imagine what it would be like.

The unstructured life of a special agent had delivered the final blow to his marriage. Judy, his ex-wife, and their daughter, Charleen, lived in North Carolina near his former in-laws. It had been difficult enough for them when he was in the Air Force, off on training missions, then seven months in Kuwait, but when he retired to take a job with INS, their patience ran out.

Immigration had seemed like a nice quiet way to make a living, until he began traveling from one hot spot to another. Southern California, of course, and any place where employers were less interested in the national origin of the employee than in cheap labor. There were alien roundups, deportation flights and legal actions. Time and again he had to testify in cases thousands of miles from home.

Then by accident he discovered that smuggling human beings could be a two-way street. Other countries were not as concerned about immigration as the United States. For a price, some foreign officials were happy to look the other way if someone was brought from the States. He had found enough evidence to support an investigation. A confidential arrangement between Homeland, Justice and the State departments gave him the freedom of a special assignment.

Day by day it became more important to be right, to show the department and his family and everyone else that there were terrible crimes that had to be exposed. This investigation was the most important thing he had ever done.

But it was the last straw for their marriage. She wanted him to choose between his career and their life together. Then other problems turned up in counseling, issues that he had never even considered or known about. Their marriage might not have been saved anyway.

The worst part for him was missing Charleen. Just 11, she was growing up fast without him. There were few enough opportunities to share her life. Now he was shut out even when he found the time. Visits were clumsy and uncomfortable. The important things went unsaid, except at the last minute when he told his daughter how much he loved and missed her. He felt so low afterwards that it was hard to return. Someday, perhaps when she was in high school or college, he would spend the time to get to know her and teach her not to hate him.

Here he was, all alone, on a special project trying to protect families. The bitter irony was that he had given up the very thing he was fighting to save. Night after night he returned to a motel room for a lonely night of television, jealous of those who had normal lives, those who had the things he did not. Could he ever expect to become the family man his wife had wanted? Right now he had a job to do. After that he would take some time and find his way.

Work had always been in the way: flying combat missions in the Air Force or finding illegal aliens for the INS. Now he was on a mission of his own, on his way to an obscure midwestern town with combat damage and low on fuel.

There was a bright side. At least he was not trying

Milk Market

to make his way through a January blizzard. It was pretty country, rich farmland with patches of oak woods between the corn and bean fields. The weather was nice, not hot, and the countryside was green.

It looked like it was going to be a good year for farmers and everyone else in Minnesota. In between farms there were towns with warehouses and factories and endless rows of new homes. Such prosperity seemed odd in a place where the winter weather was so harsh. The prairie soil was rich, but the growing season was interrupted by months of freezing temperatures and blizzards. Yet people had survived without slaves to help work the land and had passed these rich farms on to the generations that could feed the world given half a chance.

Leaving the freeway at the Riverton exit, Wells stopped for a late lunch. The Perkins near the freeway was noisy with gossip about the disappearance of a local boy. A television crew in the next booth was happy to fill in the blanks. There was a search going on for a missing teenager. Local authorities were dragging the river for a body and combing every field and woodlot. The National Guard had been called out to help in the search.

Wild rumors, encouraged by news reports, were running through the town. The boy had been kidnapped, according to a witness, and an arson cop from the city was the only suspect. There were raw nerves in Riverton. Fearful parents were keeping their children at home.

Wells shook his head in amazement. At the fire station they had said that Bennett was in trouble. The poor bastard was as good as convicted if the people in the restaurant were going to be on the jury.

"What have I walked into here?" he muttered. "There is no way this can be happening to me! Just what I need, something else in my way!"

Wells knew better than to get into the middle of such a storm without a visit to local police. They would be busy looking for the child. That was understood. If the local cops didn't want him meeting with their suspect, he wanted to know about it in advance. He knew he was right when he saw the television trucks parked along the drive to the Crow County Courthouse.

He found the sheriff's office downstairs, in the back of the building. Following a short wait in reception, he met Chief Deputy Holmes.

"I've got some business with Adam Bennett about an arson case," he said as he showed his ID badge.

"What can we do for you?" Holmes asked politely.

"Courtesy call, I just want to make sure I am not stepping on any toes out here, going out to see Bennett. I guess he's your suspect in an abduction case?"

"Yes he is." The Chief Deputy was not offering any additional information.

"The only suspect?" Wells wondered.

"I can't tell you that."

"I understand. And you haven't found this boy you're looking for?"

"Not yet, still searching." Holmes' reply was short.

"This is Thursday. He's been gone how long?" Wells knew he had already asked too many questions.

"Late Monday." Holmes stood up to finish the conversation.

"Too bad. What makes you think he is still in the area?" Wells asked.

"Tell us where else to look."

"Anyway, I appreciate your help." There was more that Wells wanted to know. What did they have on Bennett? Had it occurred to them that the kid might be long gone out of their jurisdiction?

He followed directions to the Bennett place. It was not hard to find. There were more television trucks parked along the road in the middle of the countryside. It was easy to understand why Bennett was not answering his phone. Under a media siege, he might be too distracted to worry about DeLuca. Wells drove by without stopping. He decided he wanted to know a little more about Adam Bennett before he stopped to talk.

* * *

In the millpond above the Riverton dam and in the roiling brown waters below it, the sheriff's water patrol made the last few drags. They had trolled their triple grappling hooks back and forth through the water for nearly two days. It was past dinnertime and hopeless.

"If he's in there, he'll turn up later," the searchers claimed.

They were tired. They knew that a body does not often stay underwater. Unless it was hooked on a snag, it would float up somewhere, usually far downstream. Many of them could remember the names of drowning victims whose bodies had surfaced days or weeks after they were missed. Others were encouraged by their failure to find Robin Anderson. It meant that he could be somewhere else, and that he could still be found alive. It was a dim hope.

"At least we know," one of them said, "where he ain't."

Sheriff Knowlton stood on the riverbank. He had given the order to halt the dragging operation. For some reason, the television cameras showed up. Knowlton was getting comfortable with his role as spokesperson for the search. He knew the voters of the county were listening and watching for news of the investigation.

"Sheriff, why don't you use divers instead of dragging?" There was always a reporter who had not paid attention.

"That water is too muddy, son. The divers tell me they wouldn't be able to see a damn thing down there. So we had to do it the old-fashioned way."

"Are you going to look farther downstream?" another asked. "Will you be dragging again tomorrow?"

"It's just over, that's all," the sheriff said. "This part of the search is over. I'm confident that the boy is not here. He could still be farther downriver. We just know he's not here."

In a brief moment, those who watched the evening news heard only "this part of the search is over. I'm confident that the boy is not here."

CHAPTER 7

For the first time in his life, Billy Mayes missed baseball practice. He told his mother he was too sick to go, complaining about a sore throat he didn't have. She looked into his throat and pretended to be sympathetic. It was unlike him to stay in the house for a whole day and watch television.

Billy was confused. He didn't know what to do or even how to feel. His best friend was missing, kidnapped by some pervert. Would Robin ever come back? He had been gone since Monday, three days ago. The tears in his mother's eyes upset Billy as they watched the Andersons on television.

"Those poor people!" she cried.

"If they catch the son of a bitch..." his father threatened.

"Three days! Do you think there's any hope?" she wondered.

It was strange to see Mr. and Mrs. Anderson on television. Robin's mom and dad were like other parents. Robin's mom always made lunch or an afternoon snack and tried to act cool. He stayed at their house for supper sometimes, just like Robin sometimes stayed at his. Once he had gone fishing at Clear Lake with Mr. Anderson and Robin.

Billy could not admit that he rode in Mr. Bennett's car. He was afraid of what his mom and dad would say and what people would think. If his parents found out he ever took a ride from a stranger, he would be in big trouble. His dad would kill him. His mom would cry. They would probably ground him forever. Even that wouldn't be as bad as the lectures he would get over and over again.

He was sure Mr. Bennett would never hurt anyone, but no one would believe him anyway. He was just a kid. Billy didn't know what to do about Mr. Bennett, so he did nothing.

He never wanted to play baseball again. If anyone found out he had been in the car with Mr. Bennett, they would call him a queer. It had been bad enough at practice on Wednesday. Tom, who used to be his friend, and another ninth-grader, had called him a "little faggot." Tom was just showing off. He was acting like a big man, but Billy was never going back to baseball or the park.

Detectives from the sheriff's office and the FBI questioned almost every kid in town, concentrating on half a dozen boys who had been swimming in the river with Billy and Robin. Men in gray suits came to talk to Billy and asked a bunch of embarrassing questions with his mother sitting right there.

"No, Robin would never swim anywhere near the falls," Billy said, knowing that three of them had done it only a few weeks ago.

She was shocked about skinny-dipping. They had asked if there were any adults that hung around down by the river when they were swimming. It was a dumb question because Billy had never seen anyone down there, and because if anyone could see them, they would never go swimming without bathing suits or at least underwear.

All of a sudden too many adults wanted to know what Billy and his friends did when they were down at the river. Everyone would be in trouble if their parents found out what they did away from home, how sometimes they hitched to the next town or how they got packs of cigarettes. What would happen if they found out who threw the park benches into the millpond?

He had to tell them about working on the car with Mr. Bennett. There was nothing wrong with that, they reassured him. No matter what they asked, Billy was not going to say he had been in the green BMW, that he had taken a ride with someone they thought was a kidnapper.

It was bad enough that everyone in town was afraid. The town park was deserted because children were nearly locked away in their homes. The other coaches wanted to cancel baseball for the rest of the week until Deputy Heff convinced everyone it would be safe to keep playing. Heff was the coach of the Yankees, Robin and Billy's team. He said it was better to keep kids together playing ball than to have them wandering around by themselves or shut in at home. And kids had to have something to do in the summer.

Heff knew older boys had teased Billy cruelly. It was more attention than the boy deserved. His best friend was missing, after all. When Billy missed baseball practice on Thursday, Heff came to his house.

"Billy wasn't feeling well today, that's why he wasn't at practice." Mrs. Mayes sent the deputy to the basement recreation room with a wink.

Billy was slumped in a big chair in front of the television set. "I'm sorry Heff, I'm too sick to practice."

"We missed you. We're going to need that bat on Saturday."

"Yeah, I know," Billy grumbled.

"You talked to the detectives about Robin, right?" The coach sat down across from his outfielder.

"Yeah."

"Have you got any ideas? I mean, about what happened to him?" he asked.

"No," Billy moaned. "But I know he's not in the river."

"Did you tell them that?"

"Yeah, I told them he wouldn't swim by the dam," the boy cried.

"Are you telling me that too?"

"Yeah. I mean, I'm not saying never, but we weren't anywhere near the dam on that day." Billy tried to sound positive.

"So, what do you think happened?"

"I don't know," he whined. "The last time I saw him was at Mr. Bennett's house. And I know Mr. Bennett wouldn't hurt a flea."

"How do you know that?"

"He's just a normal guy," Billy argued.

"All right, Billy. Thanks. I'll see you at the game on Saturday, Okay?"

"Yeah," he said, doubtfully. Billy was glad when the deputy went up the stairs.

* * *

Heff sat in his squad car, trying to get it all straight. He rubbed his fingers through the short crew cut that he had worn since boot camp at Pendleton. Life had been simple in the corps. As a military policeman, he never had to worry about a missing child. There were AWOLs every Monday morning, but they usually turned up within a day or two, broke, with a bad hangover.

Except for two hours at baseball practice, he had spent most of Thursday morning on the search. The sheriff had expanded it now to suspicious woodlots and river bottoms as far as 25 miles away. Even though it was miles from the Wisconsin border, the FBI was involved. If Robin had been taken across state lines it was a federal offense. Even if he were not, the FBI was there to help local authorities in a high-profile case.

Some early theories that Robin had run away were quickly discounted. It was just not that kind of home situation, and he was not that kind of boy. There was no custody issue, the motive in a lot of kidnappings. A few nut cases were still convinced it was a case of alien abduction, but most were convinced that either the river or Adam Bennett had taken the boy. There were no other suspects.

Dragging the river below the falls and dragging the millpond above the dam had produced nothing but lost public property. There was the chance that a body would turn up in a week or two. If the current snagged a victim on an underwater branch or rock, there might never be a body. These were the facts that Heff coldly analyzed until he remembered Robin's face at baseball, playing hard, running, cheering, just being a kid. If only the boy would just show up! If he would just walk into town with a story to tell! Even if it was bad story, everyone wished Robin would just come back.

Heff knew that kids still went swimming at the dam. Fear of getting caught was what made it exciting. He made it his mission to catch them at it, but he couldn't work 24 hours a day. There was no way to make them understand that the hydraulic action of the dam could suck a swimmer in and keep him under, turning over and over again with such power that even the strongest swimmer could not escape. It was worse in the early summer when the water was high, or after a few days of rain, but even now it was a hazard. After the last drowning, the town had raised a chain link fence around the dam and the boiling water below it. It only made it easier to swim there without being seen or getting caught.

It was hard for parents to believe that boys didn't fear danger. But a dare was an irresistible challenge. The thrill was in swimming as close to the boiling water as they could. They had less fear of the hydraulic action than of their parents finding out they were swimming near it.

To children in town, the possibility that Robin had

been abducted was just a story their parents heard on the evening news. Most of them knew little about what it meant to be kidnapped and molested. What they knew was limited to whispered rumors. It was better not to talk about it, a strategy that worked to hide their ignorance from their friends. Whatever it was certainly couldn't happen to them, so Robin's disappearance didn't seem real.

For their parents it was too real. They had been worried about the wrong things: drugs, gangs, dirty dancing, rap, suggestive videos and all the evils that came out from the city. No one had given much thought to kidnapping. Now Riverton parents were afraid and angry. If they let themselves think about it, they could imagine what had happened to Robin Anderson.

Heff understood their fears. He had coached most of the boys in baseball and basketball and he had a 4-year-old boy of his own. What would he do when it was his own kid? How would he feel? Parenting was always a risky business. You were responsible for your children's safety without being in control. The older they get, the less control you have over where they go and what they do.

None of that helped Bill and Marilyn Anderson. Heff had visited them twice since Monday trying to find the right thing to say. No one could feel as bad or be as worried as the Andersons, but the pain was real for Heff too. What more could he have done? He tried to keep the kids busy playing ball, and he tried to keep them away from the dam. But kids in Riverton had played along the river for a hundred years. He could remember being their age, stealing cigarettes and going down there with his buddies, smoking and talking big. Nothing had really changed.

On his afternoon shift, Heff made a point of stopping at Perkins for coffee. The waitress who served him raised her eyebrows when he asked for Carol Bennett. He learned that Carol had been laid off until the problem with her husband was settled. The restaurant was buzzing with speculation and gossip. There was a rumor that since Carol was pregnant, her husband had taken an interest in little boys. He was supposed to have confessed to the crime. Robin might still be found in the river, but that did not mean he hadn't been kidnapped first. Everyone wanted the deputy to hear their ideas, so Heff downed his coffee in a hurry and went back on patrol.

Later he stopped Bobby Johnson in Albert's truck. He knew the boy couldn't get a driver's license.

"Bobby?"

"Yes, sir." The boy was always polite.

"Why are you driving this truck on the county road?"

"My dad lets me drive the truck," he explained.

"But you know you are not supposed to be driving. You don't have a license."

"No, he says I don't have to when I drive on the farm," Bobby said brightly.

"You're not on the farm are you?" Heff tried to be stern.

"No, sir." Bobby looked down at his boots.

"You better go right home and tell Albert I told you not to drive on the county road."

Heff wondered about Bobby. Everyone thought he was harmless, but he was big and strong. Not even

Albert could know what his boy was thinking. If Robin had been kidnapped, it was as easy to suspect Bobby as Adam Bennett.

Heff didn't know Bennett very well, but he had heard Adam's side of the story when Detectives picked him up at his house. Maybe he hadn't been a cop long enough to be cynical, but felt he knew when a suspect was telling the truth and when he wasn't. He liked to think that he could tell the difference between a criminal and a speeder, between law-abiding citizens and crooks.

But there was too much public pressure in this case to go without a suspect. It was an election year. For the first time in years, the sheriff had serious challengers including a popular deputy. If Robin's disappearance involved a crime, it was the county's worst crime in a hundred years. Or ever. Knowlton needed to respond. There had to be an answer for the people and the press. The department and the sheriff looked better when there was a suspect.

Heff had tried to stay away from politics. He was too new in the department to take a position, and he was only interested in law enforcement. He was still grateful that Sheriff Knowlton had hired him, praising his experience in the Marine Corps as a military policeman. He wanted to be loyal to the sheriff, but election year politics had to explain why there was so much tunnel vision about Bennett.

He had noticed that the candidate seemed to enjoy every minute with the media, answering their questions, telling them more than they wanted to know sometimes and more than they should hear at others. They should never have learned about the mystery witness who said he had seen a car like Bennett's picking up a kid that looked like Robin. That was all the press and the voters needed to convict Bennett. The identity of the witness was still a secret. Those in the department who knew were not letting it out.

Around suppertime Heff found an excuse to stop by headquarters. He walked back to Sheriff Knowlton's office and knocked on the half-open door.

"Sheriff, can I talk to you for a minute? Can I talk to you about this case?"

"Sure Dalton, what's up?" The sheriff pushed back from his desk.

"I've talked to these kids, I mean, after the investigators."

"You're their baseball coach, right?"

"I think this is the wrong guy." Heff took a deep breath. "We're wasting our time while some asshole is getting away."

"Who?" The sheriff looked surprised.

"I don't know, but these kids don't think Adam Bennett is our man. We're putting everything in trying to prove it was him, instead of following other leads."

"Heff, don't worry, we're following up every lead that we get."

"Good, I hope so. And I just can't stop thinking about the dam."

"We've done all the dragging we're going to do." He wondered if his deputy knew he had ordered an end to the dragging operation.

"I know that, but you know there are snags under there. A body can stay under for a long time." Heff knew what everyone else knew.

Milk Market

"Do you know this guy? Bennett?" The sheriff took a different approach.

"Just his wife, she works at Perkins," he answered.

"I've seen her in there. Cute, pregnant girl. Do you know anything about her husband?"

"Nothing, but these kids are pretty sure of themselves."

"Yeah, Heff, but kids can be pretty naive." Knowlton had heard it before. "And that's what these degenerates count on. Let's just let the FBI handle this, they've got the experience. We've never had this before. Thank God!"

"I just wanted to tell you that the kids think we're wasting time trying to get anything on this guy."

"Heff, look at this. This guy admits driving the kid home, dropping Robin off a few blocks away from his house. Then he goes for a long drive by himself. The kid never shows up at home, but we got a witness who sees the car and sees the kid get into the car."

"But that doesn't add up. Why would he stop somewhere, Robin gets out of the car then back in? Something is not right." The deputy shook his head.

"Well it adds up for me. This asshole looks guilty as hell, all we have to do is prove it or get him to admit it. Just leave it to the FBI, OK? First we have to find Robin, and I can't feel very hopeful now. It's been three days."

"Sheriff, I've caught some of these kids trying to hitchhike to St. Cloud before. Robin might have done something stupid."

"He's not the kind of kid who runs away from home."

"I don't mean that, but what if he sticks his thumb

out...somebody picks him up, and we're wasting time with Bennett."

"Heff, don't worry. We're going to let the FBI kind of walk us through this."

Heff was not satisfied. The rest of his shift was quiet, a few traffic stops and a domestic at the Rivertowne Motel. At 11 p.m. he drove home slowly. There were some things about Robin's disappearance he didn't understand.

From his driveway he could hear the phone ringing in the house. He wondered who would be calling so late. As he closed the car door, he could hear Crystal just inside answering the call. She opened the screen door with the phone still in her hand.

"Dalton! Quick! Billy Mayes is missing!" she shouted.

"Jesus!" His heart sank.

He should have known when Billy missed baseball practice that something unusual was bothering the boy. Billy had always been dependable, but he had been close to Robin Anderson. Maybe he was taking it harder than anyone imagined, or he knew something that he couldn't tell. He might have been threatened. Heff knew now, too late, that he should have stayed with Billy for a while. There were questions he should have asked to find out if Billy was holding back. He had been more interested in protecting the boy than in finding the truth.

He quickly drove his squad car back to the Mayes' house. The neighbors had started to gather in support. Some had already left in their cars to drive every street and county road. Fortunately, the press, which still haunted the town, had not been informed. Then again, they might be needed to help find Billy.

Sheriff Knowlton arrived five minutes later. He learned that the boy had spent most of the day by himself in the basement family room, watching television, unwilling to talk to anyone. The basement window screen had been unlatched from the inside. It looked like Billy crawled out then replaced the screen.

"Here we go again, Heff." The sheriff looked him in the eye.

"I'll find him," Deputy Heff promised. "Don't worry I'll find him."

CHAPTER 8

It was going to be one of those doorway confrontations. On the evening news, the suspect would be seen opening his front door slightly as the reporter asked an inflammatory question. No other television crew had tried it after the lawyer warned them about trespassing. If it worked, KQTV would win the 10 p.m. news battle on Thursday night. If it was good enough, they could reuse the footage over and over again until the case was settled.

Adam didn't see them walking boldly up the driveway, but when they suddenly appeared on the porch, he flashed over. His frustration found a target.

Before the photographer could back away, the door flew open. He and his camera were thrown backwards into the driveway. The reporter, shaken but bold, tried to ask his prepared questions. He and his fistful of notes followed the photographer to the ground. After they picked themselves up, they cursed and began to back down the driveway. While the reporter brushed himself off, the photographer tried to see if his $30,000 camera had been damaged.

"Get the fuck off my property!" Adam screamed.

"Mr. Bennett..."

"Get the fuck out of here!" He threatened to throw them all the way down the driveway.

"That's assault..." They could see they were going to lose the argument for the time being, so they skulked back toward the county road to the cheers of the rest of the television crews, who had perfect videotape of the incident.

Carol stood in the doorway, speechless. She had never seen Adam so angry, and she had never known him to be violent.

The anger he had kept inside for two days was finally vented. He had become increasingly irritated at the television trucks camped at the end of their driveway. There was no good reason for the media to lay siege to their home. He didn't deserve to be a suspect. If the Anderson boy had been abducted, they should be trying to track down the kidnapper. The media should be turning the country upside down to find the boy, instead of harassing Adam and his wife.

In a few short days they had watched their dream slip away. They couldn't take a walk in the yard or even sit on the front porch. The cameras came out as soon as a door opened, so they stayed in the house.

At 5 p.m. Carol should have been asking Adam what to cook for supper, or he should have been offering to take her to one of the few restaurants in Riverton. Dinnertime came and went because they were not following a normal schedule. He looked through the kitchen cupboards and the freezer with little appetite, too angry and exhausted to have a meal.

The circumstances of the case were simple, yet he couldn't see any way to help himself. Adam's claim of innocence meant nothing because denials were expected from a suspect in a terrible crime. The sheriff's department and the FBI were convinced of his guilt, so information that did not fit their case was simply ignored. It was his word against circumstantial evidence that was enough to ruin a reputation, to make enemies of friends and to draw television reporters like flies. In the meantime, the search for the missing boy went on without success.

It was easy now, a few days too late, to wish he had paid more attention to the boys who had come to their house. At the time, Adam had been too busy to remember their names, if he had ever heard them. It would have been better to kick them off the property than to make friends. He wished at least that he had taken the boy to the door of his home instead of dropping him off a few blocks away on the road. He was guilty of letting the kid out of his sight before he was safely at home.

He had told the investigators to look in the river. Yet he didn't really think that Ace would have gone back to the river.

For now, Adam and Carol were trapped in their own house. He worried more about the stress on his wife and baby than about himself. They needed peace and quiet, but when Carol tried putting the telephone back on the hook, it rang constantly. In between obscene threats were requests from reporters for interviews.

Just after 6 p.m. several of the television trucks

drove away. There had been bright lights while reporters read their news in front of the home of the suspected child abductor. It was a relief to see them go until they imagined what had been said to millions of people watching the evening news.

Carol finally fell asleep in the early evening. Exhausted, Adam tried to sleep on the sofa to leave her undisturbed in bed. Wednesday and Thursday were supposed to be his days of rest.

Just when Adam dozed off, there was a loud knock on the kitchen door. He jumped up quickly when he heard Carol calling from the bedroom. She needed her sleep. He knew he should keep his cool, but he was tired of the reporters and cameras and obscene callers. And he was afraid. There were fools who believed everything they heard who might try to take justice into their own hands.

Looking out through the lace curtains on the kitchen door, Adam was ready to throw another reporter or cameraman off the property. His anger was rising again. He would demand consideration for his wife, who was not guilty of anything except being eight months pregnant and being very tired. He had been too patient so far.

"Yeah?" he snarled.

The anxious figure at the door tried to jump back out of the way, but Adam was too quick with a push on the door that knocked the visitor off the porch onto his back in the grass.

"Get the hell off my property."

"Mr. Bennett, I am not a reporter!" Backing away to save himself was a short black man. The well-worn suit and crooked tie could belong to a reporter, but he did not have the look of a shark desperate for a story.

Adam, still angry, didn't intend to let the stranger stand before he threw him off the property.

"Adam! What are you doing?" Carol had come from the bedroom in her robe. She looked around to see if the stranger was alone. "Let him up!"

"What do you want?" Adam growled.

"Mr. Bennett, my name is Ron Wells. I think you are innocent. I'm not a reporter."

"Not interested, thanks." Adam moved back to the edge of the porch.

"I need...I want to talk to you about your arson investigation."

"What?" The words came from far away. Arson investigation? Adam hadn't thought about it.

"I want to talk about a fatality at a fire you are investigating." Wells was standing now but keeping his distance from the porch.

"Jesus, I can't believe this." Adam didn't know whether to laugh or be angry.

"I'm sorry, I know this is a bad time," Wells explained. "But there might be a connection between these cases. I mean between this abduction and your investigation."

Adam's mind raced. He was the only connection. What was the angle here? What was this stranger's angle? As an investigator, he was trained to be suspicious. Now he was just skeptical and short tempered. "You're full of...."

"No, I'm serious." The visitor knew he was being inspected and judged by someone who knew how to read witnesses and suspects.

"Adam, who is it?" Carol was still at the door.

"I can't believe this nightmare. Carol, this guy thinks...What do you think?"

"Can I come up?" Wells stepped up onto the porch without waiting for an answer.

"Come in." Carol opened the door.

"I know this is a bad time," he repeated. "I've been following this. Let me explain. I think there could be a connection between this abduction and the case you're working."

"What's this got to do with DeLuca?"

"Just let me explain. It's just possible there is a connection. Maybe a long shot, but a chance."

Adam recognized a New York accent, but a little subdued, maybe Jersey or somewhere else in the East. It made him more suspicious.

"I've been tracking some missing children," Wells said. "Listen, some of this is really bad. I don't want to upset either of you, I mean any more than you are, but we may be able to help each other."

"Please sit down." Carol was still polite.

They sat at the kitchen table.

"What's the name again?" she asked.

"Ron Wells." He laid his identification card on the table.

"I don't get it. Do you know where this kid is?" Adam read the card, "Homeland Security Department, Immigration and Customs Enforcement." He pushed the card over to Carol.

"No, but maybe, but I'm pretty sure you're not the guy they should be looking at. From what I hear, you don't profile for it."

"Tell me something I don't know. What would Immigration have to do with this?" Adam asked.

"I don't want to waste your time. This is bad stuff. If you'd rather not hear..." he turned to Carol. He didn't want to upset a pregnant woman.

"Why don't we talk tomorrow?" Adam wanted Carol to get some sleep.

"I'm all right." She was still groggy. "Should I make some coffee? All I have is decaf."

"This is a long story." Then he added hastily, "But I'll try to keep it short."

They could tell he was choosing his words carefully. Yet he was in a hurry to say all that he had to say, anxious to make his case before Adam threw him out of the house as easily as he had thrown him from the porch.

"DeLuca was just a name. A guy from another agency gave it to me, an undercover drug enforcement agent I know. That's all I had to get me chasing all over the country. Then his name comes up on the FBI wire. I go to your police department, they send me to the fire department, and they send me to the arson division. They tell me you are the lead on DeLuca. So here I am."

"Keep going. Are you saying DeLuca was an illegal alien?" Adam was curious, but more interested in seeing how Wells could make a connection to a missing boy in Riverton. He could see that Wells was nervous and short of breath, a man who had too much to explain in a short time.

"No, this case is different. I actually don't know whether he was illegal or not, but that's not what this is about." Wells finally began to relax.

"How could it have anything to do with the crap I'm going through here?"

"I think DeLuca abducted and transported children. Maybe for disputed custody issues, at least originally, maybe for something worse. All right...probably worse."

"If this kid was abducted, DeLuca was dead before it happened," Adam stated.

"I know, I know. But he couldn't work alone. If DeLuca was murdered, he must have crossed someone. That's why I need anything you've got: associates, relatives, anyone. He had to be doing business with someone."

"Why can't this just wait until I get back to work?" Adam looked at Carol. They were very tired.

"Listen, there are bad people in this world." He ignored Adam long enough to finish his story. "Some of them are rich. They own a country or part of one. You know, a jungle, a desert, an island. They are free to indulge themselves in any way they want, and some of them are pedophiles."

"What are you trying to say?" Adam asked.

"This is bad, maybe you don't want to hear this." He looked toward Carol.

"Tell us," she ordered.

"Okay!" He cleared his throat, "I'm trying to...I'm trying to trace a white slavery operation that deals children, American children."

He waited for them to understand the horror of what he was saying. "I know this sounds bad, but there's a market for children. I couldn't believe it myself at first, but it's true. And there are plenty of people greedy enough to supply the market."

"That's awful." Carol turned away from the table. "I can't believe this."

"I know it seems unbelievable. But there is evidence."

"Why haven't we heard about this before? My God!" Adam and Carol, already living a nightmare, were repulsed by the possibility that what they were hearing was true. Yet they could no longer believe things they took for granted a few days before, so they neither believed nor doubted what was being said at their kitchen table. This travel-weary black man might believe in alien abduction for all they knew. It would not surprise them if he did. Normally Adam would be sending the bizarre visitor on his way, but these were not normal times, and Adam was no longer angry. He was just tired.

"The reason you have not heard about this is because it's a hot potato. If the public hears about this before we can prove it and arrest someone, parents are going to riot. Think about it! They are going to want to know why nothings been done."

"Well, why hasn't something been done?" Carol asked with as much indignation as she could gather.

"I have to name victims and arrest criminals first." Wells looked to Adam for support. "Then the public can find out. My assignment is to build a rock-solid case. Until I can do that, this is a confidential investigation. I am sticking my neck out to tell you!"

"If this is true, what's it got to do with this boy that's missing? Do you think he is a victim of this...operation?" Carol wondered.

"I'll get to that."

"And what's this got to do with my arson murder case?" Adam wanted to know.

"I start with nothing until I get the name, DeLuca.

I'm looking under rocks and can't find him anywhere. He turns up dead. Now I'm dead in the water again. I'm stuck. If I have to go through channels, wait for the medical examiner about the autopsy, I'm screwed for days. And I'm in a hurry. You already have a head start. You're the man on the case. So here I am."

"You've got that much right!" Adam assured him.

"I didn't expect you to be famous. Still, maybe we can help each other."

"How could this help me? Unless you think the Anderson kid is part of this? DeLuca couldn't have had anything to do with it. He was dead the day before this kid disappeared."

"Right, but DeLuca didn't work by himself. I think he was a middleman."

"Even if he was a middleman, I'm telling you he was already dead when this kid disappeared," Adam insisted.

"Just tell me, was it an accident or murder?"

Adam was not supposed to divulge details of a current case, not even with a government agent. But he had little to lose at this point. But why would ICE be interested? And was Wells really an ICE agent? It occurred to him that there were enough desperate reporters camped down the road who would do anything to get inside their house. They would say or print anything. He looked for a hidden camera.

"Homicide. The back door was forced and the smoke detectors were disabled. There were a few other things. The basement door was left open, and there was probably an accelerant used. We're waiting for lab results." Adam lied about the accelerant.

"How about suicide?"

"Suicide by arson?" Adam laughed. "That's a good one. DeLuca was loaded. Blood alcohol was almost point two. I'm not supposed to tell you all this. There was no note, and it was too elaborate for suicide." He laughed again. "Suicide? Now that was a stupid question."

"Do you have any leads?" Wells continued without embarrassment.

"The cops do the homicide investigation." He lied again. The cops would only do an investigation if he proved arson. "How does any of this help me? This town has me tried and convicted for something I couldn't do."

"They want a body. Until they get one they've got nothing. It looks to me like they gave up dragging the river, so they don't have anything. Unless there's something I don't know? Do they know about your violent streak?" Wells turned to Carol as he talked. "All they've got on you is circumstantial, weak circumstantial. No body, no case. If they find the kid, and you didn't do it, you should be cleared on physical evidence. If they never find him you will always be the suspect."

He gave them time to think, and then asked Adam, "When do you work next?"

"Tomorrow, if I go at all. I should stay home to take care of my wife." He looked at Carol. "There are things we have to talk about."

"Help me with this, and you might help yourself. I'm at a dead end. And if the kid happens to be a victim of this slave trade, there's a chance we can find him and get him back. It's a long shot but... He's been gone since Monday, right?"

"I guess so."

"Today is Thursday so it's already been three days. Depending on how it works, he might be within a few hundred miles or a few thousand."

"I know there are parents who kidnap when they can't get custody, but this stuff sounds pretty far-fetched." Adam was in doubt.

"No, sticking you as a kidnapping suspect is far-fetched," Wells answered. "But my theory is they will not find a body because the kid is still alive. Just far away. That means you will be the suspect forever, even if you are never charged."

"Still, this is just your theory, right? You don't have any more than suspicion."

"I've got victims I can't account for, just like this one of yours. And I believe it is more than a coincidence if a kid disappears when DeLuca is in the area. But you are right. Everything I have is like the case against you, circumstantial at best. Help me fill in the blanks." Wells made his final plea.

They sat quietly for a while trying to understand. Troubled and confused by fatigue, they were faced with another confusing problem.

"How many children are you talking about?" Adam asked.

"I don't know how many. It might be a few dozen, the ones I am tracking. Or it might be more. What's the difference? It only takes one to mess up your life if it is your child. Imagine what it does to a family!"

Wells continued, "Here's what I don't understand! If your house catches on fire, the fire trucks come in a few minutes. But when somebody's baby is missing? They look around the house, they call up some neighbors, take a look down at the park. Maybe five or six hours later they call the police. Maybe they wait till morning. Now if their baby has been taken away, she's long gone. If something terrible has happened, some pervert has plenty of time to hide what he's done."

"Or," he lowered his voice, "or there is plenty of time to get out of the country."

Adam, in spite of his own troubles, could not help thinking about Ace. Even more than being accused of abducting him, it was painful to think of how the boy felt if he was alive and in trouble. He looked at Carol, who was unable to speak. Their terrible nightmare had suddenly become worse.

"I hope we can help each other," Wells pleaded. "I need to know what your investigation finds out about DeLuca. Most of all I need to find out who he worked with, maybe a pilot."

"No, DeLuca was a pilot himself." Adam knew little more about the man.

"I know that, but he had to have a partner, probably another pilot. Just about anything he could fly out of the country would need two pilots. Granted, they might not care about international air regulations. That's possible too. But I believe there could be at least two pilots."

"We've got nothing. Not even family." Adam shook his head.

"Did you find any money?" Wells knew there had to be money somewhere.

"About 11 grand in a bank account."

"That's good. Interesting. Neither the IRS nor Social Security knew about any income. Where did he

Milk Market

get that much money?"

"Before all this crap started, I had some things to look at," Adam assured him.

"You know, DeLuca worked with someone. This thing probably started with exporting disputed custody children or getting fugitives out of the country. Those things are hard to pull off on a commercial flight. Then someone found out there was another way to make money."

"It is still unbelievable." Adam rubbed his eyes.

"Maybe DeLuca didn't care for what it had become. Maybe he knew too much and wanted out. And maybe we will never know. But someone knows. We've got to find out who he was working with."

Wells wrote a phone number on the back of a business card and pushed it in front of Adam. "Please call me when you know something. I'm going to be snooping around the airport in the morning. I'm sorry to bother you with this now, but if your cops out here in the country don't have a better suspect than you, we should be working on this together."

He walked down the driveway to his car, leaving Adam and Carol in wonder and doubt. Wells seemed credible enough when he was sitting in front of them, but in his absence the kidnapping of Robin Anderson in the little town of Riverton did not seem to fit.

"I don't know what to think." Adam put his arms around his wife. "Or whether to believe a word of what this guy says."

"I don't want to think about it." Carol was disgusted.

They didn't watch the 10 p.m. news. It was too stressful to think about how Adam would be portrayed. In every city fire station and every home in Riverton he would be seen as a monster that lured children to his house. Child abuse was a sensation on the news, and Adam was now its focus around the country. His innocence was unimportant. Adam was the story, and he didn't want to see himself on the news.

Most of the newscasts featured a reporter standing in the Bennetts' driveway telling the world about the suspect in the disappearance of an innocent teenager. The little farmhouse was a perfect backdrop for the story. KQTV was the only station without footage of the suspect assaulting a television crew that approached his house. Its lead story included indignation over the attack on their reporter and photographer. Charges would be brought!

If Adam and Carol had watched the news they would have seen it all along with a picture of Robin Anderson. As far as they knew, Robin was Ace. He was missing and everyone blamed Adam.

For the second night, neither could sleep, so they talked long into the night. Carol claimed she was too tired to rest. Adam was worried about her and the baby. He was scheduled to work in the morning, but he was willing to use a sick day to stay with her.

"I think you should go stay with your folks until the baby is born, or until this thing is cleared up." He knew she wouldn't leave.

"No way," she cried. "I'm staying here with you. We're staying here with you."

"This is too hard on you and the baby," he insisted.

"I'm not leaving you alone with this." She was serious. "Just go to work in the morning. I am just going to sleep all day anyway. We need to get back to normal. Whatever that is! I will be all right, and maybe this ICE agent can help in some way."

After all, if the boy were found, all of this would go away as quickly as it had come. They knew Adam was innocent and trusted that everyone would eventually know the truth. Maybe there was a simple explanation. Perhaps the boy was asleep in someone's den, or gone out of town with a family friend without asking permission. These things happened all the time. Even better, maybe he would be found playing video games at an arcade in the city. He would come home when he ran out of quarters. Carol and Adam prayed for a miracle.

Until Robin was found, they decided to try to stay calm for their own sake and for the sake of their infant. If Adam went to work, he could forget about the boy for 24 hours. She would catch up on her sleep, then try to finish decorating the living room walls. He usually called from work at 10:30 p.m. At least that was their normal routine, so Carol promised to put the phone back on the hook the following night after the news.

Adam dozed fitfully, but merciful sleep didn't come. Instead he tossed and turned, half awake and half asleep, wondering what had happened to their lives. It had never occurred to him that an innocent person could be accused of a monstrous crime. He wanted to go to work and lose himself in the job. The DeLuca case was still there waiting to be proved.

CHAPTER 9

Just before dawn, Adam got up quietly. Afraid that he was keeping Carol awake, he took his clothes out into the hallway to get dressed. The hinges squeaked when he tried to close the bedroom door.

"It's too early. Can't you sleep?" she mumbled.

"I just didn't want to disturb you."

"You aren't disturbing me," she protested.

"I'm sorry. Go back to sleep," he whispered.

Wind-driven raindrops pelted the window over the kitchen sink. The spattering was the only sound in the house as he looked out into the half-light. Low clouds and patchy rain were sweeping across the prairie from the west.

It was Friday. Three long days had passed since Adam had become the suspect in Robin Anderson's disappearance. Waking up to the reality of it was a shock even though it had been on his mind throughout the night. He didn't know that every square yard of Crow County had been searched and the river had been dragged without a trace. The boy had not been found, dead or alive, and the widely held belief was that he had been abducted. Adam remained the only suspect.

He stood in front of the kitchen door staring out at the countryside that held a dark secret. Somewhere out there was an answer. There was a criminal, a victim or the truth that could save his life. He was a helpless victim himself. For now there was nothing he could do but wait for the truth and try to put the past few days behind him.

At least he had a new interest in the DeLuca case. There were more questions now to go with the unknowns about the fire and its victim. Perhaps Wells would be able to shed some light on DeLuca's background. It couldn't hurt to have a federal agent interested in the case. Any lead would help. In the end he would love to hand over a good case to homicide just to see the look on Owens' face.

Wells' impression from the fire department was that Adam was the only one in arson who was interested in the case. They had even referred to him as the lead investigator. Adam had not bothered to explain that there were no lead investigators. Everyone in the division was supposed to share the work equally. But if the others were not interested in solving the DeLuca mystery, he would pursue it by himself, perhaps with help from the U.S. Homeland Security Agency. If Wells could provide some help with the Riverton disappearance, so much the better. The connection still seemed unlikely.

His memory of the ICE agent's visit was like a dream. They were under enough stress before Wells came out of the dark with his unlikely theory. Adam was not sure that he would even listen to a similar story if it were repeated this morning. The tale was too strange. Still, he would be very interested if it helped the DeLuca case.

He picked at some cold cereal and reheated a cup of coffee in the microwave. It was too early to go to work. He sat impatiently in the half-dark kitchen waiting for 7 a.m. Finally he went to the bedroom, kissed his wife good-bye, and left the house earlier than usual.

Leaving the driveway in the rain, he was happy to see that the television trucks were gone. Nervously, he checked the rearview mirror to see if he was followed. He began to relax when he felt like another faceless commuter on his way to the city. The anonymity was a blessing.

At work he would lose the advantage. Everyone knew him, and they would all know that he was the suspect in the Riverton abduction. Everyone in the country knew by now. On the fire department, even without television and newspapers, the word would have spread with electronic speed.

Unfortunately, there was always embellishment. Perhaps he had already been tried and convicted in fire stations from one end of the city to the other. He was innocent, and he was not afraid to look anyone in the eye and say it. He dreaded that he would soon find out who among those on the department were his friends and who were not. But friends or not, he had to face them.

At Station 9, Adam took a deep breath before he opened the door from the parking lot. It seemed oddly quiet inside. There was none of the usual loud chatter or banging of gear being changed or checked on the fire rig. Perhaps it was too early.

The building slowly came to life as he put his own boots and coat into the arson car. A door slammed. Gear clattered to the floor somewhere. There was a burst of laughter from the locker room. Three firefighters stood near the back of the engine discussing the night's work. As he walked into the kitchen to get a cup of coffee, he tried not to show that he was watching everyone closely for reactions. There were the usual morning greetings. Were they being too polite, or was he being too sensitive? No one was talking about him or about the abduction, at least not in his presence.

Stewart came into the kitchen while he was pouring coffee. They greeted each other casually. On the way to his locker Stewart patted him lightly on the back. Adam recognized the gesture of support. The hardest part was over. It was Stu who would spend the day with him, in the office and in the car.

Back in the arson office, the night's reports were being entered. Al and Tom, arguing over a detail, crowded each other to view the computer screen.

"Hey, Adam, did that ICE guy ever talk to you?" It was Tom's way of saying good morning.

"Yeah, he came to the house." Adam was relieved to have something to talk about.

"Way out there? What in the hell is that all about?"

"They've got an interest in DeLuca as a smuggler," Adam explained. "This guy has been trying to find him since January."

"Sounds like the DEA should be the ones to take

an interest in this guy."

"DEA looked at him a couple of times, then they lost track. They've got all they can handle." Adam added.

"Well if the feds couldn't get anything on him, I don't know what they expect from us."

They had done some legwork after Wells had looked at the file. Adam was relieved to find them showing interest in the DeLuca case and not in the Anderson boy's disappearance.

The discovery that the pilot worked for an air charter company based in Atlanta was not news to Adam. He listened as they repeated what Wells had told him the night before. The company didn't answer its phone. They had learned that the FAA keeps employer information on commercial pilots when they work for charter airlines. DeLuca was required to pass a check ride from the company's chief pilot. Not much of a lead, but it was a place to start.

"Here's the number. You guys better keep trying it today," Tom said with unusual enthusiasm. "They also want you downtown at headquarters first thing this morning."

"What's that about?" Stewart wondered.

"I don't know. The Assistant Chief said you guys were supposed to see him right away."

It was not unusual. Adam supposed that there was some paperwork to finish or messages that required attention. It probably meant details that had nothing to do with arson investigation. They might be asked to hold some insurance investigator's hand. He and Stewart sorted through the usual morning paperwork and then drove downtown to the fire department administrative office in the courthouse.

They wanted to see Adam. He walked into the Fire Marshal's office. "Good morning, chief, what can I do for you?"

"Come in, Adam. Close the door, will you?"

Adam did as he was asked. His curiosity was quickly satisfied.

"Adam, I...Adam, the chief wants me to suspend you."

"What?" Adam was shocked.

"You are all over the news. He doesn't like the publicity, says it reflects on the department. He wants you off until this thing is cleared up, you know, until they find this kid and you get off the hook."

"Ralph, this is bullshit. I can't believe this! You know I didn't mess with any kid! Is he so afraid for his job that this has got him running for cover? Jesus!"

"You've got to see his point, Adam."

"Do you see his point?"

"I don't have a choice." He didn't look Adam in the eye, staring out the window instead at the high-rise office buildings that shaded the courthouse.

"You aren't going along with this are you?"

"Come on, Adam, I'm not the boss. Even the boss isn't the boss. This is coming from higher up. They are looking at this as an embarrassment to the city."

"I can't believe this! What has this got to do with the fire department or the city? Riverton is 40 miles from here, in a different county. I have not been arrested, only questioned. And I had nothing to do with this crime. Hell, nobody even knows if there has been a crime. They're still dragging the Crow River. Can't you do something?"

"I'm sorry, Adam. I don't have a choice. This is what they want."

"Do you know we're in the middle of an arson homicide?"

"This is what they want," he repeated.

"I want to see him." Adam was angry.

"Christ, Adam, you don't want to go in there and piss him off. Get this thing cleared up, and it never happened. Don't go in there and piss him off!"

"I want to talk to him," Adam repeated, calmly.

Ralph slowly rose from his chair and walked out to the reception area while Adam sat in the chair and felt his face and ears redden with anger. In a minute Ralph returned, "He's in a meeting. Upstairs. It might be all day."

"Thanks, Ralph." Heavy sarcasm scarcely masked his emotion. He walked out the door and motioned for Stewart to follow. He was too upset to talk to anyone else in the office.

"Take me back to the station," he grunted as they walked toward the car "I don't work here anymore."

"What are you talking about?" Stewart was puzzled.

"I'll tell you in the car. So much for innocent until proven guilty. Here or in Riverton." He told Stewart what had happened.

Both were quiet on the way back to their office in the fire station. They were both angry with the fire chief.

"Do you suppose he would ever stand up for an employee?"

"I guess not. What are you going to do?" Stewart asked.

"I don't know. I thought I could get away and work on this case." He knew Stu didn't know what he was talking about. "I wanted to bury myself in this DeLuca business and forget about the rest for a while."

"For all it's worth, Adam, I know you aren't involved with this kidnapping."

"Thanks, but apparently being friendly with a kid is a crime now."

"How's Carol going to take this?"

"She's been good, but this is too much for anyone. Jesus, I don't even want to go home and tell her about this."

"She knows the truth. Don't worry, the truth will come out," Stu assured him.

Before Adam left the arson office, he and Stu gathered all the notes they had about DeLuca. The record search with the FAA was clean. DeLuca was a commercial pilot, licensed to fly anything up to and including small jet aircraft. He had never been in trouble with the FAA. There was no record of any enforcement actions or complaints about his flying. There was the telephone number of the air charter company in Atlanta, Rainbow Aviation.

"This just pisses me off! Finally a case to work on that means something. The one you wait half a career for, and I am off the job." Adam slammed the file drawer and kicked his locker door shut.

"What am I going to do with this stuff?" Stewart asked.

"Nothing. It's a dead end. Give it to the cops. They'll bury it." Anyone in earshot could hear the bitterness in his voice. He couldn't control his voice or his expression. But before he left the building, he reconsidered and walked back into the office.

"Stewart, I'm sorry. I didn't mean that. Stay on this. There's a reason the feds are interested in this guy. He's dirty, and he probably was murdered, so hang with it. Today I was going to go through his car. We hadn't looked at it yet, and I don't know whether the other shift did or not. Hang in there."

"Adam, they can't just suspend you without cause."

"I guess they can."

"Let's talk to a lawyer anyway. Let's call the union." Stewart wanted to fight.

"Don't you think the city knows that months will pass by the time I can do anything? They don't mind being wrong if they get what they want."

"I'm sorry, I just thought..."

"Thanks, Stewart. Just do me a favor and don't let up on DeLuca."

"I'm there, Adam."

Adam quickly turned and walked to the parking lot. He didn't want Stewart to see pain behind his eyes and the tears that were welling up out of his control. He was walking away from the job that meant everything to him. It defined him. Everyone knew that: his wife and family, friends, neighbors. No matter what happened he was all fire department. It was the source of his self-respect and the respect of everyone around him. He had made his way as a firefighter and arson investigator. Now it was all gone, and it might never return.

He drove away quickly without knowing where to go. He didn't want to go home to break the news to his wife. Out of habit he drove to the health club where off-duty firefighters met to play racquetball. He didn't want to see anyone now, but the empty parking lot was a good place to sit and think.

With the radio playing low, he tried to lean back and go to sleep. Still tired from the ordeal of the past few days, from not getting any rest, he let the weight of it all fall around him. There were no tears to shed but there was anguish for the loss of a job he loved. And there was a loathing for those who had known him during his career, but who now turned their backs. Did they really think he was a kidnapper? Years of working to earn their respect had been destroyed by the simple idea, "You're making the city look bad."

Pain and anger kept him from thinking straight as he struggled for an answer. There was nothing but a mental knot tied to emotions he had never felt before. He could not decide whether to be angry or depressed. The collected emotions couldn't be sorted out and organized. There must be some simple thing he was missing that would straighten everything out.

But he couldn't go home. In that direction he would only cause more pain for Carol. He had not been unemployed for years. There was a mortgage and bills to pay. If this didn't end soon, they would miss their house payment and eventually lose the place in which all their dreams were invested.

Carol had rejected his suggestion that she go to Green Bay to be with her parents. She was insulted by the idea that she should not be with him through their most distressing times. She wanted to support him and testify for him, if it became necessary. Besides, no matter what, if the baby came early, she wanted him to be there.

He would do anything to spare Carol this new pain, but there would never be a good way to tell her. Unselfish as always, she would be more worried about him than herself. She would feign optimism for his sake, pretending everything was going to be all right.

It would be better to use the payphone at the end of the parking lot than his cell phone. His home phone was probably bugged too, but if he could just hear her voice, perhaps the right words would come to him. Somehow he would find a way to let her adjust to one more avalanche of trouble. But he needed to rehearse a little longer. How would he tell her that they were both unemployed because he had befriended a seventh grader?

He had not given himself time to think about the boy. It had been fun having someone around to help him with the car. Ace was a good mechanic. He knew what tool would be needed and what to say when things were not going well. For a moment, Adam had even wondered what it would be like to work on a car with a boy of his own.

The thought of anyone harming a child was sickening. He didn't even want to think about what a boy would go through. Adam knew well enough that there were predators with a taste for every kind of perversion, including abuse of little boys or girls. They didn't usually turn up in arson investigations, but he did get to see the depths to which people could sink. Nothing surprised him except being a suspect himself.

It would have surprised him to know that Ace's name was Billy Mayes. Ace was a perfect witness to establish his innocence, or at least to change his appearance of guilt. Adam knew only that Robin Anderson was missing. Because he and Carol had not seen the news on television, he didn't know Robin was the boy who had left their house earlier in the afternoon. He didn't know that Ace had disappeared too.

He plugged the coins into the pay phone over and over again without success. He wanted to talk with Carol before he drove home. Besides, she could have news. If the boy had come home or been found he hoped she would know. Then he remembered. She would not put the phone back on the hook until 10:30 p.m. In a way, it was a relief that the phone was still off the hook, but in desperation he tried calling the restaurant where she had worked. It was a long shot, but she might have gone there to be with friends.

"Is Carol Bennett there?" he asked.

The voice on the other end was cold. "Carol Bennett doesn't work here anymore."

Adam gave up. He still had to think of a way to give her the bad news. Even in her condition, Carol was not fragile. But this would be the last straw. How perfect life had been for them! They just never appreciated it as much as they would now, if only... He didn't want to start whimpering there in the parking lot.

He had the card from the INS agent, with a cell phone number. Meeting with Wells would postpone telling Carol that he had been suspended. It was the easier thing to do, and he needed time to think.

CHAPTER 10

Wells answered his telephone on the first ring. "Glad you called. Got anything for me?"

Adam sat in his car next to the payphone suddenly gripped by the feeling that he was being watched. He carefully looked around the parking lot and at each building in his view. It wouldn't surprise him if a television crew or an undercover investigator from the Crow County sheriff's office was tailing him.

"Anything new?" Wells persisted.

"Not much. I'm not on the case anymore. They suspended me."

"What? Suspended! For what?" Wells was astonished.

"For being a suspect," Adam answered.

"What kind of chickenshit outfit do you work for?"

Adam couldn't think of anything to say and he couldn't answer the question.

"What are you going to do?" Wells asked. "What are we going to do?"

"I don't know yet," Adam replied.
"Let me buy lunch."
"It's too early for lunch."
"Coffee then. No problem. It doesn't make any difference. I'll pick you up and you can give me what you've got on DeLuca. Are you at your fire station?"

"No, but I can be there in a few minutes." Adam agreed to the meeting.

Fifteen minutes later, Wells pulled into the parking lot at Station 9. They stood together by his rental car for a few minutes while Adam delivered the scant information collected in the last three days. He wondered if they could get the name of the chief pilot at Rainbow from the FAA.

"Even the IRS doesn't know about Rainbow. It's like a shadow company." Wells had not been able to spend the weeks he needed in Atlanta to find the Rainbow owners or office. There was no information and no answer at the listed telephone number. "But it's always worth another try. I didn't know they had a chief pilot."

He dialed the Atlanta number for Rainbow Charters on his cell phone.

"Damn, I don't know why they have a telephone number. All they have is a damn answering machine. I've left 10 messages and never got a return call. If there is an office down there somewhere, it must be empty, or the people are all dead. The trouble with Atlanta is it has half a dozen airports that could handle a small jet or turboprop."

"How do you know what kind of airplane they would fly?" Adam asked.

"I assume they would need a jet or turboprop to get

anywhere out of the country. I could be wrong. There are piston twins that could get you as far as South America. If I find Rainbow, we know what kind of airplane they fly. Anyway, I was looking at airports that could do the fuel and maintenance work on business jets. I found nothing down in Atlanta. But Deluca was here, so Rainbow must have an airplane here. The airport here is where to start."

"If he was dead, how could he have had anything to do with the Riverton kid?"

"Remember, I said it was a long shot," Wells reminded him.

"Sorry, I guess I am working on a different case."

"We have to find out who he is working with. Did he have a partner, or was he working alone?" Wells ignored Adam's comment. "I told you, I don't think he was working alone. The airport here is the place to start. That is where I was headed when you called. When we know more...we'll just know a lot more."

"I think we may be like Atlanta here," Adam guessed. "We might have more than one airport big enough too."

"So, we just have to get started. Have you got anything better to do? Someone around here must know something about DeLuca, or about the Rainbow Charter Company."

"This is not the way I would be working it if I weren't suspended."

"Well, you are suspended. What were you looking at?" Wells asked.

"Real estate agents, county real estate records, mortgage registration. Somebody sold him the house he died in, and it took real money to pay for it."

"You might have something there, but I say the airport is where to start looking. And I still have a job. Are you with me?"

He climbed into Well's car without answering. It might be a waste of time, but there was nothing else he wanted to do.

Still, he had doubts about Wells. There was something unusual about Immigration taking an interest in abductions and arson cases. It stretched the imagination. Adam could have called the local ICE office to check up on the agent. How could Wells connect a crime in Riverton with an arson case 40 miles away? Then there was a suspicious desperation about the agent. Wells seemed to be in a rush that made the far-fetched connection even less rational.

"What exactly do you have on DeLuca?" Adam needed to know. "Have you got victims? I mean what are we going on here? Sounds like a hunch, unless you've got a victim, or at least a witness who says this is happening."

"Oh, I am the witness," Wells assured him. "I stumbled into this, so I'm the witness."

"I guess I've got the time to hear how you connect DeLuca and Riverton."

"Remember, I said that they may, emphasis may, be connected. But listen! My job is investigating minor illegals. Usually they are just like every other illegal, just younger, looking for a job. Or, they are going to join their family in the states. Lot of times it's minor women brought in for prostitution. Different reasons, anyway. Then I'm looking at a lot of missing children reports on the news. Kids' pictures on milk cartons. Everyone assumes they are all runaways or in custody disputes. But you know, the numbers just don't add up. There's too much room for slippage."

There were not enough resources to track every runaway or victim. There was no way to tell which were which. There was an organization that kept national statistics but there were too many cases that could not be explained. No one looked at them on a case-by-case basis except local authorities but Police departments couldn't afford to look past their own limited jurisdictions.

Wells had spent months looking at unsolved cases, particularly at the small percent of missing children who were too young to run away and had no custody issues. He had either visited each site or talked with the chief of police in each community. There was no pattern, but reasonable explanations had been eliminated in each case. He had charted more than 100 cases in every part of the country, and that, he felt, had only scratched the surface.

"I started to wonder if there are people going out of the country as easily as they come in. Like everyone else, I browse the Internet. Just looking for ideas or passing time, I can't even remember. I'm finding a lot of interest in children by pedophiles around the world. Remember what they were saying about Michael Jackson a few years ago? Maybe he was innocent, maybe not, but doesn't it make you wonder? How do rich pedophiles procure? I mean, suppose you've got all the money in the world. You can have anything you want, right?"

"I've never had that experience," Adam replied.

Wells was anxious to share his story. Hours of

Milk Market

searching on the Internet had only confirmed his suspicions. There was plenty of interest around the world in procuring children. Of course, it was anonymous on the Internet. Perverts had their own nicknames and knew about each other.

More than once he had seen a reference to the Milk Market without being able to determine what it was or what it meant. Child abusers shared their perverted fantasies in Internet chat rooms that he monitored; yet they were careful to avoid leaving any real evidence that would get an investigation started. There were no material clues that the Milk Market existed.

"This is sick." Adam still couldn't believe it. "Isn't there some way to trace these people?"

"They are more clever than that. They use blind e-mail and a language of their own when they are doing real business on the net."

"I just can't believe crap like this goes on."

"People don't understand," Wells continued. "There are still places in the world where slavery is common. Some countries pretend it doesn't exist, others accept it as part of the culture. We are the exception, well, the Western countries. The Christian countries are the exception, I guess. In some of these places..." He took a deep breath.

"Anyway," he told Adam, "the Internet led me to southeast Asia on vacation last year, to check out kiddy prostitution."

"Some vacation."

"I went in on a sex tour posing as a travel writer. I didn't want to say this in front of your wife. I was not a real customer, just posing as one. In Bangkok I start asking about kids. You can't believe it. They offer little girls, little boys. Literally anything you will pay for." "The boys are expensive. Seems that in a lot of cultures, girls are expendable. Their lives mean nothing. I talked to missionaries who have saved some of these little girls. You know, returned them to their families in the country, only to have the old man take them back to the city and sell them into prostitution again. I'm talking real young girls, sometimes younger than 10 years old."

"Maybe I don't want to hear any more of this," Adam worried.

"I am not buying in Bangkok, right." Wells intended to finish the story. "I am still passing myself off as a travel magazine writer. So I keep asking for something better. A guy approaches me in a bar, very polite. 'Mr. Wells, I believe I can show you what you are looking for.' I follow him to an old home, kind of run down. In a back courtyard I get a choice of girls and boys, about a half dozen. From about 12 to, I'd say, 16. White. Anglo. Speaking English, or a mix of English and something else. While I'm there, a customer comes in, makes a pick, and takes one into a room."

"Were they American?"

"That's what I'm getting at!" Wells was intense.

"Why wouldn't the victims grow up and run home, you know, free themselves and contact authorities."

"Because they end up dead or their memories burned out from drugs and years of abuse. And there are enough rich pedophiles in the world to create a market for them, so you know they might get passed around. If they are still alive, well...it would be better if their loved ones believed they were dead."

Milk Market

Wells had tried to interview them without becoming a customer. He told them he was a missionary. When they spoke at all it was in a combination of English and Thai or some unrecognizable language. They were spaced-out, or more likely burned-out on drugs. They were either American or European.

"What did you do?"

"Went right to the embassy. Told my story and left it in their hands. Of course I expected there would be action. The Thai government was supposed to investigate, but I didn't expect to hear anything more about it from them. They wouldn't be interested in finding out who these kids were or where they had come from. And I had my doubts about our own government."

"You mean no one cares?"

"They care, but it's state department stuff. We're not supposed to do anything that would embarrass another government. Nobody is supposed to be embarrassed. They will handle it in their own way. Very discreet, of course."

"I took it up through channels as soon as I got home. Fortunately, the state department did send an investigator who found a few brothel kids to interview. I listened to the tapes."

"Did these kids know where they came from?" Adam asked.

"Most of them were so burned out they gave us nothing. Two had some dim recollection of an island in Mexico. Nothing more than an island in Mexico! That made sense to me. There is only one place that could be. Cozumel. Big enough airport and big enough to harbor boats that could go anywhere else in the world."

"If my boss hadn't gone to bat for me, my part would have ended there, instead I ended up here, on special assignment. My job is to keep this away from the public until it's a winner. It has to be cut and dried."

"You know as well as I do that sooner or later some reporter will get a piece of it, so I am in a race. I've heard some background noise from 60 Minutes or Dateline. I can't remember which. Then there is the budget. I am racing against the end of the fiscal year too. I have to get to the bottom of this or I will end up swinging in the wind. You work for bureaucrats and politicians, you know what I mean."

"Right, tell me about it." Adam still wondered about DeLuca's part.

"So I started out at a dead end, this gap between what I could find here and what I had seen with my own eyes in Southeast Asia. There was nothing in this country linked to Bangkok. Then a friend of mine at DEA told me about one of their suspects, a pilot. They couldn't prove he was smuggling drugs. Thorough searches of his airplane and radar surveillance found nothing, even though he made numerous trips to points in Mexico. They dismantled his airplane twice. You know, they took it apart until there wasn't a place to hide a cigarette butt. Nothing."

"So guess where he was putting down in Mexico most of the time. You bet, the island of Cozumel. Anyway, DEA quit looking at him when they couldn't find a drug connection. They were right up against a big-time harassment complaint. You can't just tear apart an airplane every time someone flies in from another country. Even Mexico."

"I suppose not."

"So that was DeLuca, your arson victim. But all DEA could give me was the name and the Atlanta address and a link back to the FAA."

"They didn't have anything for us either," Adam added. "They are supposed to send a file, but they didn't sound too enthused about finding it. Why wouldn't they keep a file?"

"There probably is one, buried somewhere. They would have been looking at him again, at some point. But I couldn't wait."

"They gave us nothing. We asked for information from the Atlanta cops too, but nothing came back. At least not yet," Adam added.

"You probably are spending as much effort to find out about this guy as I did. Naturally DEA thinks our concern is illegal aliens or felons coming into the country. I can't get much out of them. Until they think drugs are being brought in, they really don't care. They believed this pilot was just a wealthy playboy, so he wasn't their concern. They've got enough on their plate without him. I can't get across that I think DeLuca is smuggling out of the country, not into it."

"Anyway, I had my special assignment, I knew who I was looking for, but he had to die for me to find him. That is how I got here. Deluca was not alone, but he was smuggling children, possibly even the boy that you're accused of kidnapping."

"Well, I am just an arson investigator."

"No, you are a kidnapping suspect," Wells reminded him.

"I've got to call my wife." Adam was suffering from information overload. He needed time to think about his own case, and he needed to talk to Carol. "Can I use your phone?"

"Sure. She doesn't know yet? I mean that you got suspended? You didn't tell her?"

"Nope, and our phone has to be kept off the hook."

After several busy signals, Adam searched his wallet for another number. Albert Johnson would let her know that he was trying to call. He knew Albert would do anything for Carol if he would only answer his own telephone. Finally, after a dozen rings Bobby answered and agreed to drive over and ask Carol to hang up her telephone so Adam could get through.

"Thanks, Bobby. Thanks a lot. Tell your dad what I said." He knew he'd be able to reach her if he tried again in an hour.

"I can tell you this, Bennett, We would have been working together on this whether you were a suspect in this kidnapping or not. Whether this kid was abducted or not."

"So why haven't you just turned this over to the FBI or someone who could put a dozen people on it?"

"I have all I can do to convince my own boss that I'm on to something. If it were not for a little built-in dislike for the state department, they would have reassigned me months ago. Besides, now I am close. I chase this guy down and you think I am going to let go now? Do you think I am going to turn this over to someone else? The FBI? Not on your life!"

"We do it all the time. Arson investigates, and as soon as we can prove arson we turn it over to the police department."

"Then why doesn't your police department have this one?"

"I'm like you. I can't prove anything yet."

"There you go! And you still don't believe all this that I am telling you, do you?"

"This is all pretty hard to digest."

"Remember, 99 percent of what you see around you everyday is good. I've seen that little town you live in. We don't know how good we have it here. Even a black kid raised in north Philly," he gave Adam a look to see if he understood, "has it good. Then I ran into this. I'm not surprised anymore about what people will do to other people."

"But these are children..." Adam was disgusted.

"I know, man. I know. American children, Yankee children. Babies. Don't you know there are people out there that hate our guts to begin with? And they don't give a shit about human life. They will kill their own folks without giving it a second thought. What do you think they care about little white kids from the USA?"

Adam suddenly wanted to be somewhere else. He wanted to be safe at home with his wife, but he asked, "Do you have any idea of how many? I mean, how many kids are you talking about here?"

"I've got about a hundred that need a hard look. But I put together a database with another 400 from all over the country that can't be counted as runaways or custody cases. How many are you willing to forget about?"

"None. None, but how can a human being do that? Take a kid for that?"

"Shit! Human being! Last year I opened up the back of a semi south of San Diego and found 16 bodies. These kids paid to be smuggled into California to work. Paid big money to suffocate in the back of a truck just to get into this country!"

Adam could see that Wells took his work personally. It explained why he was pursuing the DeLuca case like a madman. How would he be if he found a living witness or criminal to question?

Wells continued. "You know what the Japanese army did in Nanking? Do you know what the Nazis did to Jews? How about going over to Africa to fill up a boat with other human beings, bringing them over here to pick cotton? Just because it's modern times doesn't mean there are no more monsters in this world. Humanity is still producing them, just like in the history books, living right here among us. You know! What kind of person lights someone's house on fire when they are sleeping? No sirree, don't you be surprised."

Adam knew he had struck a nerve.

"I'm sorry," Wells said. "I didn't mean to go off on you. I've been chasing this thing, this bad thing all by myself for nearly a year. I guess I have always needed someone to hear all this. I know you've got troubles of your own, though. So, I'm sorry I unloaded on you."

"No problem." Adam knew that Wells had just tried to explain an evil world that he assumed Adam could not understand. But Adam did understand. He was the victim himself of evils that were generated, not by bad men but by unfortunate circumstances. He had befriended a child.

Now he was backed into a corner. He had to see how it all fit together: Wells, Deluca and the

Anderson boy. Or whether any of them were really connected. His choices were not good. Go home with more bad news, or work the case with Wells. The path of least resistance was to do something instead of nothing, to work an arson case that could be bigger than anything he had ever investigated.

As they approached the airport, Adam was quiet. He had decided to keep working, to pursue the DeLuca case to help his own. Wells was quiet too. He knew he had said enough.

CHAPTER 11

On Friday morning Sheriff Knowlton held a press conference to inform the media that Billy Mayes was missing. Before any rumors got started, he wanted to make it clear that Robin Anderson's best friend had simply run away from home. There was no reason for the public to panic. The sheriff and the boy's family hoped that Billy would be found quickly with the help of the media.

Heff didn't attend the press conference. He was sure he knew Billy well enough to find him quickly, but his search had failed. The equipment shed under the high school bleachers was locked up tight, and there was no sign of the boy in the old mill building down by the river. With nowhere else to look, he drove his squad car up and down each country road until he found himself stopped in the Bennetts' driveway.

Reporters had finally abandoned their vigil at the house. For three days they had been like vultures waiting for the suspect to appear. The kidnapper had

Milk Market

already been tried and convicted in the evening news and the morning newspaper.

Officially, Bennett was innocent until there was a trial and conviction. Yet the news and rumors had affected the entire sheriff's department. Most of the deputies thought the county attorney was dragging his feet on the case. The suspect should be in jail. The rumor that a witness had seen the abduction involving a green foreign car made it an open-and-shut case in the minds of everyone who was horrified by the crime.

Heff was not convinced. There were other suspects who had not been questioned, and he was not sure Adam Bennett fit the crime.

He drove slowly up the driveway to the old farmhouse. It was inappropriate for him to stop at the suspect's home. There was no reason for him to be there. It would upset the sheriff if he learned about the visit, but without television crews to track the movement of every deputy, Knowlton would never know. Even if someone saw him there he could say that he was investigating a complaint. It was easy to make up something for a report.

The house was dark and quiet. Heff walked up on the porch and knocked on the kitchen door. The dog was barking, but there was no movement inside. He was ready to turn away when Carol came to the door, opened it and looked around.

The patrol car in the driveway was a surprise. She hoped it was good news for a change, but the look on Heff's face told her otherwise.

"Hi, Heff."

"Carol." He tried a smile.

"Sorry about the dog. Mickey has been nervous with all the people around." She was nervous too. "Adam is at work today, in the city. It's his regular shift."

"I just stopped by to see how you are doing."

"Not well, but thanks for asking." Carol had known Heff since she started to work at Perkins. He had never stopped by their house before. She wondered why he would stop now. "Is there something else, Heff?"

"More bad news. It doesn't concern you though."

"What's wrong?"

"Robin's best friend is gone. I think he just took off because he couldn't handle all this."

"Oh God!" She knew that her reaction was too halfhearted, but she had become numb. The words did not sink in, and there were no more emotions to use, even for another missing child. "Have they started another search?"

"That'll be next."

She could see that he was taking it hard.

"Was he one of your ballplayers?"

"Right. He was one of the kids who was here on Monday. I just thought I'd let you know, you know...I don't know, if he came by or something. He doesn't blame your husband for Robin. He told me that he didn't think Mr. Bennett would do anything to hurt anybody."

"I hope he comes back soon," she wished.

"We hope he has just gone to stay with a friend somewhere. His folks are worried sick, naturally, with Robin gone and everything."

"If he comes by here, I'll be sure to let you know."

"Thanks. I know. But I just wanted to come by and wish you, both of you, the best. I still hope that Robin turns up. Now I hope nothing bad happens to Billy."

"I hope not too." Carol was too drained to sound sympathetic.

"I'm not even supposed to be here, but I think they're barking up the wrong tree."

"Thanks. I know they are barking up the wrong tree, but right now that doesn't help. This is so horrible."

"I tried calling before. You must have the phone off the hook."

"We have to leave it off the hook. You wouldn't believe the calls."

"Yes I would." He could only imagine. "Look, if you need anything, if either of you need anything that I can help with, let me know. Call my house. Crystal knows what you're going through."

"Thank you," Carol said, her eyes filled with tears. "Adam wouldn't hurt anyone, especially a kid."

"I know."

"Heff, did you know Robin Anderson very well?"

"Both he and Billy play baseball for me. They are good kids."

"He's been gone so long now!" Carol despaired.

"I know. This is terrible for everyone, especially his folks and his little sisters."

"I'm so sorry."

"I'd better get back on patrol."

"This might sound stupid... Heff, should I call his mother? I mean I feel so bad for her, and for all of them. I wish I could make her feel better."

"I don't know. I just don't know. Why don't you

let me talk with them first? I'll let you know how they feel about it."

She closed the door and watched through the window as the deputy walked back to his patrol car and drove down the driveway. Before his visit, Carol had assumed the whole town believed Adam was guilty of abducting and abusing Robin Anderson. She had cried enough, but this visit from Heff, who was only a casual acquaintance, brought her to tears again.

Before her was the vision of a mother she had never met, Mrs. Anderson, weeping at the loss of her little boy. She remembered the boy, all sweaty and greasy, working with Adam on the car. She had ordered them to clean their hands before they ate. To think that the boy was gone...

Her thoughts went back to his mother. In spite of her resolve to be strong, the tears came again. Detectives had questioned her. How long was Adam gone when he drove the boy home? Was he tense because of her pregnancy? We mean, sexually? Too personal! She had been insulted and refused to answer any more. The local investigator and the FBI agent had looked at each other significantly before they went on their way.

Her husband was an honest working-man. Better than anyone else could know, she knew he was not a pervert. Little boys were not objects of his desire. God knows he couldn't wait for her to be skinny again, but he was kind and patient during the pregnancy. He would be a great father.

Their love was strong. They were both healthy, and there were no problems with her pregnancy. Her strength had always been in the feeling that she and

Milk Market

Adam had done everything right. Where was that confidence now?

"Get busy," she told herself. "You've got to shake this off."

She had to stay in control and avoid feeling sorry for herself. In the meantime there were rolls of wallpaper stacked up on the sofa in the living room. Decorating was supposed to be fun. She and Adam had looked at pattern after pattern in the wallpaper section at the lumberyard, arguing until they found designs that both could agree to use. They had been so free then. It all seemed long ago and meaningless.

She could hear Albert Johnson's pick-up coming down the road. Its muffler was rusted away. The noise brought Carol down from the stepstool she had climbed to measure for wallpaper. Albert and his son Bobby pulled into the driveway. On speculation she poured a cup of coffee before Albert reached the porch.

"Adam called over to the house. He wanted to talk to you, but your phone was busy." Albert took his cup. "He said he was busy chasing some firebug so you shouldn't worry and he will call you later."

"Thanks, Albert." She was happy to hear Adam was wrapped up in the DeLuca case.

"I thought you weren't drinking coffee," Albert said.

"Its decaf, it's safe for both of us."

"Well then it don't have much of a kick. But you probably get all the kicks you want," he laughed. He knew that she had been crying.

"Where's Bobby?"

"He wanted to stay in the truck. This little boy

that's missing is really bothering him."

"Really!" she said, sympathetically.

"I wanted to come and tell ya how bad I feel, too. Adam didn't do nothing to that boy. I seen them working together here. There's nothing wrong with that."

"Thank you, Albert. It makes me feel better." Another tear came to her eye. "I know Adam will appreciate it too."

"You just remember we ain't the only ones who think so."

Carol wanted to hug the old farmer. Instead, she reached across the table and took his hand. "Thank you again."

They talked for a while about the weather and in a matter-of-fact way about the television trucks, as if they came every day. He was glad they had gone away. She was afraid they would be back. As Albert climbed back in the truck, Bobby waved at her. She waved back. When they drove away, she went back in the kitchen and slowly washed the coffee cups.

* * *

It was the first time she and Adam had met. Like so many who worked near Lake Calhoun, she often took a walk along the east shore during her lunch break. It depended on the weather. That day, she remembered, was sunny with a gentle breeze coming across the lake. Little wavelets stirred the sand at the shore where toddlers played in and out of the water.

She loved all of the city lakes, and the bicycle trails and walkways that circled them. Lake of the Isles was

Milk Market

lovely with its shady bays and islands. Lake Harriet had its busy beaches and pavilion. But Lake Calhoun was her favorite. It seemed more sociable with the constant activity of runners, walkers and bikers on its paths. There were sailboat regattas out in the lake and busy traffic on the surrounding boulevards.

To save time, Carol usually brought a sandwich from home or stopped for fast food. A walk at lunchtime was a good change from the air conditioning in the bank and the smell of the employee cafeteria in the lower level. There were plenty of cold and rainy days to spend down there chatting with her co-workers. She enjoyed being outdoors more than most, she supposed, because she was still a country girl at heart.

Adam was a city boy, through and through, but he loved animals. He had a big black dog named Mickey that loved to run around the lake. Carol met Mickey first. The big dog stopped to say "hello" and Adam quickly followed. She tried to pretend that her only interest was in the dog, but Adam had a winning smile and a sense of humor. He told her that Mickey would not go to just anyone. He was very selective, but yes, the dog did help him meet girls.

It was so long ago. They had been strangers, sitting on a park bench and talking about nothing in particular while Adam threw pebbles into the lake for Mickey to chase. They laughed together, and Carol had discovered a feeling that she was not supposed to have so soon after meeting someone. It was a feeling she liked, so she agreed to their first date.

She remembered talking to herself on the way back to work. "My God, I picked up a man at the beach."

Adam turned out to be nicer than someone picked up at the beach. After their first date, dinner and a movie, there was no doubt they would stay together. They were rarely apart after that, except when they were at work. It was a very conventional romance. They fell in love, met each other's friends and families and got married at her parent's church in Green Bay six months later. Mickey, now stretched out there on the porch looking sad, was always referred to as their matchmaker.

Moving out of the city had come naturally. Neither she nor Adam could remember how they had started talking about it or when they made the decision. At some point they both took for granted that they would find a place in the country. It would be a fresh start in a new place and a clean break for both of them. There could be no better place to raise a family than a small town. He was reluctant about commuting at first, so they had rented a house in Riverton before making a commitment and buying property. Then they found the farmhouse, and here they were. Now there was this unbelievable mess.

At least Adam had returned to work. Perhaps with the change in perspective, being away from Riverton, he would understand that his innocence would ultimately come out. Then their lives would return to normal.

There was nothing she could do to help until then. She could not go out and find the lost boy, and she could not convince anyone that her husband was innocent. Her hope was that there were others in town like Heff and Albert who were not swept up by their emotions and the hype of the television news. The frustration of her role was that she could only be a supporting player. Her job was to stand and wait.

She was anxious to talk to Adam at bedtime. He needed to know that Albert was supportive and that Heff had stopped by the house. It would cheer him as much as it had cheered her to know there were people who believed in his innocence.

She had to try to prevent all that had happened from ruining what should be the happiest time of their lives. There had to be a way for her to regain her serenity of a few days ago. Two visitors today that made her feel better. If they found the boy, "Please God may he be found alive!" Adam would be free. A lot of people, including the media, would owe them a big apology. They would owe Adam a big apology.

Tonight he would call at the usual time, if he could, and she would be positive for him. Everything would be all right.

* * *

Sheriff Knowlton sat alone in his office. It was quiet now. The day crew had gone home and the afternoon shift was out on patrol. The radio speaker on his desk crackled from time to time with routine calls between deputies and the emergency dispatcher. This was one of the few times that he enjoyed a little peace, one of the few opportunities just to sit by himself and think before he went home to supper.

Knowlton knew there were young people in his department, good people, who considered him a dinosaur. Law enforcement had changed. The assumption that gray hair made him obsolete was wrong. He had kept up better than most. When voters went in the booth, they were going to have to remember that experience counted more than anything taught from books. He knew the guys who wrote the books and could have written one or two himself.

The Mayes kid was just a runaway, but it made the department look bad, an embarrassment. It suggested the sheriff couldn't do anything right. While they were looking for one lost boy, another disappeared.

With everybody keeping their eyes open after the news conference, the boy should turn up quickly. More than likely he would come back home on his own. He had not been kidnapped, just disappeared from the recreation room through the basement window. The sheriff would be happy to give some serious verbal discipline to young Billy when he came home.

The boy was in danger until then. His parents were afraid that he would be kidnapped just like Robin. If Bennett had not commuted to the city this morning, perhaps the boy would be at risk. Even then, the sheriff had to consider the possibility that Bennett might come back to Riverton to find a boy who would certainly be a witness against him at trial. The suspect must be desperate by now.

Knowlton had never experienced so much public pressure. The voters were getting impatient. They were asking for answers. The search for Robin Anderson had gone on long enough, and they wanted someone arrested. If you can't find the kid, arrest someone, they were saying. It would get worse when the news about the Mayes boy hit the streets. If he had one more shred of evidence, one more witness or anything new he would arrest Adam Bennett. That is all it would take for the county attorney to go along. He was under the same pressure as the sheriff's department.

Each of the five county commissioners had called. One at a time they had asked for news about the search and the suspect. They applied their own kind of pressure. "Do something," they said. There were hints, not too subtle, that he was facing serious opposition in the fall election.

"You are not as popular as you were 10 years ago," he was told.

Dragging the river had bought some time even though it had yielded nothing. The media had been relentless. When he called a halt to the operation without results they wanted something more from him. They were as desperate for a story as he was to make an arrest. Knowlton knew that another event somewhere in the state would get them off his back, but now with the Mayes boy missing Crow County would be in the headlines again.

Just one more reason to be suspicious, and he could arrest Bennett and put the squeeze on him. The green car was the key. Otherwise they would be looking at the slow Johnson boy. He had been around the kids on Monday too, but he drove an old maroon pick-up, not a green foreign car. It had to be Bennett. One more bit of evidence, and the suspect might break down and tell them where the body was hidden. Then, except for a possible lynching attempt, this would all be history.

He still felt terrible about the boy and his family, but he was confident now that Robin would never be found alive.

A little more evidence, one little break in the case, and there would be an arrest.

"I've got the right man," he said out loud.

CHAPTER 12

Wells was an impatient driver. He bullied his way through traffic, following the car ahead within a few feet of its rear bumper until the other driver, in fear or anger, moved out of the way. Adam gladly helped the agent navigate to the business aviation base across from the main terminal. He was relieved when they slowed and turned into the parking lot near a large group of hangars.

"I spent the last week in Atlanta looking at these kind of operations," Wells complained. "Excuse me, but they all look the same."

From the street, the collection of buildings looked old and weathered, but inside the main hangar the concrete floors were treated and polished to a high gloss. The block walls and open trusses of the roof were newly painted white. An array of spotlights overhead reflected on a half dozen immaculate corporate jets. It was like a showroom floor with tens of millions of dollars' worth of the newest aircraft.

Mechanics dressed like doctors in white coats fussed over their spoiled patients. Company pilots expected no less than perfection in maintenance and cleanliness of the aircraft. When a president or CEO climbed aboard the company jet for a business trip, there wouldn't be a speck of dust or a splash of oil.

While Adam wandered among the sleek jets, Wells found the business office. In the reception area he flashed his ICE identification and asked for information about an airplane owned by Rainbow Charters. As Adam walked in they were being directed to a Cessna Citation jet parked outside on the ramp.

"How about the pilot?" Adam asked for DeLuca by name. The receptionist didn't have any information about the pilots.

"Did you hear what she said?" Wells was elated as they walked back into the hangar. "Pilots! More than one!"

"Do you even know what a Citation looks like?" Adam asked as they faced a long line of airplanes parked outside.

"No problem, unless there is more than one," Wells replied.

"There must be someone out here who can help us." Adam looked at his watch. It was already noon. He was afraid there would be no one around to show them to the Rainbow jet. It looked like the mechanics working in the hangar didn't come outside.

There were two rows of corporate jets and twin-engine airplanes. Adam and Wells walked together until they found what they were looking for at the end of the first row.

Milk Market

The Rainbow jet was last in line by the chain link fence. They would have seen it from the street or the parking lot if they had looked for the rainbow. The jet was painted white like most of the others except for the broad swath of rainbow colors on the tail. It meant nothing to Adam, but Wells read the number on the tail out loud and scribbled it in the notebook he carried in his jacket. Adam wondered what Wells expected to learn from looking at the airplane when a lineman drove up on a tractor.

"Can I help you?"

"We're looking for the guy who flies this," Adam responded.

"FAA?"

"No. No, we're with the insurance company." Wells was quick with a reply.

"We don't see the pilots very often. It goes overnights mostly. About once a week, we get orders to fuel it. That's about it. A charter outfit pays the bills. It must have come back in on Wednesday, or yesterday. I've got orders to fuel it today."

"We're having trouble finding the pilot," Wells explained. "He must have moved. The company can't get a local address for him."

"They should have it in the office."

"The receptionist said she didn't know anything about the pilots," Wells said doubtfully.

"Let's go see about that."

Adam and Wells looked at each other and followed Harold and the tractor back toward the office.

"Did you hear that? It made a trip this week."

"That doesn't mean we know where it went," Adam said doubtfully.

"No, but we can probably find out. The FAA is on our side, remember?"

"We know DeLuca didn't fly it." That was certain.

Back in the office, they ignored the receptionist who sat like a statue. Adam hoped she had not been paying attention when Wells identified himself as an ICE agent now that their pretext had changed to an insurance investigation.

"Here we go. It's Rainbow Charter." Harold flipped through a Rolodex behind the counter. "They list a De something, DeLucas, I guess. That the guy you're looking for?"

"We know about him. He didn't fly this week."

"Are you sure? Like I said, it was gone at least one night this week."

"There had to be another pilot," Wells insisted.

"No, that bird is legal for one pilot. Its better with two, but not illegal."

"DeLuca died last Sunday night," Adam said.

"Oh! Oh, well. I guess you're right. He didn't fly this week."

"Who orders the fuel and maintenance?" Wells wondered.

"That would be this DeLucas. But wait. There was another guy sometimes. I don't know his name." He thought for a minute, "Alicia, you got the fuel invoices? Let's look for a signature. If there's another name, that's where it would be."

Adam and Wells watched as he paged through a pile of invoices.

"Nope. Nothing here. Most of these don't even get signed. The bills go to the company and they pay them, or else they wouldn't be getting jet fuel."

"The bills go to their Atlanta address?" Wells hoped for a street address.

"Post Office Box 3925. Does that help you?"

"So we better talk to Rainbow." Wells checked to see that the telephone number he had for the charter company was correct. "Thanks for your help, Harold."

They walked back to the car in the parking lot. Wells was discouraged. It looked like another dead end. Even though there was another pilot they didn't have a name. There was nowhere to start. In desperation he tried the Rainbow number in Atlanta again and got the answering machine.

"At least," he said, "we know there was another pilot. That's the guy we have to find."

Adam reached over and turned off the ignition. Wells looked at him curiously.

"Let's look in the airplane."

"Good idea. Of course! Let's take a look in the airplane." Wells grinned.

They followed the fuel truck down the line where Harold was preparing to refuel the Rainbow jet. He could see no reason not to allow them in the airplane while he filled the wing tanks. Adam followed Wells into the cabin when the lineman unlocked the airstair door and pulled it down.

The interior of the airplane was luxurious. The smell was of rich leather from the seats that faced each other in the cabin. There was thick carpeting on the floor and wood trimmed tables between the seats. At the back was a leather seat that spanned the width of the airplane. In front, Adam admired the confusion of gauges and radios in the cockpit.

"Nothing here. Pretty clean." Wells looked over Adam's shoulder, "Wait a minute. How about a flight bag?"

He pulled the black leather case from behind the pilot's seat. "This belonged to DeLuca." He pointed at the initials engraved near the handle, "AD"

"What's in it?" Adam had never seen a flight bag.

"Charts and maps. Sectionals, approach plates. Operational stuff. Here's DeLuca's name and address inside the top flap. God, what I would have given for that a week ago!" Wells was excited. "Here we go! Logbook! If he was keeping it up this will tell us where he went and when. I've got a database of missing children with a whole lot of where and when in it. How much do you want to bet that I can match them up?"

"You might, but I bet there won't be an entry for this week. Anything else in there?"

"Nothing this good. No wait. Look at this!" Wells found a package in a side pocket. Wound in rubber bands were a dozen savings passbooks. They were different sizes and colors, fake cardboard leather with gold lettering, each from a different bank. "I didn't know you could still get this kind of account."

There were eleven passbooks in all, a few from local banks and several from small towns in the area. Adam went through each passbook in turn while Wells made notes of each bank and balance. DeLuca had amounts from a few thousand to more than $30,000 in 11 savings accounts.

"I'll bet the banks loved this guy," Wells said. "Big balances in passbook savings. You know, the lowest interest they could pay."

When Adam reached the last passbook his heart jumped. There it was! The Riverton Savings and Loan. "Look at this." He showed it to Wells.

"How much?"

"Seven thousand, even," Adam said, noticing the smug look on Well's face.

"Doesn't mean anything. It looks like he just spread money around to as many banks as he could visit. I've got a total here, let's see: $127,000 and change."

Adam whistled. "He had to spread it around."

"Right," Wells agreed. "He was making a lot of dough, and he had to spread it around and keep the deposits small."

They knew there were federal laws in place to prevent income tax fraud and laundering drug money. Bank examiners took a hard look at the source of large deposits, particularly if they were in cash. DeLuca must have known about the laws too.

"Where did he come up with this kind of money?" Adam asked.

"I can tell you that the IRS doesn't know about any income. Any legal income that is," Wells reminded him.

"So it could be drug money."

"Or it could be worse than that. Remember the DEA gave up on DeLuca for drug smuggling."

"There are a lot of illegal ways to get money that the IRS and DEA don't know about." Adam speculated, "He could be a hit man, or..."

"Or a kidnapper. Look at the deposit dates. Looks like we go back about sixteen, seventeen months."

They looked through the passbooks again. Wells

was right. None of the deposits had been made more than a year and a half earlier.

"So. One flight bag, one pilot?" Adam asked, changing the subject.

"Not necessarily. Some pilots don't let it out of their sight. Carry their lunch, you know. Man, if I had been DeLuca with all these passbooks, I would have kept mine in sight."

"What's that?" Adam noticed a book wedged between the cockpit wall and the right seat. It was a library book. *The Adventures of Puddin' Head Wilson,* by Mark Twain.

"Is there a name in it?" Wells asked.

"It's overdue at the county library. No name, but probably DeLuca's. Anyway, we might find out for sure at a county library computer."

Wells' face brightened with one more hope. There was a chance that it didn't belong to DeLuca. It was found beside the right seat, the co-pilot seat. Any other name would give them a fresh start.

Back in the hangar, they used a telephone directory to locate the nearest branch library, only a few miles from the airport.

Adam took the book in alone. Until he identified himself as an investigator, the librarians wanted him to pay the overdue fine. Then a supervisor listened as he explained it was an official arson investigation. He cringed as he said the words. If anyone found out he was still working after his suspension, he would be fired. The library supervisor took the book into an office while Adam paced nervously near the door. Was he doing a computer search or even calling the fire department to see if he should provide the

Milk Market

information? After several long minutes, he returned with a slip of paper that he handed to Adam. On it was the name and address of the borrower.

Wells could tell by the look on his face as he returned to the car that they had a new lead.

"We've got a name and an address." Adam grinned.

"Who's the guy?"

"Mark Peavey."

Wells was enthusiastic. "O.K. Now we're getting somewhere."

"Just one problem," Adam reminded him. "Maybe this Peavey ended up like DeLuca."

Wells ignored the suggestion. "Lets go find Mr. Peavey. I knew DeLuca wasn't working alone. You might get your arsonist, murderer and kidnapper all in one."

"I'm suspended, remember?"

"What's the difference? If we find this kid, or any trace of any kid... and if we find your arsonist, you're in the clear and you're a hero."

"And you're a dreamer." Adam was not as optimistic.

"Do you still have your badge?"

"Yeah, but I don't work there anymore."

"Don't they take your badge when you are fired?" Wells asked.

"I'm not fired, just suspended."

"Good. You've got your badge. That might get us in a door!"

Adam hesitated. He felt like a criminal himself when he used his badge to extract information from the public library computer. "Look, I've got no jurisdiction in an arson case, or any other case for that matter. I'm like a private citizen, worse, I'm a suspect in a case."

"Help me," Wells begged.

"You don't understand," Adam resisted. "I am a private citizen, I can't go flashing my badge around, or they will fire me. They will take it away forever."

"You're talking like you have something to lose."

Adam was helpless again. He had Carol, and their baby. Everything else had been taken away, including his good name, his job and even his wife's job. It was hard to imagine that it could ever be the same or that he could ever regain the life he loved.

His new partner was an unknown quantity who had come to his house a little more than 12 hours ago. They were pursuing a hunch that went far beyond the scope of an arson investigation. But one thing was clear: If Wells was correct, they were both pursuing the same person, a murdering arsonist who took part in kidnapping and white slavery. At least now there was something to go on. The story was coming true. And they had a name.

More important, it appeared that the airplane had been gone after Robin Anderson disappeared. Although DeLuca was dead, he had suspicious bank deposits of more than $100,000 spread out in small banks around the country.

"Do you need lunch?" Wells was unwrapping antacids and popping them into his mouth. "I'm good."

"I can wait." Adam was not hungry.

"Then let's get hold of Mark Peavey and give him a little encouragement."

Milk Market

"If he is still around. Just remember that I am low profile in this. If it becomes a spectacle, I am going to disappear." Adam was thinking instead about the terminology, squeezing information from someone and recalling that he had been the victim of an interrogation only a few days before.

"Why don't you drive? You know the way." Wells looked at the slip of paper in Adam's hand.

Adam did know the way. The neighborhood, just south of downtown, was made up of rows of apartment buildings that had been fashionable 60 or 70 years before. Now they were frayed at the edges, run down refuges for the underemployed and unemployed. The dingy brick walls sheltered shady characters and too many people who seemed to have nothing to do. Because of fires and arson investigations, Adam knew each address as if he had lived in the neighborhood himself. Most of the buildings were similar, three stories, stairways front and rear, with entry on the street and in the alley.

"This is the one," Adam said as they drove slowly past 320 6th Avenue.

"Is there any place to park around here?" Wells wondered.

There was nowhere to park on the block or on the next street. Even the spaces in front of the fire hydrants were occupied.

"Tell you what, pull around the back. Let's see what it looks like." Wells was excited. "Good. Here it is."

Each building had a row of dumpsters or garbage cans, a crude no-parking sign and the address scrawled near the back door at alley level.

"This is good," Wells repeated. "If this guy is nervous he will try to bail out on me. Pull around again, drop me off in front, then come back here and park right up tight to that exit. Really tight so no one can get out without climbing over the car."

"You watch too much television."

"Let's just say I have pursued too many illegals."

Adam followed instructions. After Wells got out near the front entry, he returned to the alley and nosed the car in between garbage cans so that the right front bumper nearly touched the door. He got out of the car and waited, expecting anytime for a caretaker or resident to object to the blocked door. The humidity was high and a light rain was falling again, so he pulled off his tie, stuffed it in his jacket pocket and threw both into the back seat.

As Wells expected, there were no names on the mailboxes. Peavey wouldn't be trying to advertise his whereabouts. They had his apartment number, 228, that was easy to find. Soon after Wells went up the front stairs, a young man in blue jeans and a T-shirt came hurrying down the back. As Adam was rolling up his shirtsleeves, he heard the footsteps in the stairwell. He turned around as the door opened. There was a surprised Mark Peavey, with Wells not far behind.

"Hold it!" Wells shouted.

Peavey desperately scrambled across the hood of the car. Adam watched in amazement while Wells climbed after him, made a leg tackle and threw the younger man against the building.

"Let go of me! I didn't do anything." Peavey had a terrified look.

Milk Market

"Then why did you run?"

"Jesus! What would you do? I didn't do anything."

"Is this the guy?" Adam wanted to be sure.

"You bet! He came out of 28."

"Who are you guys?" Peavey wanted to know.

"Get in the car."

Wells pushed Peavey into the back seat and followed himself. Adam quickly drove out of the alley.

"Who are you guys?" Peavey insisted.

"This guy lost a kid," Wells pointed to Adam

"I don't know what you're talking about. I'm a pilot. Are you IRS, FAA or who? I'm just a pilot."

"Yeah, we know. You and DeLuca," Adam told him.

"Who's DeLuca?"

"You can cut the bullshit. You talk to us now, or you'll be going away for a long time. Or we just let you stew behind bars for a few days until you decide to cooperate."

"I don't know anything about DeLuca," he whined.

"Fire department," Reluctantly, Adam flashed his badge. He wondered why Wells didn't identify himself? "Arson investigation."

He had trouble saying the words knowing that he didn't have the right to use his badge. They were impersonating arson investigators, operating under false pretenses. What could they hope to uncover? And what would they do if they found something?

He turned the rearview mirror so he could see in the back seat. There was fear in Peavey's eyes. Adam had to keep a straight face while Wells played the bad guy role from some old movie.

Peavey still thought that he could lie his way out of trouble. He hoped by giving up a little information, he could make himself look innocent and good. Both Wells and Adam had seen it too often, and Peavey was not even good at it.

"You're a bad liar," Wells told him.

Adam was trying to imagine how Peavey could fly the complicated jet they had seen at the airport. He was too much like a scared street punk and too young. It looked like he still had trouble with his complexion. Who would want to fly with a kid, especially a kid with a row of earrings?

They stopped the car in a deserted parking lot by the freeway. Wells could see the worry on Adam's face. He ordered Peavey to stay in the car so that they could talk outside near the back of the car. There was no place for the young pilot to go.

"Why don't you just tell him you are with ICE and let me out of this?"

"Because if he thinks it's federal, he'll clam up and start asking for an attorney."

"You think he's that smart?"

"He watches television." Wells turned away from the car to show Adam a miniature tape recorder. "But not too smart. He's been an accessory. Hell no! He's guilty of kidnapping. The little asshole knows what he's been doing."

"Even this guy is smart enough to know he does not have to tell us anything."

"We will have to scare him to get anything out of him." Wells tapped on the tape recorder in his coat pocket. "Just watch what you say."

While they talked, Peavey edged over to the right

Milk Market

side of the car and quietly lifted the door handle. In one quick move, he pushed the door open and rolled to the ground. In an instant, before Wells and Adam could turn their heads he was sprinting toward an alley on the next block.

"What the...?" Adam was running in pursuit.

Wells got in the car and spun the tires, flying across the curb into the street and toward the other end of the block. While Adam chased on foot, Wells caught the winded Peavey on the next street. He drove by and grabbed the young pilot by the shirt with a twist. Adam caught up in time to throw him into the back seat.

"Let's see! Unlawful flight. You just managed to get yourself in a little deeper."

"I want a lawyer," Peavey said, breathless.

"Where were you on Sunday?" Adam asked.

"None of your business."

"I think I can put you on Ridgedale Avenue starting a fire that killed Tony DeLuca," Adam contended.

"No you can't! Why would I want to hurt Tony?"

"Maybe you wanted to fly left seat." Wells suggested.

"I did fly left seat, whenever I wanted."

"How about this week? Did you make a little trip this week?" Wells asked.

Peavey's face darkened. "I don't remember. Did I?"

"You flew 719J on Tuesday. We've got air traffic control checking their logs now to find out exactly when and where you went," Wells lied.

"If it flew, that doesn't mean I was flying it."

"You know it wasn't DeLuca. Maybe Rainbow has another pilot. You would tell us that wouldn't you?" Wells had Peavey backed into a corner. They both knew it.

"I don't know who else flies for Rainbow."

"Our witnesses say you and DeLuca." Adam was sure of himself.

"You must be logging all these jet hours, right?" Wells knew something about flying. "If you aren't keeping a log book, then you're in trouble with the FAA too. But that will be the least of your problems. I think arson and murder will be enough for your lawyer to deal with."

"I don't know anything about arson and murder," Peavey stuttered.

"Well if you don't know, then you know somebody who does. Let's see, accessory to arson and murder. That's good enough. And don't forget unlawful flight to avoid prosecution. Give him his rights, Bennett."

Adam remembered the Miranda statement too well. "You have the right to remain silent, you have..."

"I didn't do anything," Peavey insisted.

"Then why are you running?" Adam asked.

"You guys are scaring me."

CHAPTER 13

"I think you should be scared!" Wells agreed with the young pilot.

They were parked on a quiet street. Adam hoped they would avoid attracting attention. The last thing he needed was a black-and-white coming by to find out what they were doing. He didn't want anyone in the city to know he was using the authority of his badge while he was suspended.

With the windows rolled up, the interior of the car was stuffy and humid. Peavey was in a sweat, pressed up against the locked door on the passenger side of the back seat. Adam was still behind the wheel, while Wells sat in back ready to prevent another escape attempt. The windshield wipers ran intermittently to clear the fine mist that was falling.

"Do you want to tell us about it?" Wells asked.

"I didn't do anything. I didn't kill Tony," Peavey whimpered.

"You knew he was dead though, didn't you? Before I told you," Adam asked.

"It was in the newspaper."

"That's a lie." Adam knew DeLuca's name had never been released to the public.

It was possible for someone to know that DeLuca had died in the fire without being involved, but his identity had never been revealed to the press. To the media, he was one of those victims unidentified pending notification of next of kin. Unfortunately in this case, no relatives had been located.

"No, I guarantee it wasn't in the newspaper. So you must have had something to do with it." Adam had the upper hand.

"I heard about it." Peavey was scared enough to talk, but he wanted to change the subject. He told them how hard it was to be unemployed. He had all the ratings and the training he needed to fly for a major airline, but with airlines merging or going out of business, there were qualified pilots coming out of the woodwork. He could never compete with pilots who had thousands of hours flying jets in the military or for airlines.

He had met Tony DeLuca during flight training in Florida. Tony approached him with an offer to fly a Citation jet to Mexico once in a while for good money. At first he declined because he would never be involved with smuggling drugs. But when he was assured that illegal drugs were not involved, he was happy to take the job. He needed the money. DeLuca helped him get the type rating needed to fly the Citation, then they took turns or flew together averaging two or three trips a month for a travel agent in Mexico. Usually it was to bring someone down for vacation. Often the travel agent flew back and forth with them. The money was good; he had made two trips in one month for $6,000.

"Man, that's pretty good pay for a couple of flights to, where did you say you landed?" Wells asked.

"Cozumel. It's an island down the coast from Cancun."

"I know where it is. How long does it take to get down there?"

"Three hours, more or less," Peavey guessed.

"So, you're getting a thousand bucks an hour?"

"I don't know, I never worked it out by the hour. It was good money," he muttered.

"Check or cash?" Adam pressed.

"What?" Peavey seemed startled by the question.

"Did you get paid by check or in cash?" Adam repeated.

Now he wanted to be vague, but he had to answer the question. "In cash."

"What about DeLuca?"

"What about him? He got paid in cash too." Peavey was very nervous about DeLuca and about cash. "I didn't have anything to do with the fire."

"Didn't you say you worked with him?"

"I don't know anything about him except he's dead."

"When did you last see him?" Wells inquired.

"I don't know. Last week sometime." Peavey was staring out the window.

"How did you know he was dead?"

"I went to his house. The neighbors told me he died in the fire. You have to talk to Carlos. Carlos told me DeLuca got drunk and burned up in a fire in his house. I think Carlos got him drunk and started the fire."

"So Carlos is the travel agent?" Adam asked.

Peavey nodded.

"Why would Carlos want to kill DeLuca?" Wells wondered.

Peavey learned from Carlos that Tony wanted more money. He was going to blow the whole deal unless he got twice as much per flight. Carlos told Peavey that the boss would not stand for blackmail, so DeLuca wouldn't be flying for them anymore. Peavey had been warned. Before he found out what happened to DeLuca, he had been happy to keep flying and to make the money they were paying.

"Why would you call it blackmail?" Wells demanded.

"It was usually kids flying down there. It was always a kid going on vacation. Like the parents were already in Mexico. Carlos was the travel agent. Kids couldn't fly to Mexico on their own, not commercial, so Carlos took care of them."

"Didn't you think it was a little odd to get paid so much, and in cash?"

"It was like...custody cases, stuff like that," Peavey explained. "They never had to clear Mexican customs or Immigration down there. We always got a red carpet at the general aviation gate. All the officials down there know Carlos."

"You thought that was legal?" Wells asked.

"We were just flying the airplane. But Tony didn't like it either. He just wanted more money."

"You're talking about kidnapping!" Adam was dismayed by the young pilot's ignorance.

"Yeah, but it wasn't right. So I quit." Peavey was a bad liar.

"No shit!" Adam could feel his face redden when he heard the lie. Peavey looked away. Adam felt a burning rage. He was too exhausted to control himself and too angry now about this case. It was too personal. Not only were kids being taken out of the country, Wells was probably right about the reason for it. Wells was right about all of this. Besides, they had taken a good kid he knew from Riverton and managed to get Adam accused of taking him.

"These wasted bastards..." Adam said, under his breath. Before this moment he had never wanted to punish a suspect himself. Now he almost hoped that the pilot would try another escape. Peavey was safe as long as he stayed in the back seat.

"When was your last trip?" Wells took control.

"Last week," Peavey lied.

"Who else flies the jet?" Wells looked the pilot in the eye.

"No one. Me and Tony."

"Where was it yesterday?" Adam asked sharply.

"How should I know?"

Years of experience interviewing suspects told them that Peavey was trying to walk a narrow line. He had been acting like a cooperative witness, hoping to get by with telling part of the truth. Adam and Wells knew that the jet had been gone. If Peavey and DeLuca were the only pilots, then he had made a trip within the last few days.

"You're full of shit, Peavey. We know you flew to Cozumel on Tuesday with a passenger. We already know that," Adam pronounced.

Silence.

"All right, where's Carlos? How do we find your

travel agent?" Wells asked.

"His name is...I can't remember the last name. Anyway he usually stays down there in Mexico. I think it's Lopez. Yeah, that's it, Lopez."

"Is he down there now?" Wells continued.

"I think so." Peavey was beginning to whine again. He didn't want to cross Carlos.

"Can you find him for us?" Wells pressured.

"Are you kidding? I would end up like Tony."

"Not now."

"Why not now?" Peavey was eager for a way out.

"We can put you in witness protection." It was Adam's turn to lie. A suspended arson investigator could not guarantee the safety of a witness.

"Why should I trust you?'

"Because you don't have a choice." Adam spelled it out, "You're up on some serious charges here. As I see it, you're stuck. You end up dead or in jail, unless you help yourself. You're between the law and Carlos. I think you've got a better chance with the law."

"I want to talk to a lawyer before I say anything." Peavey had his last line of defense.

"Stay in the car this time!" Wells again motioned for Adam to get out of the car. They stepped out into the drizzle, again walking to the back of the car while Peavey twisted his head around to watch them talk. Adam wanted to go off the record. He asked Wells to turn off the tape recorder.

"So he's given us a name," Adam said. "He might be a good witness, but we have to turn him over to the FBI. This should be their case right now."

"By the time you explain this to the FBI, especially as a suspect, your Riverton kid will be gone from the

Milk Market

civilized world, believe me!"

"Well, you're a fed. Do something," Adam insisted.

"Don't you understand? We don't have a case yet. This is still not for public consumption. We are talking to one suspect. We need the whole operation. Without the kid, without any kid, we've got zilch. Maybe we get some television reporter asking why we don't do something about this crime. There would have to be a congressional investigation. And I would have nothing for them. If we can catch up with Carlos, we may get the kid. We may not. But it's the only way we get your murderer."

"You're nuts. I've got Peavey."

"This guy is nothing. As soon as he talks to a lawyer, he forgets everything he tells us here. We scared him remember? Tainted interview! And Carlos? If he ever comes back here, he won't know what we are talking about."

"You can do this without me." Adam wanted out.

"Bennett, this is the kid they say you took. You want to get off the hook, find the kid, or whoever took him."

"This little son of a bitch took him!"

"He is just a pilot," Wells defended.

"So how are you going to get Carlos?"

"If we have to, we go to Mexico."

"Sorry, that's out of my jurisdiction." Adam knew that any investigation was out of his jurisdiction while he was suspended. Even Peavey, he was afraid, would question an arson investigation that reached into Mexico.

"I don't think we can get Carlos to come here."

"There has to be another way." Adam couldn't just go to Mexico.

Wells opened the door and sat next to Peavey while Adam got behind the wheel again. For a moment Adam just wanted to go to sleep, to lie down on the front seat and listen to Wells talk. He could hardly organize his thoughts until he turned around and looked Peavey in the eye. It was as if someone else was talking,

"Tuesday night you flew to Cozumel." Adam was intense. "Your passenger was a 13 year old boy who was kidnapped on Monday. It's now Friday. We're going to find that kid, and if anything has happened to him, you are going to hang. God won't be able to save you. I'll see to it personally."

"As far as this arson and murder of DeLuca goes, you either did it or you were an accessory. Do you know what that means? If you protect whoever did it you are just as guilty as they are. We have your skinny little ass if we get no one else. You can have it all." Adam surprised himself. "And there aren't enough lawyers in the country to save you."

Wells looked at him with surprise too. Adam had become a believer.

"You have one chance before we arrest you. This is it," Adam said.

"What's that?" Peavey moaned.

"Give us everything you've got. If it's good enough, we'll do everything we can to help you," Wells offered.

Peavey pressed hard against the car door. Adam was afraid he might be getting ready to bolt again, but the pilot was ashen gray and his hands were folded in

Milk Market

his lap, shaking.

"Peavey!" Wells had his attention. "What makes you think Carlos won't do you as quick as he did DeLuca? What have you got on him that makes you think your life means anything? The only way we can help you is if you tell us everything. No bullshit. If you don't, you are going down! One way or the other, you are going down. I mean dead or behind bars for a long time. You had to know what they were doing with these kids, little playthings for rich people. Christ, man! You had to know. No one is that naive."

The facade that Peavey had tried to maintain had disappeared. No longer just afraid, he was shaken. He squirmed in his seat, running his fingers through his hair.

"Have you got a brother, a little brother?" Adam wondered.

"No."

'Have you ever heard of the Milk Market?" Wells asked.

"No, I don't know what that is."

"All right," Adam was getting more impatient, "Do you have a family at all? Some little boys or girls? Do you give a shit about anyone?"

"Yes. I do." Peavey was choking. He tried not to whimper or cry, but he was on the edge.

"Then try to imagine where you have been taking them. Do you know what is happening to these kids?" Adam whispered.

"Sweet young thing like you is going to know pretty soon, in prison," Wells added.

"It's up to you." Adam knew they were pouring it on thick, but there was a crack that they had to exploit. Now was not the time to let up. "Think about it. You've got about a minute."

It was too late. Peavey had been thinking about it for weeks. At once his face contorted and turned bright red as he tried to catch his breath. Tears poured down, and his cheeks and dripped from his nose. "I had to work. I had to fly. I borrowed $35,000 to get all my ratings." Great sobs punctuated his breathless words.

"How did I know that there were going to be all these experienced airline pilots on unemployment ahead of me?" He continued, "It was just money and a chance to fly. A chance to build hours in a jet. I didn't know what the hell was going on until DeLuca told me. I didn't know how to quit. Don't you think I knew what would happen if I tried to quit? Look at Tony."

"Well, you did quit now," Wells replied.

"I'm sorry. Lord, I'm sorry. I don't know what to do. I wish I had flipped hamburgers or something. Anything!"

"Too late for that." Adam and Wells said it together.

"What am I going to do?" Peavey cried.

"Help us," Adam stated. "That's your only choice."

"There's nothing I can do."

"Just help us! Give us everything you've got," Wells pleaded. "How about your log book? Are you tracking all this jet time?"

Peavey didn't say anything. He couldn't control his sobbing.

"All these trips to Cozumel are documented then?" Wells asked.

"There's one other person," Peavey whimpered.

"What?" Wells had turned away. Now he and Adam looked back at the young pilot. "You don't need a copilot do you?"

"I don't mean that. There's another guy that helps Carlos. Dave. His last name is Runyan, or something like that. I don't know where he lives or anything. He helps Carlos sometimes."

"What do you mean, he helps?" Adam demanded.

"He brings the passenger sometimes."

"Tell us anything. What kind of car does he drive? What does he look like? Tell us anything you know!"

"That's all I know," Peavey whined. "Except he knows how to start a fire so nobody can tell it wasn't an accident. Carlos told me that."

On the job, Adam would have been elated to get information like this from a witness. He had to get the details and names to Stewart. Maybe it would be enough to get arson and homicide fully involved in the case. At least it would give Stewart some hope and a lead to follow. Carlos Lopez and David Runyan. If he were at work, he would already be running a record check on both names. Now he had to leave it to Stewart.

"Can you get hold of Runyan or Carlos?" he asked.

"No way. They call me when they want me," Peavey said.

"Wait a minute." Adam realized as he spoke that finding Runyan could take days or weeks. "Is there anyway we can get to Carlos?"

"No. No, he's in Cozumel."

"Where does he stay when he is here?" Adam questioned.

"I don't know."

"Can you fly us to Mexico?" Wells asked.

"Yeah, if I wanted to die!" Peavey responded.

"You're in deep shit no matter what. But we can guarantee your safety. No one will get to you," Wells promised.

"How are you going to do that?" Peavey was interested in Wells statement. So was Adam.

"Can you get us there right now?" Wells repeated.

"Sure, if the Citation is fueled."

"Don't worry, it's ready to go," he was assured. "We checked."

"Even if you went down there, do you think you could find Carlos?" Adam asked.

"He's got a bar down there," Peavey volunteered.

"Let's go." Wells was impatient. Again he motioned to Adam for a conference outside of the car. "We have to go to Cozumel."

"I can't do that. I am not supposed to even leave the state. It will look like I am guilty and trying to escape. Jesus, if I take a jet to Mexico...?"

"We can be down there and back in less than 24 hours," Wells argued.

"Sorry, it's not for me. Besides, what can you do in Mexico?" Adam asked.

"Identify, man! Find out who takes kids, or who is behind it. Find out who does murder and arson. Maybe save at least one kid."

The important thing was the boy. Adam would help Wells in any way that he could if they could find out who took the Anderson boy. The arson case was not as important. His department and the city clearly didn't care if it was solved. The rest of the arson investigators had showed little interest, and the cops wanted only what they could get on a silver platter. Adam couldn't allow himself to think he had to go to Mexico to help, but what if there was the slightest chance that Wells was right?

"I've plenty to handle here," Adam persisted.

"You've got more than you can handle here."

"I've got a wife, a pregnant wife." He had too many responsibilities to go to Mexico.

"I know you do. She normally wouldn't expect you home until tomorrow morning, right? Call her and tell her you're working with me on the case."

"Sorry, you're on your own."

"You are not doing anyone any good here. You can't work. You can only sit around and feel sorry for yourself. And look guilty," Wells reasoned.

"I didn't do anything!"

"Then help me prove it!"

"Why me? I mean, my God, why am I in this mess?"

"You have a murder case. You have as much business pursuing this as I do."

"I don't mean that. Have I been set up somehow?"

"No way anyone could set you up, unless you had some connection to DeLuca."

"No, I didn't know him. Besides he was dead before all this started."

"Right. So why are you in this? I told you up front there was a 1 in 10 chance these cases were connected. Nobody set you up, but with all the publicity you've been getting, you might be the ticket to finding out where this thing goes in Mexico."

"I don't think I can help you." Adam looked at Peavey sitting in the back seat, head in his hands. It was disgusting to think that Ace, a nice kid, was now thousands of miles from home because the pilot needed a job.

"I need you, Bennett. I need a witness to all of this. If we just could get down there and get some names and addresses, we could be back by midnight." Wells went to the side of the car where Peavey sat and knocked on the window. "How long to get down there?" he asked.

"Three hours, a little longer, depending on air traffic and winds."

"What about paperwork?"

"No sweat, it's all taken care of down there." Peavey tried to regain his self-control. "Special consideration. On the way back all you need is a declaration, and be able to pass an inspection. Carlos doesn't want any trouble with customs or the DEA."

"I'll bet he doesn't!" Wells turned to Adam. "Do you think this can be done by turning it over to someone else, by waiting around for someone else to act on this? What did you do when you were a firefighter? Did you sit around and wait for the fire to go out by itself, or did you crawl into the building and get it before the neighborhood burned up?"

"I knew when to back out, when things got too hot."

"My bet is that you didn't give up very easy. Now is not the time to back out. You have too much at stake." Wells paused. "You have to make up your own mind on this. I need your help, but I'll go ahead without you. I would like to think we are in the pipeline here. With you along, I can point to the headlines and say I've got the guy here who will give anything you want for the kid."

"All we have to talk about is price," he continued. "But I think what you should be thinking about is this kid. He's in the pipeline, but we would be right behind him. There is a chance he is still in Cozumel. Somebody has to try and get him back if there is any chance at all. Ask his parents if they would be willing to fly down there to try and get him back. I would hate myself forever if I didn't try. And this can't wait for some bureaucrat. We go now. Later doesn't work."

Adam cared about Ace. He wouldn't be able to forgive himself either if he passed up a chance to save the boy. "I must be nuts. Crazy as you are anyway. I have to talk to my wife."

"C'mon Bennett, you can call her from the airport. We have to go to Mexico." He got back in the car. "Let's go, Peavey. Take me to Cozumel!"

Adam drove them back to the airport. He was tired and confused, and he didn't want to go to Mexico. He wanted to go home. Then he thought about the boy. Robin Anderson certainly wanted to go home too.

CHAPTER 14

Near the airport, a Northwest Airlines 747 on final approach seemed low enough to land on the street ahead of the car. Adam slowed down to watch the massive airliner meet the runway, and then he accelerated again. Wells sat in the back seat with Peavey, watching carefully to make sure their witness was not tempted to make a run for it when they stopped in heavy traffic.

Adam watched in the rearview mirror. He wondered if the young pilot was sincere. Was Peavey truly sorry for what he had done, remembering his passengers and imagining their fate, or just unhappy that he had been caught? He must know that he could never redeem himself except by testimony against Carlos and Runyan and anyone else involved in these crimes.

Instead, the pilot might decide that he didn't know anything about kidnapping or arson and insist on having an attorney. He could say he was coerced into making statements that were not true or deny he had made them at all. If he had known Adam's presence was unofficial, he probably would have told a different story. Thank goodness Wells had the miniature tape recorder. It would help if Peavey's memory suddenly failed.

"Peavey, what else have you got for us?" Wells was mentally putting the case together. "Is there anyone else connected to this that we should know about?"

"I told you everything I know."

"What do you know about Carlos?" Adam asked from the front seat.

"I don't know. He's big. He must go two ninety."

"Is he a Mexican citizen?" Wells asked a crucial question.

"No. Hell no." Peavey was sure of himself. "He brags about being from Texas."

"Good, that's good." Wells grinned at Adam, who was watching in the rearview mirror. "How about Runyan?"

"I don't know where he's from. I've only seen him a couple of times."

When Adam drove into the Century Aviation parking lot, he was aware of the Rainbow jet parked near the security fence. Peavey suggested they drive to the end of the parking lot to be near the Citation. Out of the car, he quickly opened a combination lock on a gate in the chain-link fence. They were only a few steps from the airplane. No one noticed when they came through the gate, unlocked the jet and lowered the airstair door.

"What do you think of the gate?" Wells looked knowingly at Adam. "Easy way to get access without being noticed, right? Who knows how many passengers you've got or who they are?"

Peavey busied himself walking around the airplane checking for mechanical problems. Adam was assured that the pre-flight inspection was routine, but he kept track of the pilot while Wells began a thorough search inside the cabin of the jet.

Adam walked back to the hangar office with Peavey after the airplane was declared ready for flight. Peavey kept his distance, sensing Adam's hostility and disgust, but Adam was not thinking about the pilot. He wondered if anything would be gained by going to Mexico. He desperately needed to talk to Carol, and he wanted to give Stewart the information that would keep him working on the DeLuca case.

A glass wall separated a waiting room from the pilot's lounge. Adam watched Peavey work on his weather briefing and flight plan, making sure there were no calls to alert Carlos or Runyan. From a pay telephone near the door he tried calling Carol again and again, hoping Albert Johnson had relayed his message. Wells came in a few minutes later but went directly to Peavey. He leaned over the desk and talked excitedly to the pilot, who was shaking his head. Curious, Adam stood and walked into the room.

"Look at this! Here's Peavey's logbook and here's DeLuca's." Wells threw them down on the counter.

"Where did you find those?" Adam asked.

"In the bottom of the flight case. Both of them." He had taken the time to go through DeLuca's flight bag in the airplane. "Up to date too, including trips to Mexico!"

With a quick read he had found 10 different cities the two pilots had visited within the last six months. Some of them more than once.

"How much do you want to bet I can find at least an equal number of missing children within two or three hundred miles of these towns at about the same time these flights were made?"

Peavey sat at the desk with his head down. His tears streamed out of control.

"He says he needs an hour to get ready. I told him he's got 15 minutes." Wells was unmoved. "He gave me something else."

"He doesn't want to talk to me." Adam's hostility was clear to Peavey.

"DeLuca made a trip last week. It's in his logbook. Peavey didn't go, but DeLuca told him they transported a little girl."

"Oh God!" Adam was disgusted.

Adam had to admit that each shred of evidence added up, making an incredible crime seem possible. He was still angry at Peavey although he knew that another pilot would have taken the job if he had turned it down. He found it hard to imagine that anyone could be naive enough to think that such a crime could ever be forgiven.

"We have to find someone who can be trusted to hang on to these logbooks, someone who would know how important it is."

"I can take care of it. I am not going to Mexico with you," Adam declared.

Wells took him back to the waiting room where Peavey couldn't hear. "I really need you in Mexico with me."

"Remember, I've got no jurisdiction..." Adam began.

Wells interrupted. "This is still your arson case. Worse than that, it's your abduction case, whether you like it or not."

"No, I'm off the arson case, and there's a hick sheriff working on the kidnapping. My job there is to be the suspect."

"And it's a fine job you're doing." He tried to get Adam to relax.

"Thanks. Why do you need me? I can't keep people from noticing you're a fed."

"Thanks for that," Wells replied sarcastically. "I need a witness, a credible witness. I'm out on a limb here. My boss is ready to transfer me to jeep patrol on the Texas border. This is as close as I've been to proving that missing kids are going out of the country. Everyone thinks I'm nuts. Except you. And you've got your own reasons for not thinking I'm nuts."

"No, Wells, I think you're nuts too."

"I need your help. We might save two children, a boy and a girl. You could rescue this kid of yours. Now we both know they are not going to find him in a ditch or in the river. If you don't find him, they are just going to build a case against you. Even if they never charge you or have a trial, you will be harassed for the rest of your life. You sure won't be able to live where you live now. And who knows about your job. You might get it back, and you might not."

"I didn't do the crime. I know that, and my wife knows that, if no one else ever knows." Adam defended himself.

"I can't believe you still don't get it!" Wells

insisted. "What you know doesn't make any difference. It's what people think, or what a jury says. But even if the kid never shows up because he's out of the country or buried in the mud at the bottom of your river, you lose everything. You are the suspect. That means in most people's minds you are guilty. Innocent until proven guilty is a joke. It looks like this kid is in Mexico right now."

"We still can't say that for sure. And if he turns up at home, I will be in the clear."

"You hope! But I'm telling you, Peavey flew the boy out of the country yesterday or the day before." Wells demanded his attention. "His other passenger was probably the arsonist, murderer and kidnapper. That would be Carlos. When have you ever had a chance to wrap up a case like this? Man, don't you see? We have to follow this just to find out!"

"I told you, if I take off, even for the day, it looks like I'm running away. It looks like I'm guilty."

"We're going to be back before anyone knows you are gone." Wells was winning the argument.

"Remember, DeLuca was murdered," Adam cautioned. "Don't you think it would be a little dangerous to look these guys up? Do you think you can just go down there and what? Make a citizen's arrest in Mexico? Get the Mexican authorities to believe your story? You might just find what you're looking for and end up at the bottom of the ocean. No, thanks. I'd rather just be the suspect."

Wells said nothing for a moment. "That's why I need you. I'm not going to try to arrest anybody."

"Why do you need me?" Adam turned to walk away.

"I need a witness and somebody to watch my back. You would never be exposed to danger. Just stay in the background. I need to identify someone, find out as much as I can about what they do and who they are. I'm not stupid. I'm not going to walk in and commit suicide."

Adam turned around. "I hope not. Besides, you look like a cop. A crook spots you a mile away. Even Peavey tried to bail out the back door."

"Give me a break! Let's just follow this thing as far as we can take it. If we get turned around at Mexican customs, fine, we come back. If we get in to meet with this guy Carlos, we learn something. Anything helps if it leads somewhere."

"If we get into this guy, he'll kill both of us. All three of us."

"We just don't go that far." Wells had been convincing.

"But you would go all the way if you had the chance."

"I told you, I've spent over a year on this. This is the first time I've found a source. American kids would turn up here and there, either dead or burnt out so bad they didn't know where they had been or where they were from."

"I've got to stay here." Adam tried to stand his ground.

"You're screwed here unless I get lucky in Mexico."

"I don't know what you are going to do when you get there."

"I don't know either. With you along I would have some options."

Milk Market

"Like what?" Adam asked.

"I just need some excuse to get to Carlos and whoever he works with down there. It doesn't have to be good. I could even say you are the kidnapper that needs to get this kid back. Or you just pose as the pilot while I offer money to get the kid back. We leave Peavey in the airplane for his own protection."

"I can't pose as a kidnapper. Why don't we just ask for the kid?" Adam suggested. "We could offer a ransom. Find out what the price is anyway. That might get us the proof that they've got him."

"Fine, that might work. Unless they want to see some money."

"Tell them we can get anything they need."

"If we had the cash to give them anything they need..."

Adam finished the thought, "why wouldn't they just take it and kill us?"

"Let's tell them that you are a fugitive that needs to get lost." Wells tried again.

"Sorry, if they know what is going on up here, they know I am innocent and I am not going to run and hide."

"You are right, it depends on what they know about you. But I wouldn't have to identify you, just say you are hot and need to get anywhere you can't be found. Don't think it never happens!"

"You are underestimating these guys." Adam shook his head.

"There is another way."

"What's that?"

"We could tell them there is a big reward for the boy. We are after a hundred thousand. Just sell us the boy at the going rate. Or we are willing to split. We can get them their price, no questions asked, and promise to make it look like he was a runaway."

"You are dreaming. Do you think it would be that easy to scam this guy? He is smart enough to have a chartered jet and, if you are right, to be making some big money."

"Carlos and Runyan, and whoever else is working with them are probably just two-bit criminals that have figured a new angle. I've seen enough smugglers to know they are not masterminds." Wells had confidence.

"But you only know about smugglers who are bringing people into the country."

"I don't think any of them are too smart. These are just crooks with a different angle."

"Except more dangerous. If they are dangerous here, imagine what they are like in their own country." Adam was trying to be cautious.

"There is no other way to get at them. Peavey doesn't make your arson case or our kidnapping case. He will help when we need a witness, but we need more. Here is your Riverton kid to follow and a pilot to lead us right to the bad guys. We don't have any choice. You just need to reach your wife, and I have to make a call to let my boss know what is happening."

"He'll tell you to give it to the FBI," Adam answered.

"Not until I can prove something. I'm in the same boat as you are. I have to prove that I am right before anyone will believe me."

Adam was too exhausted to argue. Their cases

Milk Market

were hopelessly tangled. Adam could only help himself by helping Wells. "Well, we have another name now. I have to find out about David Runyan."

"How are you going to do that?" the agent asked.

"I still have a partner. Stewart will run these names through CID. Maybe Runyan and Carlos have criminal records." If he had not been suspended, Adam would have been turning the city upside down to find Runyan.

"DeLuca didn't. But give it a try. Your partner can probably get something quicker than I can by calling Washington."

Adam went back to the pay phone in the pilots' waiting room. His call to Carol ended with the familiar busy signal. For whatever reason, Albert Johnson had not delivered his message. Perhaps the old farmer had been confused about what he was to say.

Stewart was not answering either, so Adam made his request to the arson office voice mail. Besides asking for a criminal record check on David Runyan and Carlos Lopez, he wanted Stu to know there were leads to follow in the DeLuca arson. He wanted to encourage Stewart to keep working on the case. It was not an easy message to record on voice mail, but he hoped that Stu remembered what he said about the case in the morning. Before he left the fire station he should have said, "And for God's sake, Stu, remember to pick up the voice mail!"

Wells came from the office with a large manila envelope, containing DeLuca's savings passbooks and the pilots' logbooks. At the last minute, he added the tape with Peavey's admissions from his mini-cassette recorder before sealing the envelope.

Adam reached for the package. "I want to give this to my partner."

"There isn't time for that. We are ready to fly." Wells held on to the envelope.

"We can't just let this evidence sit here. What if we don't come back?"

"If we get the envelope to your partner, will he know what to do with it?" Wells asked doubtfully.

"Maybe not at first, but he will figure out how it relates to the arson case. I'll see if I can get him to come out here and pick it up."

"You're sure he will figure it out?"

"He'll figure it out. At least it won't get lost." Adam called the voice mail again to tell Stewart that the envelope full of important evidence could be picked up from the receptionist at Century Aviation.

"What about passports? Don't we need them to get into Mexico?" Adam was still skeptical.

"I don't know whether he's telling the truth or not, but Peavey says we will get the red carpet treatment from Mexican customs. No questions asked. Usually they don't come out to the plane."

"That's if we are expected," Adam replied.

"If they don't let us in, fine. We come back. We've got our own plane and pilot, so we make the schedule. Let's get some lunch. Maybe Ace there will be done with the pre-flight rituals and we can get out of here."

Ace. It was funny that Wells called Peavey "Ace."

It was the middle of the afternoon. Adam didn't want to go anywhere, certainly not to Mexico. He was being pulled two ways. He wanted to see Carol, but first he wanted all of this to be over.

Milk Market

"No matter what, we are back tonight," he said.

"By tomorrow morning for sure."

"No, tonight," Adam insisted.

"We will be back before your shift would have been over, if you were still working," Wells assured him.

"But I will be out of the country."

"We'll be back before anyone knows that you're gone. Try calling home again. Tell her you'll be home tomorrow. You were going to work a 24-hour shift anyway."

"I know, but I call her every evening after the news."

"Either we will be back or near a telephone, so don't worry."

"I still can't believe they would just let us in the country, without passing through customs."

"What about that, Peavey?" Wells pushed the door from the waiting room open, talking to the pilot's back. "What about customs in Cozumel?"

"Sometimes we have to call Carlos when we land, if he isn't with us. Tony spoke pretty good Spanish. Mine isn't too good."

"How did you reach him then?"

"Called his bar. It's got a funny name for a bar in Mexico. I can't remember for sure. La Chateau, something like that."

"French restaurant?" Wells was suspicious.

"I don't know, never been there."

Adam had a sinking feeling as the jet lifted off the long runway at the international airport. Was this just a mistake? It was a decision that couldn't be reversed. He was confused by fatigue. He couldn't remember when he had slept well enough to feel rested. It was in the distant past. So far this week had lasted a century. "Our own plane, our own pilot," he said to himself. "We certainly will make the schedule. We will be back by midnight or I will come back on a commercial flight."

He tried calling Carol one last time just before they taxied away, but the phone was still off the hook. There was no way to get through, and he didn't know how he could explain what he was doing or that he was unemployed. Perhaps he had overreacted. She would have been there for him as usual, but she would have insisted that he come home.

Buckled into the luxurious seat in the back of the jet as it climbed higher and higher, he could see in the distance where Riverton would be, where his wife would be sitting at the kitchen table. What if she went into labor now? What if she tried calling him at work to come home or to the hospital? He could see her trying to hang wallpaper and suddenly doubling over with labor pains. He should not have boarded the airplane. Now he was trapped, climbing and racing away from the only thing that was really important, the only person in the world he cared about.

Wells came back from the cockpit, where he had been in the co-pilot's seat. "It's like riding a bike."

"What's like riding a bike?"

"I flew A10s in Kuwait. Weapons officer, not pilot in command, but I could fly this bird." Wells was elated, happy to be going to the biggest battle of his private war.

"Really." Adam was preoccupied with his own dark thoughts.

"We're on our way. Don't worry, we'll be back before you know it."

"Are you married, Wells?" Adam asked.

"Not any more. I traveled too much to keep it together."

Adam hoped that he would not have to say the same thing. He was traveling too much today for his sake and for Carol's. Restless and exhausted, he hoped to get some sleep in the comfortable lounge seats of the jet, but he felt guilty about going on this wild goose chase. It was a mess he could not have imagined a week ago. Now he was piling one mistake upon another. Flying away, flying away from Carol! She would be left there to try to answer the inevitable speculation that he was guilty and was running away.

He finally succumbed to the week of stress. The seats were too comfortable. The sound of the jet rushing through the sky and the drone of the engines brought him sleep. Nearly three hours later, he awoke when the sound of the jet engines changed. He could feel the power being reduced as they began a descent.

Wells came back and pointed out the white sand beaches of Cancun slipping beneath the wing before he moved back up to the right seat in the cockpit. As they lost more altitude and passed through some fluffy white clouds, Adam was spellbound. Through sleepy eyes, he could see the sun sparkle on the multicolored water of the sea between the mainland and the island of Cozumel.

The island itself was a jewel in the afternoon sun. Beaches and reefs trailed away to the south, creating a patchwork of blues that varied with the depth of the sea. The approach to the airport took them over the island's only city, San Miguel, shimmering in the heat. Cozumel was just a sleepy tropical island on a hot afternoon. Its only visitors in the summer were hard-core divers, who came to explore its famous reefs.

Adam, unbuckled after the landing, stood in the aisle looking through the windshield. The concrete of the runway stretched away endlessly into the scrub jungle with a shiny water mirage at its far end. Peavey had made a smooth landing. Whatever anyone said about the young pilot, he seemed to know what he was doing in the cockpit.

When they taxied in, a short Mexican in gray coveralls met the Citation far out on the ramp and walked backwards with a red flag, guiding them from the taxiway to the parking spot near a seedy looking office and hangar.

They were a long way from the main terminal. According to Peavey, a Jeep full of customs inspectors would arrive shortly if they were coming at all. While they waited, there was no sign of activity at the customs office at the west end of the terminal building. Humidity started to seep into the airplane. Nothing moved. Even their taxiway guide had disappeared. It was eerie without Immigration or Customs officers. It was just a sleepy airport in the late afternoon sun when they stepped out onto the pavement, a strange arrival in a foreign country.

Adam had brought his gym bag, a little cash and a credit card. He doubted he would need the racquet, but the shorts, court shoes and change of underwear might be needed in the oppressive heat and humidity. He was anxious to find a telephone. He hoped Carol would accept a collect call from Mexico.

Peavey was to stay out of sight. He promised he would stay in the jet, quickly pulling up the airstair door as they walked away.

"It's going to get pretty hot in there," Adam guessed.

"It will cool off when the sun goes down," Wells assured him. "After dark he can sneak out and sit on the wing."

Wells carried a small bag into an office next to the hangar. When his English failed he used slow and deliberate Spanish, asking a desk attendant to call a taxi.

Adam was afraid of a trap. Does someone know who they are and why they are nosing into this business? Peavey had told them to find Carlos at the bar with the French name. A lengthy discussion with the taxi driver, who's English was too heavily accented to understand, eventually brought them to the Chateau.

After a short, fast ride they halted in front of the bar in a shabby slum. Adam felt his chest tighten in the atmosphere of third-world neglect. He had expected something different on a resort island. This was not the tourist area. There was nothing familiar here that he could fall back on, no way that his experience or judgment would be useful.

They were in a place where communication was nearly impossible. Only Wells' limited understanding of Spanish stood between them and total helplessness. Wells admitted he could barely understand the language when it was spoken rapidly. Adam wanted to hear only one voice, his wife's, Carol's voice.

CHAPTER 15

"We haven't forgotten about you," Carol explained tearfully. "We expected this to be over so soon, and it has been really hard. Adam hasn't done anything wrong."

Marie Bennett had been upset enough to pack her little overnight bag and drive the interstate to Riverton. If her son or daughter-in-law wouldn't answer the telephone, she would just park in their driveway until one of them explained what was happening. In spite of her agitation, she drove a sensible 40 miles an hour, convinced that the other drivers could just watch out for themselves.

The elder Mrs. Bennett was not satisfied with Carol's explanation, but she was sympathetic. She could see the stress in her daughter-in-law's face. They sat together at the kitchen table while Carol told the story. It was clearly a mistake. Her son simply wouldn't do the things they were saying about him. Perhaps she should have a talk with the sheriff!

Instead, she determined to help maintain a normal household. Mopping, scrubbing and washing, she immersed herself in housework. It was her way of dealing with a crisis, even if it meant redoing jobs that had just been finished.

"My God," Carol said to herself. "I think she is going to take the dishes out of cupboard and rewash them!" Nevertheless, she was relieved that her mother-in-law could understand why the telephone had been off the hook for three days.

Without reporters and cameras staring at her, Carol could walk outside to get the mail. From the driveway, she looked back at their little house. It meant so much to her and to Adam. Now it looked as forlorn as she felt. It was not important anymore. It was just a little house in the country where a tragedy had occurred and where a tragedy was still being played out. It was a house where a young couple had lived, fixing it up themselves, until he was falsely accused.

Mickey wanted to play ball.

"Sorry Mickey," she whispered as if someone could overhear. "I don't feel like playing right now."

Mickey accompanied her down the driveway to the mailbox. He sniffed around, aware of the crowd that had camped out by the road. Carol could see the evidence. There were soda cans and cigarette butts, fast food bags and other garbage left by the media horde. It had been like a carnival, a good time that left a mess in the neighborhood. She supposed that the trash would remain there to remind her of the past few days until she or Adam picked it up.

It was a blessing that no cars passed on the county

road while she surveyed the clutter. She didn't want to see anyone, even though Albert Johnson and Deputy Heff had given her a reason to believe she might not be shunned in town. Her hair was a mess and she was so big she felt like one of Albert's Guernsey cows, a pregnant one at that. Anyway, without traffic, she did not have to worry about being stared at standing at the end of her own driveway.

They had not picked up their mail for three days, so the box was full. She absent-mindedly looked through the stack of paper while slowly walking back up the driveway. Most of it was routine. There were bills and some advertising along with the weekly newspaper, the *County Messenger*. Its headline said: "Abduction suspected. River search for missing boy fails."

The bold headline crushed her hope. Carol didn't want them to find Robin Anderson in the river, but she didn't want him to be the victim of kidnapping either, because as far as she knew, Adam was still the only suspect.

Worse than the headline were two letters, addressed and crudely lettered in pencil. They were unsigned, of course. The first promised cruel violence to Adam if he were ever caught alone at night in a dark alley. The second was more graphic and obscene. The writer intended to rape Adam's wife and their child to pay him back for what he had done to the Anderson boy. It made her skin crawl. Carol shuddered as she crumpled them up, ready to pitch them into the ditch with the rest of the garbage. There was no way she could control herself anymore. She held the crumpled letters, standing alone in her driveway, and simply cried.

Milk Market

They were on a roller coaster ride they had never expected to take. Beginning with the news that a child was missing, things had gone from bad to worse.

She had nearly forgotten about the odd visit from the ICE agent. Wells had talked about things so out of bounds that they were unthinkable. It was just one of the side stories in this nightmare. How could all of this be related to a case of arson in the city? Adam had said that it was impossible for the arson victim to be involved because he was dead when the boy was kidnapped. At least it was something Adam could investigate.

If there was any hope, even hope that the boy would be found, it was lost in the contents of the mailbox. They had been violated through their own mail. How could people be so cruel? What kind of demented characters sent penciled dirt through the mail?

She wanted to call Adam at work. It would help just to hear his voice. He would reassure her. He would tell her that everything would be all right, that she could return to being happy and pregnant and excited about the future.

The afternoon passed slowly. She tried to nap and forget, wishing that Adam had not gone to work. A can of soup would have been enough for dinner but her mother in law insisted on cooking a full meal.

The *County Messenger* detailing the abduction of Robin Anderson was on the kitchen table. Carol avoided looking at the article. She was ready to throw the paper in the trash when she saw the picture. It was a seventh-grade school picture of Robin Anderson, dressed in a nice shirt and sweater with his hair combed, showing his best smile.

She looked again and again. Then she picked it up and examined it closely to be sure. Robin Anderson was not the boy that had been with Adam on Monday afternoon!

"My God," she said out loud. "This changes everything! Mother, look at this. Look at this, they have made a big mistake."

"We know that, dear."

"No. This is a different boy, different than the one that Adam was with on Monday!" Until seeing the pictures in the newspaper, she never realized that the kid Adam called Ace was not the missing boy, Robin Anderson. If the other boy could be located, he and Carol would be able to account for all but a few minutes of Adam's time on Monday afternoon.

She couldn't wait for Adam to call at 10 p.m. With a little luck, she would be able to reach him at the fire station. If he were not back in the arson office, the firefighters would know whether he was busy at a fire scene or not. She still wanted to keep the phone off the hook, so she hoped he would answer.

"Hi, Stewart. Can I talk to Adam?" Thank goodness they were in the office.

"Carol? I'm sorry..."

"I know it's early, I'm glad I caught you."

"He went home. Adam went home." Stewart was confused.

"He did? Great! Why? How long ago?"

"Carol, they suspended Adam first thing this morning. He left here about 9."

"What?" Now she was confused. "Stewart! You must be kidding. Suspended? Suspended!" The word

Milk Market

was clear and sharp as a knife.

"I'm sorry Carol, it's crazy, but you know how they are downtown."

"But it's after 6. He was coming home?" She was bewildered.

"As far as I know. For Christ's sake, he didn't go home?"

There was silence on the line. Neither she nor Stewart knew what to say. Her hands shook. Mind reeling, she tried to imagine some logical reason for Adam to be suspended. And even then, why would he take all day to get home?

"Car trouble. He must have had car trouble," she guessed.

"But he would have called," Stewart supposed.

"No, he knows the phone is off the hook. He may have tried." For a moment, at least, she felt better. Adam was stuck somewhere with car trouble. He had not driven the BMW back and forth to work in a long time. Maybe it was not that dependable.

"Should I go looking for him?" Stewart didn't know what to do.

"He is in the clear about the Anderson boy. You know, the boy that..."

"I know, Carol."

"No. He was working with a different boy that day, not the same boy! I wanted to let him know that. But now I am scared."

"I'll track him down. Don't worry Carol." Stewart couldn't keep the worry out of his voice. He was willing to take the freeway to Riverton to see if he could find Adam or his car. "You just stay there. Maybe he will call if you leave the phone on the hook.

I'll tell the boss I'm going, then I'll be on the way."

"Thanks, Stewart. Thanks a lot."

"Wait, Carol. I've got another idea. Maybe he went to the club to work out or play racquetball. You know, he might have picked up a game with someone going off duty this morning. Maybe he stopped for a few beers."

"That is not Adam. He doesn't do that."

"I know, but he was really stressed out. I'll check the club and ask around. You stay there and wait for my call. Or his."

"Thank you, Stu."

She put the phone on the hook. There was a sick feeling in the pit of her stomach. Adam suspended! She couldn't believe it. Why did Albert say that Adam was chasing some firebug if he was suspended? Would he go looking for this boy on his own? Would he run away? That was ridiculous. He would think of her and the baby first. He wouldn't do anything dumb, but maybe he needed some time to himself. No, it had to be car trouble. That was it. It had to be a problem with the car. He was getting it fixed and had been unable to get through on the phone. How could he depend on a car that had been in the garage for almost a year?

When the phone rang she picked it up quickly. It was Stewart.

"Did you find him?"

"No, I'm sorry Carol. The BMW is parked here at the station. I don't know where Adam is at all, but I did get a voice mail message. He asked me to run a check on two guys that might be involved in this arson case we've got. Do you know anything about a federal agent who was in town to look at the DeLuca case?"

"Yes. There is an agent named Wells. Would he be working with him?"

"I don't know. He was pretty discouraged this morning. But maybe he will call again. In the meantime I'll start looking. I'll ask around. Keep your line open."

"Where could he be? I'm coming into town. I don't know where to start, but I've got to find him."

"No, you should stay put. At least we know where you are." Stewart calmed her. "Don't worry I'll find him. I knew he didn't have anything to do with that kid."

"Thanks again, Stewart. I can only put the phone on the hook once an hour on the hour, otherwise the calls are terrible, but then I'll be waiting for your call."

* * *

Heff parked his patrol car and walked toward the field house. Riverton Park was nearly deserted. In the play yard, a young mother watched two toddlers on the swing set. The ball diamond and soccer field were empty. Heff intended to change into his sweats and run some laps around the track. It would give him a chance to think.

His summer recreation office was in the field house. Next door was a locker room used for park sports, baseball in the summer and football in the fall. In the winter it was the warming house for the skating rink heated by a banged up old stove in the corner. When the building was open, kids liked to hang around the vending machines next to the stove. It was the most popular place in the park.

The moment he put his key in the lock, he heard a noise inside. He walked into the locker room to find Billy Mayes hiding behind a locker. Empty soda cans and potato chip bags littered the benches.

"Billy, we've been looking everywhere. Your parents are worried sick."

"I know," he moaned.

"How did you get in here?"

Through his tears Billy admitted there was a secret way that only kids knew. A stick between the door and frame could be used to work open the bolt.

"Let me take you home."

Billy didn't resist. He knew he was in big trouble. Heff brought him home in time for supper. The boy was hugged and chided amid tears of relief that came faster because he had done what they hoped Robin would do.

He just walked in the back door looking tired. He hugged his Mom and Dad and cried with them. His mother offered to make him his favorite, macaroni and cheese. Oddly, he was not very hungry. They sent him to the basement shower and kept watch on the basement door to make sure he would never again leave the house without their knowledge. When Heff asked, they guaranteed that the basement windows were secure.

"After his shower I would like to talk to him again." Heff went to his car and made a call on the radio to report that the Mayes boy had been found. Billy's mother welcomed him back into the house. Still in tears, Mrs. Mayes pointed to the basement

Milk Market

stairs. He went down to wait in the recreation room.

Billy took a long time to shower and get dressed in the clean clothes his mother brought down for him. They sat together for a while before Heff asked him if he had told everything he knew about Robin. Billy was a tough kid, but while he pretended to concentrate on a television cartoon, he began to cry again. "Don't tell my dad, please, Heff."

"I can't promise anything, Billy, but you have to tell the truth no matter what. Were you guys swimming down by the dam?"

"No, nothing like that."

"Do you know where Robin is?" Heff demanded.

"No!" he cried.

"Billy, help me out here. I can't read your mind." Heff got tough, a strategy that would not have worked for anyone else. He knew what would work with any of his ballplayers, and he got an answer.

"The only thing I know is that Mr. Bennett didn't do anything."

"How do you know?"

"He was with me."

Heff's heart sank. Could it be? "What do you mean he was with you?"

"I mean he and I were working on his car. Robin left way before Mr. Bennett drove me home." There, he had said it. Everyone in town would know that he had been in the car with someone they thought was a pervert.

"Thank God!" Heff was relieved he had not heard anything that he didn't want to hear.

"Billy, you need to tell this to the sheriff. Mr. Bennett is in big trouble because you didn't tell them everything that you know."

"I know," he whined. "But if I tell anyone, my dad will kill me."

"No he won't."

Robin had left the Bennett place early. Both of them had been there together but Billy had stayed to help Adam with his BMW. Unlike Billy, Robin was not interested in cars or working on them.

Heff now understood the discrepancy between the truth and the allegation against Adam Bennett. It seemed simple now, a question of timing. Billy Mayes had been working with Bennett for several hours after Robin disappeared. It was hard to believe that none of the investigators, including the FBI, had worked out the time factor. Nobody had asked, assuming it was all in a summer afternoon to the kids.

Heff looked at his watch. They had to meet the sheriff right away. "Come on Billy, let's go for a ride."

The Mayes family stared as their boy came up from downstairs. Billy was home for less than an hour and was leaving for headquarters in Heff's patrol car. They didn't know that Billy could prove the sheriff had the wrong suspect in Robin's disappearance.

The sheriff came from home to meet them in his office. "So this is one of our missing boys!"

"Sheriff, this is Billy Mayes. Tell Sheriff Knowlton what you told me."

"Sir, I was with the guy, Mr. Bennett, till almost supper time."

"What? When? What is this Heff? Where have you been Billy? Do you have any idea how worried we were about you? How worried your folks were?" The sheriff didn't understand. He was buying time with his questions.

"Billy, tell the sheriff what you told me...."

"The other night, Monday, I got home late. I was in trouble, so I couldn't say anything. I got a ride home from Adam in his Beamer. We tested the brakes and everything. He didn't do anything wrong. Robin left while we were still working on the brakes."

"Heff, you should have brought his parents with you. Get them in here right now." The sheriff was in a foul mood. "Holmes! Where's Brooks? Get them in here! I don't care if it is suppertime."

"All right, Billy, I am going to have you tell your story again. Someone will come in here to write it down. Then Mr. Brooks will want to ask you a few questions, after your folks get here."

"Yeah. OK." Billy knew he was in more trouble with his parents. Now they would be coming to get him at the jail.

"Did you find Robin yet?" he asked.

The sheriff just grumbled. "We're still looking. It would have helped if you had told us what you knew a long time ago."

"I'm sorry." Now he was in trouble with everyone.

Deputy Heff was in trouble too. The parents should have been there with the boy. Chief Deputy Holmes arrived from his dinner table to lecture him on juvenile procedures, and then patted him on the back for his good work.

Heff had only one question, "Who's going to tell Bennett that he's no longer a suspect?"

"We aren't going to tell anyone yet. The sheriff will deal with that, with the media and all of that.

Besides, the word of one kid...well, you never know. Let's not burn any bridges here. Bennett might still be our man."

"I really don't think so, Dwight."

"Well, you just keep a lid on this until the sheriff and the FBI figure out how to handle it from here on."

"OK, but it's been pretty hard on these people."

"You did a good job here, Heff. Take a break."

He was not on duty, but he did take a break, driving directly to the Bennett place to tell Carol that Adam was no longer a suspect in the Anderson abduction. Billy Mayes had provided a solid alibi.

"I know." She was pleased, but the news didn't create the relief that Heff expected to see.

"You know?"

"I just saw the newspaper," she said. "It's not his picture. It's not the boy that was working here with Adam. I fixed them a late lunch after I got home from work."

"Great news isn't it?" He was choosing his words carefully; ready to explain that the department was not going to let Adam off the hook immediately. "Is something wrong?"

"I can't find Adam!" She broke into tears.

Heff tried not to show his surprise. He recalled that if Adam ran it would be a sign he was guilty. Had there been time on Monday for Adam to pick up Robin? Not if Billy and Carol were telling the truth. She would be expected to cover up for her husband, but Billy had no reason to lie, even if he had his reason for keeping the truth to himself.

"We'll find him, don't worry." Heff had never been less sure of himself.

"I'm waiting for him to call. Or for his partner to call. They're looking for him in the city. They're checking the health club. Maybe bars where some firefighters hang out. I don't know. He doesn't go to bars. Usually."

She had to tell Heff that Adam had been suspended first thing in the morning because he was suspected in the abduction. His car was still at the fire station, but he was nowhere to be found. She had never known him to do anything foolish, but he was distraught. As she spoke she tried to control herself. "He was so tired, I don't know if he was thinking straight."

"There has to be a simple explanation. If your telephone was off the hook, he just couldn't reach you."

"Why wouldn't this boy come forward before?"

"He was afraid."

"Of what?" she asked.

"He was afraid of what people would think, and afraid that his parents would punish him for taking a ride with a stranger," the deputy explained.

"Oh my God!"

As she leaned on Deputy Heff and Marie Bennett, she could no longer maintain a facade. Desperate for help, she cried again. Adam had to be found! They had to tell him he was in the clear.

CHAPTER 16

Adam was surprised to find the Chateau clean and cool, a welcome contrast to the neighborhood streets. A bartender and waiter stood at the bar, smiling cordially, and two customers played at a backgammon table. Ceiling fans provided a gentle breeze in the late afternoon heat. A television set mounted high on the wall carried a baseball game with an announcer commenting excitedly in Spanish after each pitch. At the back of the bar, double doors led to a cool patio and a walled garden.

Wells suggested they sit outside for privacy. They chose a shady table near the edge of the garden and asked for Carlos.

The waiter's grasp of English was limited to the menu. Until he took their order for cold beer, he made no effort to understand what they were talking about or who they wanted to see. Adam felt foolish and self-conscious, wondering whether they had already reached a dead-end until a heavyset man appeared at the door.

The man they wanted to see surveyed the garden with a scowl and rasped some orders in Spanish to the waiter, who hurried to close the double doors. Before he introduced himself, they knew they were locked in the garden with Carlos.

"You were asking for me, gentlemen?" There was no trace of an accent.

"We've got some business to discuss," Wells answered.

Adam didn't want to be included. He tried to hide his shaking hands.

"My friend has a problem," Wells gestured toward Adam. "He wants to retrieve something that was lost from his neighborhood in Minnesota."

Adam could feel his face and ears flush with embarrassment. He expected Carlos to laugh in their faces.

"We came in the place of DeLuca," Wells said, in response to the cold reception.

As Peavey described him, Carlos was a big man of 280 pounds or more, a little overweight perhaps but obviously powerful. Sweating profusely, he mopped at his forehead with a red napkin as he pulled a chair up to their table. Carlos was in control. Why were they bothering him in this heat? He didn't have to admit he knew what they were talking about.

"Am I supposed to know this DeLuca?" he asked with the look of a cat playing with a trapped mouse.

"We understand he did some work for you."

"So you are a pilot then? You have a cargo?"

Wells didn't hesitate. "We are interested in buying a cargo to bring back with us."

Adam's stomach took a turn. Looking around the

bar, he wondered where to run or how to get away. Where would he go in a foreign country? Now he was sure he should never have come. He was a firefighter and an arson investigator. Nothing could happen on the job that could be worse than what might happen here. It was foolish to think they could just walk in and expect a criminal to do business or even take them seriously. He hoped Carlos wouldn't take them seriously. Then they could get a taxi back to the airport and go home.

"Who is this?" Carlos gestured in his direction.

"Adam Bennett. Back at home he's the man in the evening news; unfortunately, accused of taking something that does not belong to him. He hopes the merchandise is here in Cozumel."

"What makes him think that the item is here?" Carlos seemed amused by the intrigue.

"Mark Peavey assured him that it was delivered here."

"And where is Mr. Peavey?" he asked, with emphasis on "Mister."

"We were in contact with him, but he seemed too nervous for this kind of work."

"I know people who would like to get in touch with him." The big man pretended to be polite. "It would be helpful if you could tell me where to find him."

"Wish I could help you there, but he told me he just wanted to travel for a while," Wells replied with equal courtesy.

Adam wondered how Wells could carry on so confidently. Then again the agent was a scam artist who had conned Adam into coming to Mexico. Now Adam was afraid they were playing a game with life-

or-death consequences.

"You can trust him?" Carlos looked toward Adam with some disgust.

"I wouldn't have brought him if I didn't trust him. Anyway, if the property is not returned, he can't go back home."

"And why is that?" Carlos raised his eyebrows.

"Because he will probably go to prison."

"What do you care? Are you his brother?" Carlos asked sarcastically.

"I have a different interest. There is a reward for the return of this...item."

"Really! So you are a bounty hunter. How much is offered for this cargo?"

"The owners are very desperate. I would pay $10,000." Wells made a bold offer.

"Señor, how much would the reward be?" Carlos was no longer amused. When the subject was money, he was very serious.

"If necessary, I would share part of $50,000 to get the item back."

"So this is negotiable?"

"To some extent," Wells responded.

"This cargo, are you talking about the boy or the girl?" Carlos took them by surprise.

"We are only interested in the boy," Wells lied, trying to hide his astonishment.

"I see." He pushed back from the table. "I am only a travel agent and barkeeper. This is none of my business, but I will get in touch with the person who deals in this merchandise. You know, everyone has a boss. Will you be staying where DeLuca usually stays?"

"Where is that?" Wells asked.

"Oh, I'm sorry." Carlos gave a little laugh. "DeLuca always stayed at the Coral Reef. Not far from where you will meet my friend."

"Sounds OK," Wells replied casually. "Can we get a lift?"

There was no reply. On his way out, Carlos talked to a short dark-haired man at the bar who then beckoned to them.

Adam was happy just to see the doors open again, relieved to wait outside for a few minutes until a taxi arrived. The attendant said something in Spanish, and they were on their way to the Coral Reef Hotel.

When the taxi reached the coast road, the poverty of the Chateau's neighborhood was well behind them. The sea glittered, shades of blue and turquoise in the sunlight. Boats anchored just offshore were swinging gently at their moorings. Soft white clouds floated overhead. Waves brushed the sand that curved between coral outcroppings, part of the reef that had raised itself from the bottom of the sea to create a scenic coastline.

The Caribbean breeze was a relief from the heat and stifling humidity at the airport and in the side streets near the Chateau. The taxi was not air conditioned, so the wind was the only relief from the heat. Adam had to take his bare arm away from the armrest to keep from being burned by the sun. He thought about Peavey suffering inside the Citation at the airport.

Their driver turned north, away from the town of San Miguel. The coast road followed the shore closely, winding through an area of small hotels and condominiums. Although lined with palm trees, the boulevard was worn and neglected, a public works project from more prosperous times now gone to seed. On the right, toward the interior of the island, was a thick scrub. It was not the lush jungle of movies, but scrubby underbrush that was nearly impenetrable. The valuable real estate here stood between the coast road and the beach.

Adam felt safe in the taxi. He wanted to talk, but Wells was watching the driver's eyes. He signaled Adam to keep quiet while he commented loudly about the beauty of the ocean and the heat of the day. The driver merely grunted in response, then drove past the Coral Reef, made a U-turn across the boulevard and returned to the driveway.

The Coral Reef was a luxury hotel. A grand lobby overlooking the sea had floors and walls of polished marble in pink and gray. In the center stood a lavish marble fountain. Terraced above the beach was a dark blue pool, uncrowded in the off-season heat except for a few swimmers staying cool at a swim-up bar. Neatly lined up around the pool were rows of unused chaise lounges. Just off the lobby, a small bar was clean and deserted.

A bellman in a spotless white uniform treated them courteously, handling Adam's gym bag as if it was fine luggage. They checked in at the front desk while their small bags were loaded on a cart and brought to a room on the fifth floor. From a small balcony overlooking the pool and beach there was a magnificent view of the sea.

Adam studied the telephone on the nightstand, trying to understand how to make an international call. Carol was now the focus of his every thought. Could she feel that he was in danger? If only he could get through, if only she had the telephone back on the hook.

An operator completed the call but heard the familiar busy signal. When Adam asked her to try again, she claimed the call wouldn't go through because of a problem with the international lines. In frustration, he asked for a supervisor who claimed there was a problem with the international lines, insisting that he try again in an hour. Adam was assured they would be able to make the connection. He looked at his watch and promised to try again in exactly an hour.

Wells was excited when he came into the room. He had been unwilling to talk during the cab ride, afraid the driver worked for Carlos. "We made the connection! All we have to do now is wait, and we will find out who steals little boys and girls."

Adam thought it would be a great thing to know, except that it would be buried with them. "Let's call the Mexican authorities right now."

"Can you believe it?" Wells was too thrilled to listen. "There are two kids somewhere on this island! Carlos slipped when he told us that."

"Then let's call the Mexican authorities," Adam repeated.

"But we can't give them anything yet. And remember, we are here illegally. We're illegal aliens, we better have the evidence to back up any accusations against a Mexican citizen."

"Peavey said Carlos was from Texas."

"But we don't know who he is working for," Wells

enthused. "Not yet."

One thing was clear to Adam: Wells had delusions of grandeur. He was a divorced man with no responsibilities except to some bureaucrat back in Washington. How else could he be fearless in dealing with deadly criminals? If Wells wanted to commit suicide, why couldn't he do it alone? Why did he have to bring Adam into this mess?

This was all a mistake. They should never have come, and they should never have brought Peavey. The pilot belonged safe in a lockup as far away from Carlos as he could be. Protecting the witness was protecting the case. He was going to be a key witness if anyone was ever brought to justice for these crimes. Together they had promised Peavey that he wouldn't be in danger. Now Adam wondered if any of them would ever leave the island. Why didn't they just get back to the airport, fly home and notify the proper authorities?

Even the mission to rescue the Anderson boy was unrealistic. There was still a chance that the boy had been found at home, asleep in his room maybe, or halfway across the country on the interstate. Or his body was snagged underwater in the Crow River.

"What do we do next?" Adam was afraid to ask.

"Just wait. They'll get in touch."

"Wells, why don't we bail out before that? Take a cab to the airport and get the hell out of here."

"Come on, we're in no danger. When they come for us, we'll find out who the client is, who's the boss. If they were going to kill us, we would never have left the Chateau."

"Maybe they didn't know what to do with us then.

They had to check with the boss."

"What have they got to lose? They know we can't hurt them. Of course if they find out who we are..." Even Wells had to admit there was some risk.

"And you trust Peavey with our lives?" Adam wondered if they could depend on Peavey's conscience now that he clearly understood the crime he had committed. "Do you really think he will stay out there in that heat until we are ready to go home? He's not exactly a strong character. What if he decides the best he can do is to give Carlos a call himself."

"I don't think we would have been allowed to come this far," Wells reasoned. "And Peavey is going to stay out of sight. He's scared, and more scared of Carlos than of us. Besides, he knows we left evidence for your partner."

"How do we know that Carlos won't be out there looking for Peavey?"

"Bennett, we have to put our faith in the little wimp. He has to keep his head down."

"All right, how about just leaving me out of it. You make a deal, you find out who the bad guys are and I'll wait here until we can go home."

"I don't know whether they will let that happen." Wells hoped they would.

"You were doing all the talking. You don't need me," Adam said.

"I'll see if you can just stay here, you know, for security."

"Good." Adam was tired. Checking his watch, he propped pillows up against the headboard and laid back. The blue sea washing against the wall of coral below was the only sound in the room. He closed his eyes and worried about Carol, alone in the country, thinking that he was just at work. He tried to nap, but there was too much noise in his head. He wanted at least to be able to talk with her.

In other circumstances Carol would love this place. She had vacationed in Acapulco before they met. They had never been out of the country together, and now their life had taken a turn that made a vacation or even a good night's sleep seem like a distant hope. He wanted only to get back to her, even if going home meant he would be arrested for kidnapping.

Yet here he was, thousands of miles away, and too tired to remember why they had flown to Mexico. Adam regretted the choice. Perhaps his judgment had been clouded by fatigue. It had become more and more difficult to focus. A few days ago he had never heard of Wells, and now they were partners in a dangerous adventure in a foreign country. Worse, they were dealing with a powerful criminal who probably could make them both disappear, never to be seen or heard from again.

While Adam tried to sleep, Wells sat on the balcony and stared out at the ocean. He was too nervous to rest as he waited for the phone call he hoped would bring him to the end of his mission. They both jumped when the telephone rang. Wells answered, listening intently, a nervous smile on his face. They were going to pick him up in half an hour. Adam was expected to stay at the hotel.

They waited together at the lobby bar, sitting at a breezy table on the deck, until Carlos arrived and took Wells away in a black Cadillac. Adam watched as it turned around in the driveway and took a left, following the beach road to the north.

He walked out by the pool, alone, an illegal alien in Mexico. His situation was worse without Wells. For better or worse, international hoodlums had just taken his Spanish interpreter for a ride. Carlos and those he worked for placed no value on human life. Whatever happened to them was not going to be an accident.

Calling home from the phone in the lobby, Adam got the same hopeless message from the operator. "I am sorry, Señor. I cannot make that connection."

He could hear the busy signal in the background. Back in the bar, he tried to think of a way to contact her. He might again have Albert Johnson go to her and tell her to hang up the phone. But then everyone in town would find out he was in Mexico. He decided to wait until 10 p.m. before trying again, when he knew she would be waiting for his call.

He took a table in the corner. Wells had taught him how to order beer in Spanish. "Cerveza, por favor."

While he nursed the Dos XXs a tall Mexican sitting at the bar smiled and nodded in a friendly way.

"Fine. Now I'm in a Mexican gay bar," he muttered to himself. "Things are getting worse."

"Señor?" The waiter told him that two men wanted to talk to him. They came to his table and in heavily accented English identified themselves as federal policemen. Adam could barely understand what they were asking. They seemed uncomfortable in ill-fitted suits and ties. He noticed their rough hands. Mexican cops apparently worked in the fields on their day off.

"What is your business here, señor?" one of them asked.

Adam was suspicious. They did not look or act

right and offered no identification. He was not going to ask them for badges.

"I am a pilot. I flew a businessman here to see a customer." He surprised himself with an easy lie.

"I see. Where is this businessman?"

"He is with the customer," Adam responded, trying to slow things down to decide how to answer.

"Do you know the customer's name?"

"Nope, it's none of my business. I am just a pilot." He hoped there would be no technical questions about flying the Citation.

Were these really Mexican authorities, possibly the customs officers who should have checked the airplane on arrival? Maybe in Mexico, policemen were not required to identify themselves. Perhaps they worked for Carlos and hoped to get more information from him than from Wells.

"Señor, how long will you be staying with us?" It was their last question.

"As long as it takes to finish the business, I guess," Adam answered quietly. Out of the corner of his eye he could see the tall Mexican who had nodded to him standing near the door of the bar. He was too interested in other people's business. Was he with these guys? Or just a gay Mexican?

He could not decide whether he had said too much or not enough. If they were really policemen he might have thrown himself on their mercy. Take me out of here. Wells could screw himself without taking Adam down with him. He ordered another beer but couldn't pay for it. The tall Mexican had paid.

"Good afternoon," he said, in perfect English. "My name is Roberto."

Adam was uneasy. "Nice to meet you, Roberto."

"Do you know who those gentlemen were?"

"Federales, Mexican FBI," Adam answered.

"Really! I don't think so."

"How do you know?" Adam couldn't trust anyone.

"I know they work for a certain criminal who lives about a mile north of here on the beach," Roberto said. "I saw your friend go with them an hour ago. If they tried to take you with them, I would have tried to stop you."

"You're American?" Adam wondered how Roberto knew so much.

"Yeah, I'm from Texas originally, El Paso. If I were you, I would get back to my airplane."

Adam wanted to say that nothing would make him happier, but he asked, "My airplane?"

"The airport I mean. The weather could be bad tonight. You might have trouble getting off the island. It could be very dangerous," Roberto warned.

"I have to wait for my friend, otherwise I would love to get out of here."

Although the warning was clear and he was more than willing to leave Cozumel, he could not go without Wells. He considered taking a cab up the beach to wait for the agent. When he came out, they could go to the airport without even returning to the hotel.

Adam tried not to show that he was nervous and confused. He was too tired to sort it all out, so he tried to be nonchalant, continuing with small talk for a while before he excused himself. Afraid that he might be followed to the room on the fifth floor, he kept walking past the elevators out the side door. If Wells was only a mile up the beach, he could casually walk up to find out what was going on. Maybe he could signal Wells that they had to get out of there. Or maybe it was too late.

He was too preoccupied to notice the beautiful sunset over the sea. Enough light remained for a walk on the beach, where he would be alone and safe. With shoes in hand, he walked on the patches of sand between rocky outcroppings. It was not the brightly colored coral seen on the Adventure Channel. Instead it was dark and hard, with sharp edges that tore at the soles of his feet. He tried to stay on the sand, but as he walked north, the shoreline gave way to more solid rock and he had to put his shoes back on his feet.

There was a large house in the distance, bright and clean in the last light of day. It appeared to be the only building along the coast stretching away to the north. Maybe a mile away, Adam guessed. When the sun set, the sky darkened quickly. Picking his way through the sand and coral became more difficult. Looking back to the south he was reassured by the lights of the hotel. He could always go back.

Watching the white crests of the waves that crashed on the beach, he trudged along until he came to a wall. It extended far into the water and all the way back toward the beach road. He searched for an opening, walking along the wall back toward the boulevard. It was like a fortress, perfect, Adam supposed, for confining kidnapped children or nosy ICE agents. He needed to know if Wells was in trouble or simply making a deal over cocktails. Perhaps he should he try to contact the real Mexican authorities on his own. Back at the beach, he found a hiding place for his shoes and waded into the sea.

When the water reached his chest, he realized that he couldn't get past the wall without swimming so he turned back. He tried to be careful, searching for footing on the rocky bottom, but on shore he slipped and fell. The sharp coral sliced into the palm of his left hand. He couldn't see the cut, but he could feel the warm blood dripping down his arm. With his right hand he held pressure to slow the bleeding. He pushed his wet feet back into his shoes and made the long trek back along the beach to the hotel.

Soaking wet and bleeding, Adam slipped through the side door to the front desk. "Slipped on the coral," he tried to explain.

The desk clerk understood and gave him several Band-Aids and a towel to wrap around his hand. Again he used the stair instead of the elevator. No one in the lobby or the bar needed to know where he had been. In the room, he was trying to bandage himself when there was a knock on the door.

Two well-dressed Mexicans identified themselves as federal policemen. They flashed picture ID cards. Polite and businesslike, their English was nearly perfect.

"Is anything wrong?" Adam asked.

"You came to Cozumel on the private jet, sir? The Rainbow?"

"Si, Yes." He shuddered as he told the truth. These were real policemen.

"We regret to tell you that the person who came with you to Cozumel has been murdered."

CHAPTER 17

"We are with the federal police. We wish to inquire about your business here."

Adam stood at the door in shock. Wells dead! The worst had happened. He knew he would be next on Carlos' list. But if he ever wanted to get out of Cozumel, he could not tell these federales anything. Adam couldn't be part of an investigation. Telling the truth would start an inquiry that could keep him in Mexico for weeks or months.

He and Wells had strayed into someone else's territory, where they didn't have the protection of American law or even the comfort of familiar surroundings. What did they think they were doing? Neither of them had any business being in Cozumel.

If these two were really policemen they would be evaluating his reaction. They would expect him to be startled by the news. Instead he looked worried.

"What was your business in Cozumel, señor?"

"We were going to do some diving," he lied.

"Your friend going to join you at the hotel then?"

"Yes, he was here and left. I don't know where he was going. Arranging for the dive, I think."

A puzzled expression came over the face of his questioner. "We understood that he never left the airport, but you say that he was here with you? He was supposed to be the pilot of your airplane. On his passport we have the name of Mark Peavey."

Adam almost laughed out loud, and then checked himself. He took a deep breath. Suddenly, there was hope, but he had to be careful about his response.

He had been angry with the pilot for his crime, but now, to think the young pilot was dead! Poor Peavey! What he had done was unforgivable, but he had tried to redeem himself. And they had guaranteed his safety!

"Can you tell me what happened?" he asked.

"Mr. Peavey was stabbed to death in the rest room of the terminal building."

"Can you assist us with this, señor?" the second detective asked.

Adam was safe only as long as he stayed with these Federal policemen.

"Can you assist us with this, señor?" The question was repeated.

"Yes, of course." Still shaken by the news, Adam hoped he could hide his fear. He felt bad about Peavey, but that was not his problem for the moment. If Carlos or his men were able to find Peavey at the airport and kill him, what chance did he and Wells have? For Wells it was just a matter of time. He could be dead already. Then they would be coming after him.

"Perhaps you know who to call and what

arrangements to make."

"Of course, of course," Adam lied. He had no idea what to do. He wanted Wells to be there. Yet he could not assume that he would ever see the agent again.

There was a safe way out standing in front of him. If he leveled with these Mexican cops, told them the truth, he might be protected. He would have to insist on being taken into custody. Then they would discover he was a fugitive from the states. It would be better to wait and see what their intentions were and to try to find Wells himself. He desperately needed a friend here now. There had to be someone he could trust.

"By the way, do you have any idea why Mr. Peavey's passport was not stamped on his arrival here?"

"I don't know. I didn't think he had his passport. We were told they were unnecessary," Adam answered, innocently.

"I would suggest, señor, that in view of all these complications, that you find an attorney here in Cozumel to assist you. It will make these things easier for you."

"Tomorrow, perhaps, will be soon enough for the identification of Mr. Peavey," added the other. He handed Adam a card with an address and telephone number.

"Thank you. Of course I'll be glad to help."

He was shaking behind the door as he listened to their steps on the ceramic floor in the elevator lobby. It was a relief to hear the elevator door close. They were right. He needed an attorney. More than they knew, he needed an attorney to help him figure a way out of this. A good attorney now could name his price. Carol would agree. If they could just have a second chance!

The face in the bathroom mirror looked desperate. He wished he could go to sleep and awaken from the nightmare, but it was too dangerous to stay in the room where he could easily be found. The bleeding had stopped but the palm of his right hand throbbed with pain. His khaki slacks were still damp from his encounter with the reef, so he changed into the shorts in his gym bag. Still shaking, he walked down the back stairs and slipped out of the side door behind the lobby. He intended to stay out of sight in the shelter of the dark. Alone, sitting at the edge of the beach in the twilight, he feared for his life.

Wells had been wrong. This was not just a game but dangerous business. Peavey's body had been found at the airport. Carlos was so secure on the island that he didn't even have to worry about hiding the crime. How did Carlos know the pilot was out there hiding in the airplane? Next, he supposed, Wells' body would turn up in the jungle somewhere. But even if Wells was still alive, they were marooned on the island 2000 miles from home without a pilot.

He had only himself to blame. This was the price to be paid for being unable to face Carol about the suspension, trying to protect her from more bad news and his own shame. Going to Mexico made it worse instead of better. It had been naive to think they would be back before morning. Now he couldn't be sure he would ever return.

For their own reasons he and Wells had taken the case too personally. Wells was driven by a desire to prove an outrageous crime and Adam by a need to prove his innocence. Of course he also wanted to make the DeLuca case. That paled in importance to finding the boy and proving to everyone he had not kidnapped, raped and murdered a child.

He could see himself sitting on the beach. It was an odd feeling, staring at his body from 10 feet away. There he was, a forlorn being, lost among the stars and the sand. His life and spirit were in a farmhouse back in Minnesota. If only he could have it back again.

He had a credit card. He could sneak back to the airport and book a flight back home. He would still be in trouble, but all that mattered was his wife and baby. He had nothing to do with the Anderson boy's abduction. If the people of Riverton thought he did, a move would put it all behind them. He could find a job anywhere, doing anything. The middle of North Dakota would be fine. Or they could move to Green Bay so Carol could be near her family. The two of them could fly away from all of this. But she was not here.

Now he knew that his life was insignificant without Carol and their baby. Without them his life was as meaningless as the waves that lapped at the shore disappearing into the sand, soaked up as if they never existed.

Wells had been gone several hours. Peavey had been murdered by the same people that Wells had gone to see. What could he have been doing all this time if he was not dead? Adam was next, as soon as they could find him. If Wells didn't show up soon, he would have to stay out here in the dark until he could find his way to the airport. He couldn't even trust a taxi driver.

There were still the Mexican authorities. Because he had already mislead them, they would probably just throw him in jail until they could sort it all out. Then they would find out he was a fugitive. The options were few. He could choose between death and a Mexican jail unless he could slip onto a commercial flight back to the states.

Suddenly there was only one choice. He had to know what happened to Wells. Even if he could escape to the airport, Adam would not leave the agent. Like it or not, Wells was his partner and his only witness. If Wells was never found, the authorities would think he was just a guilty fugitive with an unconvincing story. "What federal agent?" they would ask. The truth was beyond belief. Wells had to be alive.

Adam would have to have another try at the walled house up the beach. No one would see him as he stumbled up the beach in the dark through thick shrubs and outcroppings of coral. If he could avoid being cut up on the rock, he could swim around the wall. If it looked too dangerous, he would swim back without being noticed. This time he would have more respect for the coral.

The wall was even more formidable at night. It was higher and seemed to extend farther into the water. For the second time, he found a place for his shoes and wallet where they could be found again in the dark. At least swimming would be easier in the gym shorts.

With only the stars to guide him, tiny reflections

dancing on the waves, he waded out. This time he kept his balance in the swells that threatened to pitch him down onto the sharp rocks. The gash in his palm of his hand stung when it touched the saltwater. When it was deep enough to swim, he gave the wall itself wide berth. He worried about sharks or some unknown danger that might be in the water. Was there something else in the sea to keep intruders away from the house?

At the outer end, his feet found a metal pipe that extended under the surface beyond the concrete. Treading water he surveyed the house. There was a wide sandy beach, then a rock wall that supported a dimly lit terrace. The house was bright and inviting. Too inviting. Too much like a trap.

There were murderers waiting for him. If Wells were already dead, what good would it do to give himself up to them? Even if the agent were still alive, Adam wouldn't be able to help. This was his last chance to back away, to swim back to his shoes and make his way to the airport.

A chill went through his body. It was too late. He had to find out what went on behind the walls, even if he found out Wells was dead. They had come too far together.

Swimming quietly, he reached shore and waited at the water's edge for any sign of alarm from the house or grounds. He hoped there were no dogs. Nothing moved, so he climbed slowly among the decorative shrubs close to the wall and took cover behind the sharp rocks of the sea wall. Alert for a guard or for any eyes that would catch him trespassing, he was ready to dive back into the sea and swim away.

Hiding on the sandy beach he tried to catch his breath and quiet his pounding heart.

The house was open to the sea. In the shadow of the rock wall, he was only a wide patio away from the front of the house. The stone floor at his eye level extended all the way to the open sliding doors. High above the first floor, a crystal chandelier glistened. Every light in the house appeared to be on, but no one was in sight.

He used the cover of the landscaped grounds, palm trees and tropical shrubs to move slowly around the house. In the street side courtyard he spotted the long black Cadillac that had picked up Wells at the hotel. There were two men sitting nearby on a step, smoking and talking quietly in Spanish. He thought they were the two that had posed as policemen in the hotel. If only he knew the language! They could be pretending they didn't know he was there, preparing to jump him. They kept talking as he moved back to the side of the house, checking each window that had a light.

Strangely, he was not afraid, even though his heartbeat pounded in his ears.

Then he saw Wells, still alive, sitting across a table from a tall bald man. It was a relief to see his unmistakable black face. He was leaning back in a chair, talking with the bald man who was apparently the master of the house.

Adam moved closer, trying to hear the conversation. What could they have been talking about all this time? Then he saw that the side of Wells' face was swollen and that his left eye was nearly closed. There were bloodstains on his shirt, and he spoke as if his jaw was broken.

Milk Market

"No...cargo...nothing locked in the airplane," he said, in a voice barely audible to Adam. Wells could hardly speak.

"And who was your pilot, where did you say he was?"

"At the hotel, probably wondering where I've been." Wells struggled with the words.

"How about Peavey? You know Peavey?"

"My pilot's at the Coral..." He couldn't finish.

"Yes, my people talked with him."

"He's got nothing to do with this." Wells mouthed the words, painfully.

"Peavey didn't come here with you?" The bald man was impatient.

"No, he told me to come here."

"You told Carlos you were ready to tell the truth. Now why are you lying to me?"

"I don't know what you mean," the agent mumbled.

"Peavey was found dead at the airport. Before he died he told Carlos about you and the other, Bennett."

"What? Why?" Wells appeared to be confused. He realized that he would not live through the night.

"The authorities believe you and your friend killed him. I want to know who you are. And everything Peavey told you."

"Nothing. Nothing."

"Mr. Wells, you are trying my patience. When Carlos talks to your friend Bennett, I will learn the truth."

"Bennett knows nothing about this." Wells continued to protect Adam.

"We will see! He will be here soon."

Wells closed his eyes and groaned.

Adam groaned with Wells. He wanted to get far away as quickly as possible.

"Now I owe you something for bringing Peavey to us." The big man walked to the door and shouted something in Spanish. Two thugs came in and snatched Wells up from the chair, hurrying him to the door and to the waiting car.

Adam was now sure they had murdered Peavey and they would soon murder Wells. He would be next.

It was chilling to look at the men who would probably be sent to kill him. But his thoughts went immediately to Carol, thousands of miles away, and the baby she carried.

Wells was trapped. Adam was still free, and he intended to stay that way. He would figure out his next move as soon as he got away from the beach house. He had to get away and stay out of sight. It was not going to be easy for them to find him, at least while it was still dark. He moved quickly back to the beach, slipping into the water as quietly as he could. His shirt and shorts were heavy, dragging at his exhausted body. Swimming sapped his energy. It seemed farther now, back around the wall. He tried to hurry, taking air in gulps to avoid swallowing the salt water. He was afraid to look back for fear his escape was being watched. They might be waiting to capture him on the other side.

When he reached the end of the wall, he dared to look back. Treading water, he rested with his feet just touching the metal. The house looked the same. No one seemed to be watching. The waves carried him away, and in one last burst he swam to shore. Groping for the bottom he slipped again, catching himself with a fist to avoid ripping his other hand on the rock. He was grateful that no one was waiting for him.

Out of the water, he grabbed his shoes and ran across the vacant lot toward the road, the quickest way back to the hotel. If there was any traffic he could hide in the ditch. Halfway across the lot he tripped on an old wall, landing hard on his shoulder. On his feet again, he staggered, wet, tired and covered with sand.

In all of the dangerous situations he had faced as a firefighter, he had always known the enemy. He had always been able to help himself. Now, along with the pain in his shoulder, his legs wouldn't respond. The harder he tried, the more difficult it was to run. His legs felt like lead. Out of breath, he finally reached the road and looked back for the headlights from the Cadillac limousine that would be taking Wells on his final adventure.

Adam's hand throbbed and his legs ached. For some reason he remembered that his last meal, if it could be called a meal, had been a stale ham sandwich from a vending machine early in the afternoon, hundreds of hours ago.

He had not slept well in nearly a week. Today a catnap in the airplane and another at the hotel had not been enough. Fatigue had robbed him of his ability to think clearly. Now, when his life depended on thinking straight, he had no answers. His intention was to call the police and tell them everything when he reached the hotel.

He wondered if he would ever get back to the hotel. It was so far away. And would he be safe there? Could he walk into the hotel and avoid being seen or captured by... he couldn't even identify the enemy. He would have to find a way to slip into the building and get to the room. There, at least, he could try to use the telephone.

Even if he could explain to the Mexican police why he needed them, it would take too long for them to come. They wouldn't be able to save Wells.

If he could get to the airport, he would know what to do. He would get Mexican Immigration from the main terminal to arrest him for illegal entry. To hell with the hotel room. He had figured it out. He would have to explain to someone, hire a lawyer, call the American consul, but he couldn't be murdered if he were in custody. Somehow he would get a commercial flight back to the states. Somehow he would get out of this mess. With or without Wells, Adam was determined to get to the airport.

When he saw headlights behind him on the road, he dove into the jungle underbrush. The Cadillac whooshed past at high speed. He waited a moment then crawled back on the road and began to run hard. The harder he ran the more difficult it became. He seemed to go slower instead of faster. As he ran, he was nearly hit by a second car that was speeding along without headlights. Adam rolled into the bush again just at the last moment.

A taxi came to screeching halt, and a voice yelled for him. He vaguely recognized the driver, and started back toward the beach.

"Mr. Bennett, Adam! Get in quick. Hurry, quick!"

He came out of the ditch slowly, peering into the car trying to see who was calling him. It was Roberto, the tall Mexican from the hotel bar. He didn't want anything to do with Roberto. There was no way that he could be trusted. He had come from the direction of the big house. Perhaps he worked with the big bald man that Adam had seen with Wells. If that was the case, he was caught.

"It is Roberto." He identified himself as Adam turned to run back toward the sea.

"Stop! DEA, DEA, Bennett, I'm DEA. Get in the car!"

Adam stopped and looked back. He was tired and bloodied from his fight with the reef and too scared to understand. He wanted to run, but DEA stopped him. Could it be? Could Roberto be one of the good guys? He walked back toward the taxi.

"Hurry, get in, we've got to catch them."

"Who?" Adam was confused.

"Wells, they've got Wells." Roberto reached over to unlatch the door.

"I know. They're probably stopping at the hotel for me."

"I don't think so. Get in! Quickly!"

"No way." Adam wanted to go to the airport.

"Look, there is no time to argue, Wells is in danger. Look here," he reached into his coat pocket for identification. "I'm DEA! I'm on your side. There is no time! Get in quick!"

Reluctantly, Adam opened the front door and climbed in. It was a relief to sit down. "I've got to get to the airport."

"Bennett, you can believe me. I know what Wells is doing here. I was watching the house." Roberto tried to convince him that he could be trusted.

"What's DEA got to do with this?" Adam asked.

"Wells and I go way back. We were in Desert Storm together. I turned him on to DeLuca. I still don't know what you are doing here."

"I was trying to get Wells." Adam was still breathless.

"No, I mean you're supposed to be in your hotel room." Roberto was calm. "You are lucky I spotted you on the road!"

"We have to get to the airport before they kill him."

"What are you going to do at the airport?" Roberto asked.

"Customs, I was going to give both of us up to Customs or Immigration."

"Wow, good thinking, unless they are on the payroll. Almost everyone around here works for Hector. But they won't be taking him to the airport."

"Where are they going?" Adam was too confused to think for himself.

"Hector's got a ranch. We've got to follow them."

Adam watched the hotel fly by on their right, in a daze now, in pain, not sure that he could trust Roberto. "Who's Hector?"

"Big brother to Carlos. He's the guy who just had Wells taken away. He's the boss and the brains."

"How do I know you're not one of them?" Adam was still suspicious.

"Jesus, Bennett, figure it out for yourself. I am undercover DEA. I'm supposed to be baby-sitting you for Wells. I told him to give this shit up, but he wanted to play it out. He hoped you would be safe at the hotel, but one of their guys has been watching the hotel since Wells left. You gave all of us the slip. I expected you to stay in your room, not wander up the beach. Wells said you were tired."

Adam's head was swimming, back in the water over the reef. He didn't know now whether he was safe or in danger. Somebody had to save him. Whether it was Roberto or the U.S. cavalry, he didn't care. He was used up, aching to return to the farmhouse and Carol and to sleep. Now Roberto was talking about a ranch house. Could it be the same place? He was too exhausted to think.

"I thought you were in your room. Wells wanted me to keep an eye on you!" Roberto was going through the gears of the Toyota, speeding down the deserted road.

Adam reeled. Unable to catch his breath, he was headed off to some danger greater than he had ever known. His mind was out of control. It raced, and then retreated, unable to string two coherent thoughts together. Just when he needed to think clearly, he was unable to gather himself.

"Are we going to the airport?" Adam was still confused.

"They won't be at the airport," Roberto repeated. "Hector has a ranch out in the jungle. If they still have the kid you are looking for, that's probably where he is."

"Two kids. There are two kids, a boy and a girl." As he said it he realized there could be more than two.

"What? Wells said you were looking for a boy."

"Carlos let us know there was a boy and a girl. At least."

"Jesus!" Roberto drove as fast as the taxi would go. They sped through the narrow streets of San Miguel, at one corner just missing another taxi that braked and turned sharply to avoid a collision.

Wells had never mentioned Roberto, but the DEA agent seemed to know everything. Too much, perhaps. But Adam had no choice; he would have to trust Roberto. And watch him closely.

CHAPTER 18

"I don't think Hector is going to let either of you leave the island." Roberto pulled an Army .45 from a holster under the driver's seat. "Can you handle this?"

Hands trembling, Adam took the automatic and checked the clip. He was familiar enough with the weapon to pull the slide, loading a round in the chamber.

"Good." Roberto approved and pushed the gas pedal to the floor.

"Is this all we've got?" Adam was less suspicious with the .45 in his hand, but he considered putting the gun to Roberto's head and ordering him to drive to the airport. Turning himself in to Mexican customs would guarantee his safety. But if Roberto was not a DEA agent, why would he trust Adam with the loaded gun?

Without speaking, Roberto reached into his jacket and showed a smaller automatic handgun, silvery in the glow of the dashboard light.

"Why did you think they would go to the airport?"

Roberto asked. He dialed a cell phone as he drove. He was speaking to someone in Spanish before Adam could answer.

"Wells probably told them we had cash in the airplane." Adam wondered how Roberto could carry on two conversations in different languages.

"Jesus, what did he think they would do when they found the airplane empty?"

"They know that already. They killed Peavey." Adam was confused.

"Who's Peavey?" Roberto knew only that Wells had left a pilot at the airport.

"The pilot. He flew us down here. He was implicated..."

"Who told you he was dead?"

"Mexican cops, federales, I think." Adam was unsure.

"Not the same guys I saw you with in the lobby! They were Hector's boys."

"No, these guys had I.D. cards and acted like cops. At first I thought they were talking about Wells when they said my friend had been killed. Then they said it was Peavey. He was stabbed in the men's room at the airport."

"Jesus! Anyway, you can be sure they won't be going to the airport. What would be the point?" He shifted into top gear. "OK! Jesus! Then we need to find a pilot just to get you out of here!"

There was a better solution. At the terminal he could try to buy a ticket for the next flight to the United States. Even if they found another pilot, Carlos was not going to let them leave in his chartered jet.

The sign for the airport road flashed by and Adam

felt a panic rising in him. He was one step farther away from home. He wanted to escape from the island, but he owed Wells a chance, even if he had no idea where they were going or how they could help.

"Just please get me out of this," Adam begged, without saying anything out loud.

Roberto slowed before they reached the town square. He was on his cell phone again, speaking English now, although Adam could hardly make out the words. "Good, I caught you!" He glanced at Adam, then began speaking rapidly again in Spanish. There was a pause.

"Can you fly that Rainbow? No, right away. Pronto. Two passengers. Maybe just one." He hung up and glanced at Adam. "I think we got you a pilot."

They hurried past the bright lights of the town and then turned away from the beach on a dark paved road. There were no streetlights or signs and no houses or farms.

"Where are we going now? Where is the ranch?" he asked.

"We can't just go there, we have to sneak in and hope for a break. There's a Mayan ruin in the woods about a kilometer or so from the ranch." Roberto slowed to find the entrance, a hidden break in the scrub jungle that lined the road. "Maybe we can get close without being seen. Or heard..."

A sliver of moon had appeared. It shared a sky full of stars providing the only light when the headlights were switched off. Adam wondered how Roberto could see where they were going. The road they followed was little more than a jeep trail, nearly grown over and deeply rutted. If they slowed, even for a moment, they would sink up to the axles in sand.

"We should have four-wheel drive for this." Roberto struggled with the wheel.

Finally, they emerged from the deep shadows. The bottom of the taxi scraped the sand and the steering wheel jerked sharply in Roberto's hands. The dim light revealed a clearing in the jungle growth. They coasted to an abrupt stop in the sand. Adam could make out a low-lying structure, the remains of a Mayan temple or stone altar. It was an eerie scene in the dark and shadows.

Could this really be the way to save Wells? If Roberto thought the Anderson boy was being held in the ranch house, they should wait for help from the authorities. Then Wells and the boy could be rescued at the same time.

"Which way to the ranch?" he asked.

"Stay here and get the car turned around," Roberto ordered. "Quietly! Don't get it stuck."

"How far away is it?"

"We might have to be out of here in a hurry." There was no time for Roberto to explain. "I'll go see what I can do, if anything!"

"But you've got help coming, right?" Adam was confused. Everything was happening too fast.

"There's no time. If anyone comes in here, just tell them to go to the ranch. If it takes that long, we are going to be too late!"

"What should I do?"

"Just turn the car around!" Roberto hurried away.

The cold metal of the .45 gave Adam some comfort, yet he felt naked and alone as Roberto went off into the jungle.

His eyes gradually adjusted to the starlight and he began to hear the sounds of thousands of jungle insects. The dark sky was filled with bats swooping low over the gray stone ruin. He could see their dark shapes, swooping everywhere, around his head, between the ruin and the car. Their chirping joined the insects. Then, in the dark at the edge of the clearing, a large creature moved quickly away. He hoped it was just an iguana and tried to remember whether or not they were dangerous.

It was safe back in the taxi. Without turning on the headlights he carefully rocked the Toyota back and forth in the narrow rut until it faced back toward the paved road.

For all Adam knew, Roberto had captured him for Carlos and Hector. The taxi, after all, had come from the direction of Hector's house. He didn't know if there was really a ranch or if Roberto had gone toward or away from it. Perhaps Roberto knew everything because he was a friend of Carlos, not Wells, and he was on his way to the ranch to tell Carlos where Adam could be found. Adam was like a sitting duck, stranded at this strange place. The .45 could be a prop to earn his trust. It might not even fire, or it could be loaded with blanks. He could become a human sacrifice on this Mayan altar. Buried in the deep sand, his body would never be found.

If he had been betrayed, they would come up the narrow road or at least back from the way Roberto had gone. Bats or not, insects or not, there had to be another place to hide. He looked at the ruin itself, but it was little more than a stone platform. Straining to see, he found a little used track opposite from the one

Roberto had taken toward the ranch. It could hardly be called a path. He walked a short distance then stumbled and fell forward in the dark. The jungle underbrush tore at him until it pulled him into the thickness of it and he was too tangled to take another step. He had gone no more than 10 yards. Out in the clearing he could still see Roberto's taxi through the underbrush. Tearing himself free he tried again, walking carefully. His eyes adjusted well enough to take him a hundred yards before the trail stopped.

Adam was now more lost than before. Alone in the dark, he listened intently, but there was no sound. Fatigue clouded his mind. He slowly retraced his steps back to the ruin. His only hope was in the jungle shadows. Sitting on the steps of an ancient altar, he cried and prayed.

Over and over his attempts to think straight were swept away by thoughts of Carol sitting in their kitchen waiting for his call. Every fiber of his being longed to be there for her. He had never been so far from where he knew he should be. He had never been more wrong in his life, never felt more mistaken.

This was not the time to make promises to God. He had already failed a promise to be with his wife and their baby. His survival was less important than the possibility that she would be left alone. How would they live without him? If he could talk to her, he would explain how he had ended up here in this mess. Would he ever get the chance to tell her? No job, no accusation would keep them apart after this was over. If it could just be over!

He could not rely on the Mexican authorities. Visions of a Mexican jail and months of trying to

Milk Market

explain how he had gained entry into the country crossed his mind. No, he needed an ambassador or someone who would believe him. There had to be an American consul or some representative of the United States government on the island. Wrong! He was a fugitive, a kidnapping suspect. He had nowhere to turn.

* * *

Carol wouldn't sit down. With aching legs, she walked from the kitchen to the living room, back to the bedroom, between the front door and the telephone. It was late on Friday evening.

Maria Bennett sat at the kitchen table with Deputy Heff and his wife, Crystal, watching her nervous pacing. The suggestion that a pregnant woman should try to sleep went unspoken. They knew that she would not be able to sleep until Adam had been found, until she could hear his voice and know he would come back to her.

How could everything in her life change so quickly? She had been happily pregnant, living in the country with a wonderful husband. She was still pregnant with all of its pains and hopes, but there was no Adam and no life. Even in the company of friends and her mother-in-law she was alone.

But the loneliness didn't trouble her. It was Adam. He couldn't possibly know that Billy Mayes had cleared him in the Anderson abduction.

Thank goodness for Stewart. He had spent the afternoon trying to find his partner, calling every hour to see if she had heard from Adam. It was a great help, but his last call had been the most troubling.

Stewart believed Adam and the INS investigator named Wells had boarded a private jet on a flight plan to Mexico. He didn't want to tell her until it was confirmed, but she needed to know the truth. Adam had left a package for him at the airport that indicated he was still working on the arson case. The brown envelope had DeLuca's log books and financial information. There was a mini audiocassette that he had not had a chance to play. It all seemed to fit the voice mail that Adam left earlier in the day with the name of a suspect in the DeLuca arson.

"Adam knows what he is doing." Stewart tried to console her. He didn't know the connection between the arson case and the kidnapping. He hoped the audiotape would have the answer.

"In the meantime I know Adam must be as desperate to hear your voice as you are to hear from him. But they must think they are close to apprehending someone: an arsonist or a kidnapper, or more than one."

"This is not like him. He usually calls at 10:30."

"Unless we're not in the station," Stewart reminded her.

"But he told Albert he would call then."

"Carol, I think Adam knows what he's doing."

* * *

Even in the dark, Roberto could follow the path from the ruin to Hector's ranch. He had walked it before in the daylight. He had been able to get close to the ranch several times without being noticed by acting like a wandering tourist with a camera strapped over his shoulder. Hector was engaged in some kind of illegal activity, but surveillance of the place, a small concrete house and a few outbuildings, had produced nothing, not even a clue.

It was not really a ranch. As far as Roberto could tell, there were no cattle or crops. A previous owner might have grown vegetables or kept a few animals. Hector could only need it for doing something that had to be kept secret. The ranch house itself was a mystery, built of solid masonry with a few high windows in the back. It didn't look like anyone could live there. Some fencing behind the house kept the jungle from overgrowing the pasture and yard.

When he reached the edge of the clearing he stopped, making sure he couldn't be seen. An old-fashioned single-bulb yard light and a little reflection from the windows of the farmhouse provided more shadow than light. He could just make out what was happening in the near darkness.

Roberto recognized Carlos' Cadillac parked behind the house. Its engine was running and the radio played softly. Wells was being forced away from the car while his guards argued in Spanish. They demanded that he dig his own grave. Wells refused to cooperate.

"You, dig!" They ordered.

"Dig my ass! What are you going to do if I don't, shoot me?' He could say almost anything. They understood little English, and he wouldn't take the shovel.

Wells was either very brave in the face of death, or he had a desperate plan of his own. Perhaps he wanted to start a fight between them. It might be his only hope.

Roberto hated to turn his back on his friend, but he needed to go back for Adam. Together they would have to act quickly. At any moment the argument could end.

"Dig, Wells, dig!" he whispered. "Dig slow. Buy us some time!"

He quickly and quietly returned to the ruin, listening for a gunshot that would tell him they were too late to help.

Adam was sitting on the lowest part of the stone altar to avoid the swooping bats. He was startled as Roberto appeared out of the jungle without a sound.

"Are you all right?" Roberto asked. He hoped Adam was ready to help.

"I just need to get out of here." Adam could think of nothing more important than getting to the airport, regardless of what happened to Wells.

"I know. I know, but I need you now. They've got Wells digging a grave."

He brought Adam to the back of the car and opened the trunk. A flashlight revealed a collection of handguns, automatic weapons and ammunition.

"The drug war, you know. You familiar with any of these?" Roberto selected an Uzi for himself. Adam picked up a second government model .45 automatic and a handful of loaded magazines, which he stuffed into his pockets. They had enough ammunition to start a war.

"We have to hurry!" Roberto whispered. "Or we are going to be too late."

"What are we doing?" Adam's pockets sagged with the weight of the ammo.

"We are going either to the rescue or to war."

Roberto was still listening for the sound of a gunshot.

"You've got to be kidding. What are we up against?" Adam was too tired to fight.

"I don't know how many there are, but if Wells is quick, he will come to us when we start shooting. Our only chance is to surprise them."

"Is the boy there? I mean did you see anything else?"

"There's nothing we can do about the kid unless we can save you and Wells."

Adam's only choice was to follow his leader down the dark path. Roberto had to be trusted. Their lives were in his hands. The stars made it possible to see the sky over the narrow opening that marked the path through the jungle underbrush. He was noisy, too noisy, but he had to keep up with Roberto, who knew the path well. Suddenly, Roberto stopped and Adam nearly ran into him.

"Quiet," he whispered. "When we get close, I'll move away a little to the left. When I start shooting, you open up with everything you've got. Aim high, we don't want to shoot Wells! But, if you get a good shot at one of them, if you're sure, take it! Stay low and move around because they'll shoot back at your muzzle flash. Keep shooting! If I have to, I will try to go in and grab Wells. If we surprise them, we might pull it off. This is the only chance we've got. If it goes sour, get back here and take off. Don't even wait for me!"

Adam was light-headed. He wasn't sure he understood. He wanted to hear the instructions again, but there was no time. His breathing was suddenly louder than the metal that clanked in his pockets, and he was sure the pounding of his heart could be heard for miles. Arson investigators were not trained for this.

His qualification with handguns had been a short course at the police range, never with the thought that he would have to use a gun to kill someone, or to keep from being killed.

He could make out the block building that Roberto had called a ranch house. Except for the light coming from a few windows, it looked like a prison. Inside, if Roberto was right, Robin Anderson could be asleep, unaware that anyone was trying to find him. He would be afraid, like Adam, if he knew what was happening outside.

Roberto showed him a position near the edge of the jungle by an old wooden fence. They could hear talking in Spanish that sounded like an argument. There was a glow from a cigarette. As Adam's eyes adjusted to the light he could see figures standing by the car. One of them was Wells.

"Are you going to be OK?" Roberto whispered. "Start shooting when I do. Just don't shoot Wells!"

"Here it is," Adam said to himself, "this is where it ends." Certain his pounding heart would give him away, he tried to hold his breath.

In the yard, Carlos got out of the car, apparently annoyed that the argument between his thugs and their prisoner had gone on too long. He was agitated, in Spanish, then in English. "Finish it, I don't have all night. We have to get the other one!"

Roberto didn't wait to hear more. He fired a burst in the direction of the house, and then ducked away to the other side of the path to avoid a barrage into the brush where the flash of his weapon had been. Instead of return fire, there were confused shouts as Carlos and his men ran for cover. Roberto fired again and moved quickly.

Adam had expected to have time to calm himself, but the sound of the first shots came as a shock. It seemed to take minutes to react, in slow motion, even if it was only a few seconds. He emptied the first magazine from the .45 and without thinking pulled the next from his pocket, smoothly slamming it home, then releasing the slide to shoot again. Now there was less shock from the noise and the muzzle flashes. With his left hand he pulled the other .45 from his belt and kept shooting. After the first two clips, he remembered to move away to the next fence post. Then he loaded another and kept shooting.

Carlos' large frame was unmistakable even in the shadows of the yard. At the first shot he dove for cover. "What the fuck?" he screamed.

Roberto was still firing short bursts from the Uzi. If he had been able to see a target, he would have been happy to kill any of them. But he had to worry about Wells. In the excitement, the shouting and the shooting, he knew Carlos would have been well covered. He couldn't be sure about Wells until he heard the Cadillac tear away down the driveway.

Like Carlos, Wells was surprised by the attack. He didn't know who was shooting, but he knew it was his chance to escape. Reacting quickly, he dove for the open car door and slammed the Cadillac into gear to speed down the driveway toward the road. The spinning tires threw gravel against the side of the ranch house.

In the yard, there was panic, shouted in Spanish and English. The surprise was complete. Carlos and his thugs had been safe in the dark on Hector's property, miles from San Miguel. Yet somehow an army was attacking them.

Laying face down in the yard, they were not ready to shoot back. The nearest weapons were the shovel and some rifles that had clattered to the ground when Wells drove away.

Carlos was out of sight behind the shed but he could be heard cursing and shouting orders to his men. There was no one on the island who would dare to attack him. And no one knew anything about the operation. He was astonished to hear bullets whizzing over his head, to see muzzle flashes coming from the edge of the pasture. Did Hector have enemies he did not know about? He barked a few more commands in Spanish, making it clear to his toughs that they must find and kill anyone who dared to interfere with the business. The shooting came from several places and many different weapons. Then it was quiet.

The advantage of surprise was slipping away. Roberto knew that Carlos was getting organized. Finally, a volley of shots was fired into the bush dangerously close to his prone body. He shouted at Adam, who was already up and running. To add to the confusion, Roberto sent a few more rounds back toward the ranch house as they ran, tripping and stumbling, back to the path. He wanted to keep shooting, but they needed to put distance between them and their pursuers. Adam found the path and ran. Roberto was not far behind.

They heard more shouting and wild shooting into

Milk Market

the brush. Carlos could be heard ordering his men to give chase. The shots being fired were farther and farther away. Carlos' soldiers were afraid to come into the brush, but it wouldn't take long for Carlos to think about cutting off their escape by blocking the road to the ancient ruin.

Adam reached the ruin and the clearing first. Looking back he was afraid that Roberto had been wounded. "Are you all right?"

There was more shouting in the distance behind them. Then they heard a truck churning gravel away from the ranch house.

"Go! Go! Let's get out of here!" Roberto jumped into the driver's seat and Adam was barely able to close his door as they jerked down the sandy ruts back toward the pavement. "He got away in the Caddy! All they got to chase with is that ranch truck and a Jeep."

They were halfway back to the highway in the rutted sand when they saw the flatbed truck speed by, followed by the Jeep. Unless he had set a trap for them at the road to the ruin, Carlos was more concerned about catching up with Wells than fighting the enemy army that had escaped into the jungle.

"They never even saw us. Did they see you?" Adam couldn't remember when he didn't trust Roberto.

"No, but they sure heard from us," Roberto laughed excitedly. "They didn't know what hit them. But Wells was smart enough to get away when the shooting started. I couldn't see shit. I'm only guessing, man!"

"Did you shoot anyone?" Adam was excited too.

"I don't know. I don't think so."

"Where will Wells go?"

Roberto was still breathless. "I don't think he would leave you, but he thinks you're safe back at the Coral Reef, thinking I've still got you covered. My bet is he goes to the airport. To customs to give himself up. Or to the airplane to get away, if he thinks your pilot is still out there."

"He knows Peavey is already dead."

"How do you know that?" Roberto wondered.

"I was there when Hector told him."

"What?" Roberto couldn't believe it. "When did you meet Hector?"

"Why do you think I was soaking wet when you found me? Anyway, Wells can fly the jet."

"What?" Roberto was more puzzled.

"He flew in the Air Force."

"Then he gave himself a promotion. I was with him in the Air Force. He couldn't fly then." Roberto shook his head. "Anyway, he thinks we might have people at the airport."

"In the middle of the night?" Adam asked.

"Especially in the middle of the night."

"Doesn't Carlos know that too? If he owns the customs inspectors out there..."

"I know, but they probably won't stick their noses into this." Roberto answered. "It's not what they get paid for. They get paid for keeping their noses out, not sticking them in."

"Just get me out of here." Adam wanted to go home.

* * *

Inside Hector's ranch house, Robin Anderson was

half awake. He lived in a dull dream that lasted day after day, even when the bright sun streamed through the high windows. At night the room was dark and stuffy in the heat. After the first few days, he had stopped sobbing and let himself succumb to the drugs that made it easy to sleep hour after hour. He slept on an old blanket near the door, where there was a breath of fresh air.

It took him a few seconds to wake up, to realize there were shots being fired. Pop! Pop! Pop! Then there were many more in rapid fire. There was shouting in Spanish and a car roaring, gravel flying as it sped away. He remembered seeing the ocean in a dream. The shots were far away and just a dream.

CHAPTER 19

San Miguel was asleep. The shops that lined the square were closed and shuttered. Near the deserted waterfront, a driver dozed at the wheel of his taxi. The last ferry to the mainland had been gone for hours. Adam couldn't tell if it was midnight or 3 a.m. Miles behind the chase, he knew they had to catch up to Wells and that they would never be able to surprise Carlos a second time.

The sandy ruts from the ruin had slowed them down. When they reached the town, there was no sign of a Jeep or truck ahead of them, so Roberto gripped the steering wheel and pressed the accelerator to the floor. Adam braced himself against the dashboard as yellow painted speed bumps sent the Toyota airborne at each intersection.

They could only guess where Wells would go with his life at stake. Roberto was not convinced he would try to reach the airport where he could turn himself in to the Mexican authorities. But there weren't many

Milk Market

other options. Adam didn't think the agent would leave him behind.

"He thinks you are safe back at the hotel," Roberto assured him. "He will escape any way that he can."

"Then who does he think started all the shooting?"

"He's not thinking about that now." Then Roberto added, "He's not going to stick around long enough to find out."

At least the airport was one step nearer to Carol. Unless Carlos and his gang of thugs waited there to prevent his return, he could catch a flight back to the states tonight or tomorrow.

Roberto slowed the taxi when they arrived in the airport circle. There was no sign of the Jeep or the Cadillac. Had they guessed wrong?

"Look!" Roberto had spotted the ranch truck just inside the gate near the general aviation hangar. "Reload! There are more mags in the glove compartment," he ordered excitedly.

"What?" Adam's thoughts had been far away. "Mags?"

"Loaded clips! Stay with me!"

"I think I dropped one of the guns in the jungle." Adam could find only one .45, but he finally understood. There were four more loaded magazines next to a box of ammunition in the glove compartment. He pushed one into the remaining automatic and released the slide. The gun was ready again, even if he was not.

Shooting into the air from the safety of the jungle was different than what they might face now. It was one thing to fire over the heads of faceless people standing in the dark, quite another if Roberto expected him to confront someone in the light and shoot to kill. This was not like questioning suspects who were trying to cover up insurance fraud. It was a matter of life or death. And the short course on the police range didn't qualify him to face anyone who could shoot back.

Adam felt the cold steel of the gun in his hand and again wondered if he could use it. He remembered that Peavey, their pilot, was dead. "If it's them or me," he said to himself, "it's going to be them."

He had lost all sense of time. It was still Friday, or Saturday morning, although it seemed like a week had passed since they had interrogated Peavey.

The terminal was quiet. There were no scheduled flights in the middle of the night, but a taxi could come and go without being noticed. They drove to the main building, deserted except for customs officials and maintenance workers who worked during the night.

There were several taxis parked in the driveway. For the drivers on the late shift, the airport was a quiet place to sleep with little chance of being disturbed by passengers. Adam thought he saw one of the drivers wave them through, as if he knew what they were doing there. The others awoke briefly as they passed, then nodded off again. He hoped they were DEA agents like Roberto, ready to help when the time was right.

Roberto let the car coast to a stop just past the main terminal doors. He was straining to see any activity around the private planes parked away from the terminal. The ranch truck was parked a few hundred yards to the left of the main building where there was an open driveway gate in the chain-link fence. Fifty yards past the gate was a large hangar and the flight office. A few small airplanes were parked near the jet.

With lights out, Roberto inched the taxi slowly toward the hangar. A row of palm trees and shrubs provided cover, but it blocked their view. For a moment they were not sure the chase had ended at the airport. Wells was nowhere to be seen. Then they heard a shot echo across the field.

"We are walking in from here." Roberto said, matter of factly. He was checking the 9mm. in his belt. The Uzi he carried had a fresh magazine. He made sure Adam's .45 was loaded and ready to shoot.

Adam was too exhausted to feel afraid, but his stomach churned. Only the sight of the jet that could take him home kept him on his feet. Hours of stress without sleep or food made him feel cold and nauseous. His hands and legs were shaking. "Just take me home," he whispered to himself and to the jet out in the shadows.

"Let's go, Bennett. I hope we're not too late." Roberto shook his head. "And I am supposed to keep you out of trouble."

"Thanks," Adam replied.

"How am I doing so far?" he joked, nervously.

A second shot rang out from the direction of the hangar and airplanes.

"We've got help coming, right?" Adam didn't want to do any more shooting.

"It's still coming. With your pilot."

"How about in one of those taxis back there?" Adam was numb. "You said you had people out here."

"Still coming. One Mexican agent and a pilot."

The opening in the fence was a few hundred feet ahead of them. They closed the car doors quietly. In the bright lights of the parking lot they were naked, exposed without cover until they reached the dark just inside the gate. The ranch truck was parked in their way, just inside the fence.

When they slipped through the gate they could see both the Jeep and the Cadillac. Wells had stopped the limousine near the tail of the Rainbow jet. Desperate enough to try flying the Citation by himself, he had hoped there would be enough time to start the engines and fly away. Instead he was trapped behind the car.

Using the shadows for cover, Carlos and his men warily approached from the Jeep. A muzzle flash from behind the Cadillac and the echoing sound of the shot sent them scurrying into the darkness. Wells had found a gun in the car and meant to fight Carlos off until help came or he could fly away.

Carlos himself stood in the faint light behind the Jeep almost invisible to Adam and Roberto. He shouted orders in Spanish to two gunmen who separated to go around the car.

Two thugs with assault rifles stood guard next to the truck by the fence. Roberto quietly approached from the rear of the truck and put the Uzi into the ear of the nearest. Quickly following his lead, Adam put his .45 to the head of the other. When Roberto quietly muttered something in Spanish, both guards gently lowered their rifles to the pavement. Another guttural command and they reached into their belts for handguns, which were quietly placed next to the rifles on the ground. Then they turned and ran past Adam into the brighter light of the parking lot. Adam continued to watch them with suspicion, but they never looked back. They wouldn't stop running until they reached the town of San Miguel.

Without its guards, the farm truck provided cover for Adam and Roberto. They listened to angry words between Carlos and Wells that echoed from somewhere in the dark. Wells had escaped once. He didn't intend to be captured again.

"Where did he get a gun?" Adam asked.

"Good question," Roberto whispered.

"Why aren't they just taking him?"

"I don't know. I guess Carlos doesn't want any holes in his Cadillac."

"What are we going to do?"

"Wells can't have too many rounds left. Carlos is just going to wait him out." Roberto understood everything in a few seconds. "Stay here, make sure those guards don't come back."

"Where are you going?" Adam didn't want to be left alone.

"I'm going to try to even things up. I'm going to go in there blazing away. I hope Wells knows when to duck."

Roberto backed quietly away from the gate and sprinted back to the taxi. Adam crouched behind the truck and watched in amazement as the Toyota, tires screeching, skidded out onto the airport pavement.

This time Carlos was not surprised. In excited Spanish, he shouted orders to shoot to kill. Blazes of light and a deafening roar of gunfire were aimed at the taxi.

As Roberto raced onto the airport ramp, he could see the flashes from their guns. There was no sound at first. For a moment he didn't believe they were actually shooting. Then the lead began to hit the car doors with dull thuds and the side window shattered into diamonds that reflected the lights from the parking lot. Ducking down below the door, he fired wildly as he drove, spraying the asphalt and the shadows with bursts from his Uzi. It forced Carlos and his men to return to the cover of the Jeep, a small victory that briefly stopped their shooting. Roberto drove around the jet, sliding to a stop on the other side of the Cadillac. He rolled out of the driver's seat to reach safety behind the big car.

Wells was waiting. He pointed a big revolver in Roberto's eye, then his face lit up as he recognized his friend in the half-light. "Shit, man! Shit! So it is you!"

"You look scared." Roberto was shocked by the look on Wells' swollen face.

"No shit! They're coming for me, man. If they can count, they know I got just one shot left."

"Not any more." Roberto pulled another magazine for the Uzi from his belt. "Can you get in the trunk of the taxi?"

"What for?"

"Something to shoot."

Crouched low, Wells tried to sneak around to the back of the Toyota, staying in the shadows. Before he could reach for the trunk latch he was forced to the pavement by gunfire from the Jeep. He crawled back to the safety of the car.

"No way. They can see me as soon as I get back there."

"We can't stay here very long unless we get in that trunk!"

On the other side of the ramp, Adam had moved away from the truck, back into the dark near the fence. When the shooting began, he raised the .45 to cover Roberto, but at the last moment he decided to hold his fire. He could shoot at the shadowy forms, but the crossfire would endanger Wells. For now, it was better that Carlos didn't know he was there.

He couldn't see what was happening in the shadows between the hangar and airplanes. Hopefully none of the shooting had damaged the airplane. It could not take off with flat tires. Even now, if Wells managed to escape in the jet, Adam would chase it down the runway. There was no way it was going to leave the island without him!

Behind him, Adam could see the terminal building. If there were any security or customs officers who heard the gunfire, they were staying out of sight. Roberto was right. They were not going to have anything to do with shooting.

There was already one body on the pavement. Carlos and two or three of his men were crouched behind the Jeep halfway between the truck and the Cadillac. Roberto had changed the balance of power for the moment.

Adam shivered in the humid night air. His only cover was darkness. He was surprised at himself for being calm. Yet there was everything to fear. They were still outnumbered and he was alone, separated from Roberto and Wells. If Carlos or any of his thugs found him there, he would have to defend himself with the .45. If one or both of the guards returned, he would have to shoot to kill.

Now the Toyota and the Cadillac stood between

Wells and Roberto, and Carlos and two or three of his gunmen. Roberto watched closely as Carlos' men moved from shadow to shadow nearer the big car. He sprayed the ramp with a few short bursts of machine gun fire to force them back toward the Jeep.

"Hey, Mr. Wells! And whoever the fuck is with you! I hope you can dance because otherwise I'm going to shoot your feet off."

"Yeah, Carlos, let's make some holes in this Cadillac piece of shit."

"Fuck you! Your aren't worth the ashtray in that car!" Carlos' voice betrayed his anger. In a roar, he ordered his soldiers to shoot into the pavement under the Cadillac.

Wells and Roberto, each covered by a wheel, escaped the hail of bullets while the tires of the Cadillac went flat in four great rushes of air. The big car settled several inches, enough to provide better protection than before. Then Roberto put the Uzi up over the hood and gave them a few bursts of automatic fire to convince them that the battle was not over.

"Who is this mother fucker that thinks he is going to help you?" Carlos screamed. "Is that Bennett? That would be good. You saved me a trip back to your hotel."

"You would look good pulling up to the Coral Reef in this piece of shit with four flat tires," Roberto answered.

"I can get another car, anytime. You mother fuckers got more to lose. You're gonna be planted in my garden pretty soon!"

"You don't have anyone who will dig a hole!"

"That's OK. There won't be so much digging. Both of you are going to fit in the same hole."

"Your cemetery got closed down tonight." Roberto laughed.

"And we gonna be short one taxi driver too. That's OK. Cozumel got too many already."

Carlos was seething. He was a bully, used to getting his way. The time for cheap talk was over. There would not be another escape. He was too annoyed by this great inconvenience. Wells and whoever was in the taxi were going to die, here at the airport or back on the ranch.

Quietly, in Spanish, he ordered the Jeep rolled forward and turned toward the car. In the same moment, its headlights were turned on and the first rounds hit the Cadillac with heavy thunks and crashing glass.

When they stopped shooting, two carefully aimed shots were returned from behind the car, each to a headlight of the Jeep. Although irritated that his Jeep and his Cadillac would have some bullet holes, Carlos was angry that a simple job was taking so much effort. Sooner or later the authorities would have to respond. But he still had the upper hand. It would be over soon. How much ammunition could they have? And Carlos had not yet played all of his cards. He expected to have two more rifles in the fight.

Still hiding by the fence, Adam watched as the big man worked his way back through the shadows toward the ranch truck. Carlos didn't find what he expected. He angrily screamed a name in Spanish, then another, and got no reply. The two guards who were supposed to be at the truck must have deserted when the shooting started. Furious, he snapped one of the AK47s up from the ground without noticing that Adam was standing behind him.

"Don't move. Move one muscle and I'll blow your head off!" Adam made sure his voice was loud enough to be understood.

Carlos was frozen in his tracks. He did not turn around. "Who the fuck is this?" He was more irritated than afraid.

"One move, and you will never know." Adam was in control now. Not just of Carlos, but of himself. His hands were steady. He had found the strength, not consciously but from somewhere deep inside. He was awake, and he knew what he was doing.

"Tell your goons to drop their guns and hit the road."

Carlos yelled something in Spanish. Adam could see two Mexicans coming back toward the truck. They had not dropped their weapons, but they were confused. He jammed the .45 into the back of the big man's head and ordered him to the ground.

"On your knees!" he ordered.

"Fuck you. You're a dead man!" Carlos slowly got to his knees.

"On your face!"

"Shoot this asshole, now! He's not going to shoot back. He's not going to shoot anyone."

Carlos was on his hands and knees. Adam crouched behind him, close enough to Carlos to keep any of them from risking a shot.

"Shoot him!"

"On your face! Move!" Adam crouched even lower as Carlos finally went facedown to the pavement.

"Now, tell them to put their guns down and walk out of here."

"Fuck you!"

Adam moved the muzzle of the .45 a foot from Carlos' ear and blew a chunk of asphalt the size of a fist out of the pavement. The shot ricocheted off into the night air and shocked Carlos into silence.

"Tell them to put their guns down."

Carlos said nothing.

One of his men was wounded or dead on the ramp. The rest didn't know what to do. One moved toward Adam and raised his weapon to shoot, but a shot from behind the Cadillac spun him around, his automatic shooting wildly into the night sky. As he dropped to the pavement, the other dropped his weapon and raced into the parking lot. Another, lurking in the shadows, ran for the chain-link fence past the hangar and climbed into the darkness of the jungle on the other side.

Roberto and Wells warily left the cover of the Cadillac, then sprinted past the Jeep toward the truck. In a moment they were at Adam's side. Now three guns were pointing at Carlos' head. Adam felt the cool and calm ebb from his body. He began to shake uncontrollably, his heart pounded and a wave of nausea swept over him.

"Good job!" Roberto grinned.

"All right! All right!" Wells was still in shock and disbelief.

"Quick, give me a hand." Roberto and Adam pulled Carlos up off the ground, pushing him over the front fender of the truck. "There are cuffs in the back of the Toyota."

At gunpoint Carlos marched to the taxi. Roberto rummaged in the dark trunk and produced wrist ties. Wells had managed to open the airstair door to the jet. Before Carlos could resist, he was shoved up into the cabin of the airplane. He had been quiet, his ears still ringing from the warning shot Adam had put near his ear.

"Where do you think...? You can't take me," Carlos protested.

"We're going home. Don't worry, you'll get your rights," Wells barked.

"Rights for what? I didn't do anything. I want an attorney here, in Cozumel," he argued.

"You aren't under arrest until we get to Texas. Then you can have a courthouse full. And you're going to need them."

"This is against the law!" the big man screamed.

"Right. It's almost like kidnapping isn't it? Now shut up, or you can chew on a pillow until we get to Texas." They strapped Carlos into the seat with his hands behind him.

"Just to be sure, you have the right to remain silent, you have a right to an attorney. If you cannot afford an attorney, one will be provided. Anything you say may be used against you in a court of law." Wells looked around at Roberto and Adam. "Did I forget anything?" Then a figure appeared in the shadows. Wells was ready to shoot. Adam reached in his belt for the .45, unsure now how many rounds were left in the magazine. He was certain of one round in the chamber, but he was confused about how many times he had fired. He had used only one round.

Roberto pushed them aside. "It's all right! This is

your pilot. The one I called."

"Only if you haven't shot this thing full of holes." A thin figure in ramp attendant coveralls walked toward them. "I'll be surprised if it flies."

"Angie girl! Glad you could make it." Roberto turned to Adam, "She's one of ours."

"I'll take it from here. But first I have to make sure there's no damage from the lead that was flying around here." She gave a little laugh.

Carlos was securely cuffed and buckled into a seat. He offered to spare their lives in exchange for his freedom. They ignored him, standing outside while Angie carefully checked the Citation for damage. Roberto kept a wary eye on the customs office in the terminal building.

It was hard for Wells to talk. He was holding his jaw, sore from the beating he had taken. He couldn't tell if the jaw was broken, but it was badly swollen.

"I wasn't going to leave you alone. I knew Rob would take care of you. I didn't know where you were." Wells didn't need to apologize. "I just hope Peavey was right. I hope this asshole is a U.S. citizen."

"Don't worry. He and his brother are both citizens," Roberto assured them.

"Have we got anything?" Adam wondered.

"What do you mean? Have we got anything?" Wells asked suspiciously.

"Have we got enough to charge him? We need victims." Adam wanted to fly away as quickly as possible, but he had remembered the children.

"We lost Peavey, but we have his tape. DeLuca's log books. Bank accounts. And Hector gave me plenty. Don't worry, we'll put it all together."

"Roberto! What about the boy? Do you think he was at the ranch?" Adam asked.

"I'll take care of that with the local authorities. If they are not awake by now, I will get them up." Roberto knew who to call. "I'll get them out to the ranch and to Hector's house. If there are kids, we don't want anything happening to them now."

"Then take me home." Adam was not going to worry about proving a case against Carlos if Wells thought it was covered. Besides, that job belonged to someone else. Attorneys could finish what had been started.

"You look like dogshit. Are you sure you want to go home?" Roberto joked. "Looking like that?"

"Just take me home." Adam looked down at his torn shirt and shorts. His face was dark with dust from the ranch battle. He looked at Wells' swollen face. "What is keeping you going?"

"I don't know. I've been waiting a long time for this. Besides, I've only been up a day or so." Wells tried to smile. "I think you've had less sleep than me."

Roberto saw the squad of customs agents assembling in front of the terminal. He knew they would be coming as soon as they were confident the shooting had stopped.

"We are good to go." Angie carried her flight bag into the cockpit. Adam and Wells followed her into the cabin while Roberto helped close the door.

"See you, buddy. Good job. Now get the hell out of here!" Roberto gave Adam a big grin. "Come back when you can stay longer!"

As they pulled the door shut, Adam could see the

customs agents parked near the fence, unloading from their Jeep. They were in no hurry.

"Get out of here!" Roberto screamed over the whine of the jet engines.

As they taxied to the runway, Adam was breathless. "Just get this thing airborne!"

Were they really going to get away? He sat back in a seat across from Carlos, too tired to stay awake but unwilling to sleep until they were off the ground. At liftoff there was a feeling of relief he didn't think would ever come.

He hoped Carol would forgive him for going so far away. In his present state, he would have a hard time explaining it to her. What could he say? He couldn't fathom what he and Wells had done. Somewhere back in the darkness, perhaps a boy would be safe, not because of them, but because Roberto managed to rescue them all.

Adam drifted into the sleep of one too tired to sleep and his dreams brought him back to the jungle, where he fought desperately in the dark to get away and find his way home. Would the nightmare ever end?

Wells was screaming in delight as the Citation lifted off the runway. "Yes! Yes! Yes! We got the son of a bitch! Yes, yes!"

"You got shit! You got nothing but a big problem. My brother will squash you like a bug," Carlos sneered.

"No, I got you, you son of a bitch! You're going to be put away for a long time."

"For what? For being a travel agent?"

"Let's see, who was that just shooting at me?" Wells shot back.

"I don't know those guys. I was trying to stop them, to save you."

"Stick with that story, asshole. Lots of luck." Wells laughed.

"What am I arrested for?" Carlos asked.

"Shut up!" Wells went into the cockpit to help navigate across the Gulf of Mexico. Turning back to Adam, he said, "He shuts up or we gag him."

"I am saying nothing to you pricks." Carlos laughed darkly. "My lawyer will have your ass!"

Across the aisle from a man who had been trying to kill them minutes ago, Adam was not awake. Before the dim lights of San Miguel were far behind them, he was sound asleep, snoring.

"There she is!" Wells shouted an hour later from the right side of the cockpit. Ahead of them, looming out of the dark Gulf of Mexico were the welcoming lights of Galveston and Houston.

CHAPTER 20

"I understand you are extremely anxious to return home." W. Bruce Hawkins looked squarely at Adam with a hint of a smile. The U.S. attorney for the Houston district was in a hurry himself. He had a 7:30 a.m. tee time. "I am just as anxious to get you on your way."

Adam was not really awake. He could only say, "Thank you." His nap during the flight back to Texas had not been long enough. Still, he was impressed that the U.S. attorney was there so early on a Saturday morning.

"So I won't be holding anything up here," Hawkins continued. "But I needed to take your statements in order to hold the prisoner. The news from Mexico is this: Mexican federal police have detained Hector Lopez at his yacht. He was apparently leaving for an extended cruise in the direction of Belize. We will start extradition proceedings immediately on Monday morning. Right now, I can't even tell you where this will be prosecuted. I can tell you that we will be able to hold them without bail until they are put on trial. Clearly the brothers would try to leave the country if they were released. And we are dealing with international law here."

Hawkins was not sure Carlos would get a preliminary hearing before the following Wednesday. By then he hoped Hector would have been brought to Texas.

"Mr. Bennett, I understand the news you are waiting for is that two children were discovered at a rural ranch on the island, a ranch owned by Hector Lopez. There was a boy and a girl, both heavily sedated but apparently unharmed. Indications are that they are the American children that were abducted by Carlos Lopez and others. Arrangements are being made for their return to Houston. Once they are positively identified, I am sure their parents will be on their way to Houston for them."

It was a relief to hear the news, of course, but Adam was too tired to be excited. He wanted only to go home, to beg forgiveness from his wife and to sleep. He had wanted to call her as soon as Carlos had been taken into custody but Customs and Immigration had sequestered them until the arrival of the U.S. attorney, who insisted on the debriefing session.

He and Wells had been allowed to shower while agents found them a change of clothing. In gray work uniforms, they looked like a pair of airport custodians that were tired and battered.

A drowsy crowd of officials was gathered in the conference room. Most were irritated. They had been unexpectedly called in on Saturday morning. In addition to ICE, there were FBI special agents, a DEA representative, along with Angie, the DEA pilot, and several unidentified officials from the airport. The room was buzzing as the collected federal agents and attorneys began to hear about the case.

Hawkins enjoyed being the center of attention. "We have a name from the boy, Robin Anderson. Nothing more than Jeanette from the little girl at this point." Hawkins went on to give a sketchy account of the abduction operation, the suspects and the events of the night before in Cozumel.

"The body and effects of a Mark Peavey will be returned to Minneapolis." In bureaucratic terms he was matter-of-fact and routine. Hawkins had a sleepy looking assistant who would have to take care of the details after his boss left for the golf course.

"Now, from a procedure standpoint, I am not too happy with this operation. But from the sounds of it, you both should get a medal. And the undercover DEA agent in Cozumel deserves one too."

Adam wondered if Roberto had managed to maintain his cover. He was the hero who had rescued them: Adam, Wells and the two children.

"Procedure standpoint?" Wells leaned over and whispered to Adam, "Who gives a shit? We got the job done."

It was a moment of personal triumph for Ron Wells. Two children had been rescued, saved from fates worse than anyone wanted to imagine. More important, how many more would Carlos and Hector have taken to sell? Maybe he had not been in time to save a lot of them, but he could account for those who were now safe. And from now on the government and its bureaucrats would have to remain vigilant. This must never happen again.

When it was his turn to speak, Wells was modest. His battered face was his badge of honor. "This is Adam Bennett. He's a Minneapolis arson investigator. I had been following this for over a year on special assignment. He had an arson case and a personal interest. Our break was finding the pilots who were responsible for flying the victims to Mexico. One of the pilots was dead, we believe killed by Carlos or someone working for him. The other was persuaded to tell us all he knew."

The assembled officers laughed knowingly, as if they knew how Peavey had been persuaded.

"That witness was murdered in Cozumel. He brought us down the kidnap pipeline as far as he could take us before he died. Bennett and I were never supposed to leave the island, but with a big hand from DEA, we stayed healthy and got our man."

Wells sat back in his chair. His eyes were bloodshot, his hands shook and his face was swollen, but he was too elated to be tired. The doubters in his department would soon learn what he had known from the beginning. Bosses in government agencies were good at covering their tracks, so they would escape unharmed, but they would have to admit he had been right. The FBI would have some excuse, a reason why they didn't know what was going on, why they could not account for missing children. Instead, they would try to find a way to take credit for breaking up an international kidnapping ring.

He had done what had to be done. It was worth it for at least two families who were getting their children back, if not for his family. His ex-wife, Judy, was sleeping peacefully this Saturday morning without a thought or dream of him. His daughter Charlene might be sleeping too, but once in a while during the day he hoped she would think about her dad.

Wells looked at Adam, nearly asleep, slumped in a folding chair trying to find a way to get comfortable. Bennett was still the lucky man. Poor bastard had been through it all in the last few days, but he was saved too. His wife would understand and be grateful, even if she never forgave an odd government agent who came to her door with a wild tale of juvenile white slavery. However it washed out, even through all of this, Bennett didn't know how lucky he was to be married to a brave lady who would be thrilled to hear her husband's voice on the phone.

Adam stirred uneasily in his chair. He had heard enough from the U.S. attorney and couldn't stay awake. It was cruel for Hawkins to stretch out the debriefing while every federal agency received an update. Carol needed to know he was alive and he needed to know that she was all right. Staggering to his feet, he excused himself and walked out of the conference room.

He found an empty office with a desk and telephone. It was almost 6 a.m. when his mother answered the phone. She sounded more irritated than surprised to hear his voice. They had been awake all night worrying about him.

"I'm sorry, sorry. Mom, let me talk to her."

"Hi." Carol was crying.

"Hi. I'm sorry. Are you all right?" He tried to say everything at once.

"I don't care about me. Are you all right?" They were both in tears, too happy to speak, with too much for either of them to tell.

"I'm safe. In Houston. I'll get a flight home as soon as I can. Robin Anderson is safe. The FBI should be notifying his parents by now."

"Oh my God!" she gasped.

"It's a long story, but we got the guys who took him."

"Then you know that he was not the boy you drove home. You weren't a suspect anymore! Ace was a different boy. His name was Billy Mayes. He came forward and cleared you. I have been trying since yesterday to find you and tell you."

Adam was too tired to understand. He cried as he listened to her lovely voice.

"Stewart and half of the fire department were looking everywhere for you. At first we thought you just had car trouble on the freeway. Then Stewart picked up some package at the airport. He figured out what had happened. Are you with Wells? Are you both OK?"

"I tried to call, over and over again."

"Where did you go? I am just happy to hear your voice," she sobbed.

"I didn't think it would take all night. We followed the Anderson boy to Mexico. On our way back..." It was hard for him to think straight. "The Anderson kid and a little girl were rescued by Mexican police at a ranch. We were there. At the ranch. We didn't know if the kids were there. I can't tell you about the rest, not yet. Not now! I love you. I just want to be home with you, and I don't care what anyone thinks."

"I love you! Just come home as quick as you can!"

"How is the baby?"

"Fine, just come home, please," she pleaded.

"I'll call as soon as I know which flight..." Adam started.

"I'll be at the airport waiting. I love you."

"I love you." Adam couldn't stop crying. There was nothing left inside that he could use to resist. His strength was gone. He didn't want to see anyone or hear another word. There was some relief in laying his head down on the desk to doze off for as long as they would leave him alone. In half an hour Wells found him.

"Anyone happy to hear from you?" He didn't wait for an answer. "Good news. The government will be flying both of us back to Minnesota. Commercial. First class. We get the first available flight."

"I just want to know what time we leave. Or what time we get there."

"I wouldn't miss this for the world." Wells was not listening. "Hawkins says they will have a press release out within the hour. By the time we get to Minneapolis, the media will be on us like a chicken on a June bug."

"I can't deal with the press. I want some sleep. I want to go home. When do we leave?" Adam repeated.

"As soon as there's a flight."

"Wake me up when it's time," he mumbled.

"How about some breakfast?" Wells was too excited to sleep and he knew they both needed to eat. There was no sleeping through this victory for him. "Right now I am hungry. How about you?"

"After that I have to get some sleep." Adam was not sure he could keep anything down, but he knew that he needed food and that he would be able to sleep better with something in his stomach. He couldn't remember his last meal.

"I am tired too, man. But I can't sleep now anyway," Wells said as they walked toward an airport restaurant. Cable television throughout the Houston terminal carried Headline News:

"Two children are rescued as suspects in an international kidnapping scheme are captured in Mexico. The U.S. attorney in Houston reports that Mexican authorities, with the help of an undercover DEA agent, have freed two children who were held captive at a ranch in the jungle. They are being flown to Houston where their parents are expected to meet them. The two were abducted in the Midwest and transported to Cozumel, Mexico by chartered jet. They were tracked to Mexico by an undercover ICE agent and an investigator from Minneapolis who was in pursuit of a suspect in an arson case."

"They got it mostly right," Wells commented. "It doesn't take long for the bandwagon to get rolling does it?"

Adam could hardly swallow the bacon, eggs and toast. The meal tasted good, but it made him even sleepier than before. He didn't expect the hot coffee to keep him awake. He stayed with Wells long enough to book the first direct flight to Minneapolis. It was scheduled to leave Houston in only three hours, at 11 a.m., but not soon enough for Adam. He had been away from home more than 24 hours.

"Why don't we just find a pilot and take the Rainbow jet home?"

"I think it was confiscated by customs. Why don't you just find that office you were in and try to get some sleep?" Wells said. "I'll wake you up when it's time."

Adam needed no persuasion. He found his way back through a labyrinth of hallways to the empty office and stretched out on the floor behind the desk. Wells stayed awake, wandering the terminal and the Customs and Immigration offices. Even after they boarded the Delta 757 for the flight to Minneapolis, he stayed awake while Adam settled into a window seat to sleep.

Unshaven and wearing donated work clothes, they both looked tired and ragged when they met the media hoard in Minneapolis. The railing on the ramp to the concourse was lined with television cameras and reporters. Thanks to Hawkins' news release, the press had heard all the good news. It occurred to Adam that some of these same reporters and photographers had besieged his home only a few days before.

"There's my boss." Wells tugged on Adam's shirt as they walked up the ramp. "How do you get out here from D.C. on such short notice?"

Wells' department supervisor was waiting with the reporters. He had arranged a press conference right in the middle of the concourse.

Even though he had been warned in advance, Adam was not prepared for a hero's welcome. He pushed the reporters aside to be with his wife. Carol had never looked lovelier. He tried to apologize for making her worry but knew that he couldn't explain.

She put a finger to his lips as they held each other close.

"I was never in danger," he lied. He would have to tell her later, when the time was right, and when he figured out for himself what really happened. For now it was enough to understand how important she and the baby were to him and how much he needed them. Without thinking clearly, in the noisy terminal, he tried to explain about North Dakota, that if they had to move, they could go anywhere and be happy as long as they stayed together.

"North Dakota? What would we do?" Carol didn't understand.

"It's just that we don't have to stay in Riverton. I can work at something else, anywhere, wherever or whatever it takes for us to be together."

"But I love Riverton, I love our house. Everything is going to be all right. You have friends you didn't even know about."

He thought that time would tell. She was sure.

A few feet away Wells was enjoying the hero's role, fascinating the press with details and answering questions. His boss stood happily by his side, ready to provide the Homeland Security Agency's perspective.

Adam noticed Stewart's red hair near the back of the crowd and managed to edge over his way, keeping his arm around Carol. "I have to talk to Stu."

"Hey, hero!" Stewart grinned.

"I can't thank you enough, for looking for me. For taking care of Carol." He shook his partner's hand.

"We picked up Runyon. Got his prints on those smoke detector covers. Oh yeah, and you're back on the job."

"We'll see, we'll see," Adam turned back to his wife.

He had wanted no more than to solve an arson case and to live in peace in the country. Now he was not sure about what to do with the rest of his life. He had seen the other side, and he knew the things that really mattered to him were not his job or his house or car. Even his reputation didn't matter anymore. He had something that the Lopez brothers and even Wells did not. He belonged to someone and with someone.

Peavey wished he had just flipped hamburgers for a living instead of getting into trouble. Adam could flip hamburgers too, if he had to.

"Are you really all right, I mean the baby and everything?" he asked, as they walked down the concourse. "I am sorry I was not here. It must have been really uncomfortable for you to drive all the way in."

"I'm much better now that you are here," she said. "And I have a chauffeur."

Waiting in the drive just outside of the terminal was a Crow County squad car. Deputy Heff opened the door for them and shook Adam's hand warmly. "Sheriff Knowlton asked me to provide the escort."

"Thanks."

"Thank you for saving Robin. Thank you from the whole town. I wish you could have been there this morning, I mean when the FBI told Bill and Marilyn that Robin was safe."

Then Heff let them be alone on the ride back to Riverton, nearly asleep in each other's arms.

They rested at home on Sunday and Monday, rarely out of each other's sight. A small army of reporters stayed behind a driveway barricade provided by the sheriff's department, and their telephone stayed off the hook.

On Tuesday and Wednesday Adam tried to tell her what he had been through, but even then his memory was a blur except for some details he would keep to himself. He didn't want to scare her.

On Wednesday afternoon, a small procession of cars came up the driveway. Sheriff Knowlton and Deputy Heff stayed in the background while a young man came to their door with his parents. Robin Anderson was a handsome boy in a white shirt and tie. Bill and Marilyn Anderson stood behind their son as he presented himself to Adam.

"Thank you." Robin said, simply.

Then his parents added their thanks and shook Adam's hand. There was nothing more that could be said. Marilyn hugged both of them and cried again. Adam was embarrassed, but Carol, as usual, had the right words to make everyone feel more comfortable.

Sheriff Knowlton came forward to shake Adam's hand. "Thank you," he said. "Thanks from everyone in the community."

Adam and Carol stood on their front porch as the cars turned around and went back down the driveway. Robin Anderson waved from the back seat of his father's Suburban as they drove away.

Later that evening, Stewart's call came through. "I need you to come back. There's something I think you should take care of."

It was hard for Adam to refuse. He had to work because there was still a mortgage to pay. It seemed pointless now to resent anyone or the job he loved.

"They located Mrs. Peavey," Stu continued on the telephone. "She's a retired school teacher, coming in tomorrow to claim her son's body."

On Friday afternoon, a week after the trip to Cozumel, Adam and Stewart waited together on the concourse. The Northwest jet taxied across the ramp and parked. In a few minutes passengers started to exit.

"How are we going to recognize her?"

"I'll know her when I see her." Adam was sure of himself.

Mrs. Peavey walked slowly up the incline to meet two strangers, investigators in a city far from her home in Buffalo. It had been a long trip for an elderly woman, changing planes in Detroit. She was weary from the travel and from the news she had received only a day before. Here was where her son had lived and where she would receive the body of the boy she had carried in her belly and on her hip. She had raised him by herself.

Adam greeted her and introduced himself and Stewart.

"You knew my boy?" She looked hard at Adam.

"Yes, I did."

"He was a good boy." She was proud. "He borrowed money from me to be a pilot. He paid it all back, with interest."

"He was a good pilot," Adam assured her.

"Can you tell me about it? About what happened?"

"Mark was helping us capture a gang of smugglers down in Mexico. He flew the jet down there. We promised to keep him safe, but we couldn't keep our promise."

"I know you did the best you could," she said, sadly. Adam and Stewart could see her pain. She was being brave and polite. Mark was her only child. Unless she closely followed the federal trial of Carlos and Hector Lopez and David Runyon, she would never need to know how her son had earned the money to pay his debt. She could, instead, tell friends and neighbors her son had helped to capture dangerous criminals.

* * *

"Adam, it's time." Early in the morning on August 15th, Carol Bennett pushed herself up out of bed.

With practice from responding to thousands of fire calls, Adam got to his feet quickly and pulled on his pants. "Really? Are you sure this time?"

"This is it." She was positive.

After several hours of labor in Riverton Regional Hospital, she gave birth to their baby girl. As he promised, Adam was with her the entire time. He felt her suffering as if it were his own, worse than any he had experienced in his life.

The baby's name had been decided days before. A girl was to be named Emma Lynn. It was not a family name but a new name for a new life and a fresh start. Emma Lynn Bennett. Her parents knew about fresh starts and second chances.

THE END

About the Author:

Dennis Leger and his wife Lynn are winter residents of Teton County, Idaho, where they enjoy downhill and cross country skiing. During the summer they tour the country in their diesel motor home, making stops in Minnesota and Michigan to spend time with their three children and five grandchildren.

For the author, writing rounds out a wide variety of life experiences that include a climb through the ranks from Firefighter to District Fire Chief in Minneapolis. In addition he was elected Mayor of a small town for 4 terms. He was an Officer in the National Guard, a Junior High football coach and private pilot. A work related disability forced his early retirement from firefighting but does not keep him from running a marathon in Duluth, Minnesota each summer.

Made in the USA